I0526431

PAUL DOT GO

First Edition

Published by The Nazca Plains Corporation
Las Vegas, Nevada
2011

ISBN: 978-1-61098-169-9
Ebook: 978-1-61098-170-5

Published by

The Nazca Plains Corporation ®
4640 Paradise Rd, Suite 141
Las Vegas NV 89109-8000

PUBLISHER'S NOTE
Paul Dot Go is a work of fiction created wholly by *Robin Anderson'*s imagination. All characters are fictional and any resemblance to any persons living or deceased is purely by accident. No portion of this book reflects any real person or events.

Cover, Blake Stephens
Art Director, Blake Stephens

DEDICATION

In Fondest Memory of **DAVID LLOYD-LOWLES**

Bella Italia – Bella Casa Padronale!

PAUL DOT GO

First Edition

Robin Anderson

CONTENTS

PROLOGUE   1

CHAPTER 1   3

CHAPTER 2   11

CHAPTER 3   19

CHAPTER 4   23

CHAPTER 5   28

CHAPTER 6   34

CHAPTER 7   38

CHAPTER 8   46

CHAPTER 9   52

CHAPTER 10   63

CHAPTER 11   71

CHAPTER 12   77

CHAPTER 13   88

CHAPTER 14   100

CHAPTER 15   106

CHAPTER 16   118

CHAPTER 17   127

CHAPTER 18   124

CHAPTER 19   143

CHAPTER 20   150

CHAPTER 21   157

CHAPTER 22   166

CHAPTER 23   177

CHAPTER 24   185

ABOUT THE AUTHOR   189

PROLOGUE:

LONDON:

The big man stood patiently waiting between the weathered tombstones, one massive hand gently stroking his formidable erection, a long, thick, heavily-veined uncut shaft luminous in the dim moonlight; his trousers bunched around his feet, his underpants tight around his knees.

'C'mon! C'mon,' he whispered, 'Where are you my hooded friend?' His reference being to the hooded man he'd agreed to meet. Eyes darting anxiously around the eerie and shadowy Brompton Cemetery, a notorious gay cruising area in London's exclusive Chelsea, he whispered to himself once more. 'Two nights ago you gave me a blow job to end all blow jobs and, having swallowed all of me muttered "same place, same time day after tomorrow" before running off! So, my gobbling friend, where the fuck are you?'

A searing burning pain shooting up through his right buttock caused the big man to cry out. Turning his head sharply he looked down emitting another cry – this time in sheer terror – on seeing what appeared to be an overlarge head, its face nuzzling and biting greedily against the flesh of his arse.

'No!' screamed the man as he gave the untidy head a massive swipe with his clenched fist. 'No!' he screamed again as the head – attached to a grotesque, stunted body – jerked back ripping off a portion of flesh in its yellowed teeth.

Glaring defiantly up at his shocked victim stood a naked dwarf no more than three and a half feet tall. With hooded eyes glittering, his short stumpy hands resting defiantly on his crooked hips and a shred of bleeding flesh hanging from his bloodied mouth, the dwarf broke into a crooked grin, the released sliver of flesh falling onto his wide, gnarled bare foot.

Before he blacked out the man was given the unprecedented viewing of a gross, pumped up penis and a pair of hugely distended balls, his last thought being, 'Christ, they're the same size as his fucking head!'

CHAPTER 1:

LONDON – THREE YEARS EARLIER:

'Good morning Harry!' chirruped Susie, 'Good weekend?'

'If you call stuck in a traffic jam on the M1 for five hours then I suppose it was,' snapped Harry peering up from an estimate sheet on his cluttered desk. 'Sorry,' he added with a glimmer of a smile, 'Still pissed off about it. And you?'

'Oh, the usual,' laughed his secretary, 'Endless sucking and fucking. Most boring!'

'You dykes amaze me,' laughed Harry leaning back in his chair. 'Tell me Suze, how *do* you dykes actually fuck? I mean, apart from your fishy fingers it simply has to be a tried, true and very tired old dildo! Or a cucumber if you're green inclined,' he added with a snigger.

'Filthy queer! How you underestimate us lezzies, the glorious daughter of Lesbos!' Susie gave Harry a lewd wink. 'Just because you have a dick, *dear,* doesn't mean you have all the fun.'

'Far better being able to make a *splash* than being lumbered with some dreary old gash!'

'Charming, boss, absolutely charming! Coffee?'

'I thought you'd never ask and, as it's a filthy day outside *plus* a Monday, why not a hefty dollop of the old B?'

'I knew there had to be another reason why I love you, Harry dear.'

'Oh? So there are two?'

'Of course. From hearsay even a daily *dyked* dyke can dream!' Susie gave her grinning employer a mischievous smile. 'Rumour has it you possess a gigantic dick so how could I not but love your much talked about flesh and blood substitute for a super dildo?'

'Maybe I'll get it hard and take a plaster cast of my quote – "gigantic dick" unquote – which means you could then have several Harrys – all in different colours – for your extra-large Christmas stocking!'

'Many a word spoken in jest! And before I nip out to buy some plaster of Paris, let me get that coffee!' Susie looked at the closed diary alongside the pile of papers in front of Harry. 'Typical and no doubt unread.' Leaning over the young woman opened the diary to where the day's marker could clearly be seen. 'I left a message in your diary late on Friday. Someone called moments after you'd left to begin your lonely – apart from your hands – sojourn on the M1.'

'Fuck! I haven't looked at my diary as yet. I was so relieved to find Steve's bloody belated estimate shoved through the letter box sometime over the weekend I immediately began going through it.' Harry opened the dairy. 'William Wandsworth, please call. Who the fuck is William *Wandsworth*?'

'Had it been *Wordsworth* I would have been a tad worried!' camped Susie making here way to the small kitchenette.

Harry Humphries, one of London's most exciting and original young interior designers and darling of the *beau monde,* sat staring at the mysterious name and number written down in Susie's neat handwriting.

'William Wandsworth? Who the fuck may you be?' he muttered. 'A potential client? Must be. The name certainly doesn't ring any bells. A one night stand? Haven't hand one of those for ages and besides I never, ever, give out my telephone numbers, especially my office one.' Thanking Susie for the mug of coffee he reached for the telephone.

'Before you make any calls,' Susie interrupted, 'Do remember you have that new ballad singer here – the young man currently sending everybody into an orgasmic frenzy…' She glanced at her watch, 'In twenty minutes time to be exact.' Seeing Harry's blank expression she gave an exaggerated sigh of exasperation. 'Honestly Harry! Tommy Tyler, the one who's been in all the tabloids recently having bought that gigantic derelict candle factory in Battersea. He wants you, and nobody else but you to design the fucking place!'

'Candle factory?' Harry gave a snigger. 'Maybe you should deal with him Suze and demand a lifetime of extra-large altar candles in lieu of commission!'

'Very funny, Harry *dear*!' Susie gave a toss of her head. 'I'm quite happy with my bumping Bunti, thank you!'

'Just another considerate little thought from your always considerate boss, *dear*!' laughed Harry reaching for the phone. 'Alan and Giles not in yet?'

'Again, read your meticulously up to date diary, boss *magnifico*! Alan is on an early site meeting and Giles was going straight from home to *his* meeting with the elegant Mrs Behar in Eaton Square. Jesus Harry! You've only been away for a weekend, not a fucking year!'

'So elegant, my lady PA,' murmured Harry peering at his diary once again. Looking up at Susie standing and sipping from her mug of steaming coffee he added disarmingly, 'Put it down to the *Being Stuck on the M1 Syndrome*! Guaranteed to make you one hundred and ten per cent numb *and* dumb!'

'So I see!' Susie gave a grin. 'Ring the mysterious Mr Wandsworth whilst I check out the showroom for used condoms, old KY tubes and maybe even the odd abandoned dildo. We wouldn't want innocent Tommy Tyler getting the wrong impression now, would we?'

'Before you undertake such a mega task Suze, my sweet, another C and B?'

'From what I've heard about Master Tommy *Tinkerbell* Tyler you'll be needing it!'

'Sounds fun,' responded Harry drily. 'Sooo... before we meet Master TTT let's get *Mister* Wandsworth out of the way.' Glancing again at Susie's note he punched in the relevant number, the call being answered after two rings.

'William Wandsworth,' said a deep, resonant voice.

'Mr Wandsworth? Harry Humphries returning your call.'

'Ah, Mr Humphries! Thank you for coming back to me. Can you hold on a sec?' There was a click as the call was put on hold. 'Bloody long sec,' muttered Harry after a minute's silence. 'So fuck you too Mr W,' he added, slamming down the phone.

'Swig some of this down!' hissed Susie handing Harry another steaming mug. ''You won't believe this but TTT was already sitting in the showroom when I went in to do a final recce while the kettle boiled. I got quite a shock. There he was, sitting silently and simply waiting for his appointed time.'

'That's a first! A bloody client not only on time but early.'

'But so *charming,* Harry! Apologised profusely for being early but didn't want to disturb us until, and now it's my time to quote something – his "allotted time" – unquote.' Susie gave a giggle. 'And another TTT gem – again I'm quoting – "Walls have ears and from what I've heard about Harry Humphries and his temperament it'll be TTT needing the slug in *his* coffee when offered some!"'

'He said that?'

'He did indeed so I'm about to do his bidding.'

Harry gave a soft chuckle. 'So that's why you're whispering! What's he like, this swooner crooner?'

'Absolutely fucking gorgeous!' giggled Susie. Putting on a spectral voice she added, 'Be afraid, Harry Humphries, be very afraid as it's still a case of *your* plaster cast I'll be wanting instead of Tinkerbell Tyler's! Now go on, go through like the impossible designer you're meant to be while I get the beautiful boy his C with lots of B!'

'Mr Tyler,' said Harry in his most charming manner and dulcet tenor as he began making his way elegantly across the aubergine-coloured carpet of the small but exquisitely appointed showroom with its matching aubergine lacquered ceiling and walls, window blinds and upholstery, the only accent colour being the designer himself. Although of slim build and of medium height, Harry epitomised the words self-assurance and style. Blond, pale and with a face endlessly described as Pre-Raphaelite the designer sported an immaculately tailored white twill suit ("the Tom Wolfe of the interior design world" as he billed himself) accented by an open-necked aubergine silk shirt and a gleaming pair of tasselled aubergine-coloured loafers.

'Mr Humphries' said a shadowy figure rising from a gleaming Barcelona chair (upholstered in aubergine-coloured leather), 'Tommy Tyler. Pleased to meet you.'

Harry did a double take. As he was to later say to Murray Harbourd, not only his best friend but PR to the company, 'Imagine Michelangelo's David combined with Peter Pansy – though still, I should think, without a decent dick! – standing in the Piazza della Signoria dressed in an open-necked red silk shirt, blue blazer and beige chinos, for that is *exactly* what stood up to greet me! And camp as a row of tents I have to add!'

'Sorry about the earlier comments!' Harry gave a self-deprecating laugh as he shook hands with the fey, dark haired, olive complexioned, green-eyed young man smiling at back him. 'But as they say, listeners etcetera etcetera…'

'Ah, and hopefully it will have gotten me, with out doubt, a delicious mug of coffee,' laughed Tommy Tyler man giving Susie a dazzling smile as she traipsed in carrying three steaming mugs on an aubergine-coloured lacquer tray. Helping himself to one of the proffered coffees he gave another dazzling smile and a murmured, 'thank you err …?'

'Susie, Susie McBride. Mr Tyler,' said Susie with a giggle.

'Tommy please, or TTT if you prefer!' Tommy Tyler gave a light laugh. 'I must say I'm rather taken by your nom de plume! I've never been referred to as a Tinkerbell before but I take it it's a compliment of sorts?'

'Oh yes Tommy,' simpered Susie blushing furiously and not daring to look at Harry as she seated herself down on one of the sofas (aubergine suede) facing the young singer.

Christ! thought Harry. Knowing her penchant for diesel dykes don't tell me even old pussy in boots Suze is genuinely bedazzled by this piece of techicoloured campery?

'And I'm Harry,' said Harry thinking, but, my friend, never likely to be your Dirty Harry though I have a feeling Murray, on meeting you, would be more than willing!

'Right Tommy.' Harry sat back on a matching Barcelona chair, 'The candle factory. I know the building well. In fact I looked over the site some months ago on behalf of a middle-eastern princeling who subsequently got himself into a bit of trouble with a couple of rent boys. Not only did they beat the hell out of Prince Ali but they also smashed up his hotel suite. Needless to say the bruised and battered – not forgetting somewhat humiliated – man has subsequently been put off the so-called hidden delights of London!'

'Just as well I'm not into rent boys!' giggled Tommy, 'So I won't – if you'll excuse the expression – be *pulling* out as it were!' Giving Harry a knowing look he continued, 'And before you do a bit of thrust and *Harrying,* yes, I'm gay (Really? said Harry to himself, not daring to look at Susie, *what* a surprise!) as I know you certainly are, Harry, your notoriety precedes you! So let's get down to business.' He took a long sip of his coffee giving a murmured 'delicious' and flashing Susie another dazzling smile.

'I'm planning to *come out* publicly at the start of my next spectacular concert being held at the O2 next month. Therefore I'm going the whole hog. Being gay I will be supporting business-wise anything and everything gay, hence the top gay designer of the decade! (Harry gave a modest nod at the compliment, his blond locks falling decoratively over his pale forehead) I will only use gay trades' people – please don't take that as a double entendre! – suppliers, builders, the works. Are we on?'

'What a wonderful commission,' breathed Susie on her way back to the office to answer one of the three ringing phones. 'Are you into candelabras, Tommy?' she asked, laughingly tossing the question over her shoulder as she exited the showroom.

'Candelabras? I *hate* candelabras!' laughed Tommy. 'Ah, I see, the candle factory bit.' He gave another laugh. 'I take it Susie's also gay?'

'Hence the candles crack!' Harry gave a snigger, 'Another rather unfortunate turn of phrase!'

It was decided the two would meet again on site in three days, Tommy being committed to his recording studio and unable to put aside any time until the Thursday. The meeting, scheduled for noon, would give Harry and Alan, the company architect, a good hour beforehand to discuss any immediate building problems concerning the Victorian structure.

Having said a smiling goodbye to Susie the singer was then walked to the door of the showroom by an even broader smiling Harry. Turning again to survey the front of the smartly aubergine painted-brick building set in a side street close to the impressive Chelsea Design Centre at Chelsea Harbour, Tommy gestured towards the gleaming, gloss finished aubergine bricks and the neat white pointing.

'Very smart, Harry.' Tommy gave another laugh. 'And I've only just realised you not only match the *inside* but the *outside* as well! Brilliant!'

'Touché!' laughed Harry pointing to the navy and red coloured Bentley coupé. 'A car to match its owner's ensemble? Now that's what I call an extravagance.' He gave another laugh on eyeing a uniformed chauffeur emerging from the luxurious motor. 'And a driver to match! *Tres tres* camp!'

'Not all that extravagant, Harry!' came the quick riposte as Tommy began climbing into the back of the car. 'I only wear red and navy! Damn!' Turning to Harry the young man made a face. 'I've slipped up Harry, the interior is plain navy! Maybe next time? However, it all depends on HH Incorporated and what they decide for my new home.' Tommy gave another laugh and a further dazzling smile. 'So why not a new Bentley to match?'

'Why not?' laughed Harry. 'As the old saying goes, *In for a penny, in for a pound*!'

'A *pound*, Harry?' questioned Tommy looking out from the rear window, a mischievous grin on his perfect face. 'From what I've heard that sounds somewhat modest for a Harry Humphries dream home!'

'Tommy, I can assure you I've *never* been modest,' laughed Harry giving the young man a friendly wave as the big car pulled silently away.

'Wow and double wow,' muttered Harry as he stood looking at small building which he had inherited from a former textile manufacturer and long-suffering lover. 'You, TTT are not only a walking wet dream but – if my vibes are right – a fucking dream client!' With a camp salute at the aubergine and white-fronted edifice Harry re-entered his own mini empire.

'Isn't he a positive little dreamboat?' chortled Susie.

'Yes, a fluttering of tinselly fairy wings little dreamboat!' laughed Harry. 'What always amazes me is the fact all those screaming fans out there haven't twigged he's even a more of a screamer than they are!' He glanced down at the note Susie was holding out in front of her, 'Ah, our rude Mr Wandsworth again.'

'Yes, and most apologetic about keeping you waiting! Could you call him back ASAP please? His words, not mine.'

'I don't see why not, oozy Susie! With Mr TTTT – note four tees Suze! It now simply has to be Tommy, Tinkerbell Tinselly Tyler! – Mr Wandsworth had better have something definite to propose or, as his names implies, he can just *wander* off!'

'That's very polite for you, boss dear?'

'I don't always have to use four letter expletives, Suze,' laughed Harry, 'So where's the shit cunt's fucking number then?'

'At the bottom of the fucking note where it's meant to fucking well be,' said Susie with a syrupy smile, 'Another C and B?'

'Mr Wandsworth, Harry Humphries again.'

'Mr Humphries, I'm *so* sorry about my appalling rudeness earlier.' The man gave a deep 'down from the balls' chuckle. 'Now, do *you* have a few minutes?'

'I'm all yours, Mr Wandsworth,' said Harry camply, 'for the next five anyway.'

'Five may just do it,' came the bland reply. 'Mr Humphries, let's get down to the nitty gritty! I've seen your work and can only express my admiration for your boldness and your truly mind blowing concepts. I'd very much like the two of us to meet. I'm a painter, by the way (But of course, thought Harry, I *knew* the name meant something. *Bigger than Bacon* is how you've recently been described) and I have recently become the proud owner of a property – no, make that a *challenging* property – abroad.' The deep voice paused for a few seconds before continuing. 'I recently visited some friends who have a villa above Portofino, Italy, and fell in love with the area close to this enchanting coastal town.'

'You mean Liguria? The Cinque Terre?'

'You know it?'

'Know it? I love it!' enthused Harry. 'I have friends who own a marvellous old house in Monte Rosso.'

'But this is uncanny! Uncanny and marvellous!' said the deep voice breaking into a delighted laugh. 'Just before the start of the five Cinque Terre towns, just before Levanto, I spotted and fell immediately head over heels in love with a derelict fourteenth century castle. I did some sleuthing, found it to be up for sale and without giving it a second thought, *or even properly checking out the place,* simply went ahead and bought it!' There was another pause and the sound of a match being struck.

'However, I should warn you Mr Humphries, *Castello Paradiso del Inspirazione* is nothing like the appallingly translated name, the "Castle of Heavenly Inspiration," which I've already given it. If anything, it's a heavenly wreck! Goodness gracious but now I'm rambling and our five minutes must nearly be up!' This time there followed a deep, rich chuckle.

'I really would value your opinion on the place. I realise it's asking a lot but if you could spare even a couple of days to fly out there I would really appreciate it. Obviously I will expect to pay you for your time away from London, an initial consultation fee and all expenses.'

'When were you next thinking of going back to Italy?' asked Harry clicking the call onto speaker so Susie could make notes.

'It's probably out of the question,' said Wandsworth, 'but is there a chance you could manage this coming Friday? This would see you only being away from your office for one working day and the weekend. We'd fly to Genoa on Friday and I'll have you back in London by Sunday evening.'

Harry took a deep breath. 'Mr Wandsworth, may I call you back? Or, if it's not myself it'll be Susie, my PA. I do have a somewhat vital meeting scheduled for Friday but, if possible, I'll see if this can be changed. Ten minutes OK?'

'Ten minutes it is, Mr Humphries.' There was another pause. 'I would really appreciate you changing that meeting. Tell you what, Mr Humphries, why not make it half an hour which will also give you time to calculate your daily charges to cover your three days away plus a preliminary consultation fee you would be happy with. As I've already said, all other additional expenses will be taken care off.'

'Half an hour then, Mr Wandsworth. Many thanks for contacting me. Good bye.' With that Harry hung up

'Christ Suze,' he said looking at his equally stunned secretary in disbelief. 'Talk about it never rains and then it fucking pours!' he added before giving out a loud chortle of delight.

'*Pours* being the operative word,' grinned Susie. 'So why don't I *pour* us a celebratory glass of two of chilled *vino bianco* while you get busy with your little calculator!'

CHAPTER 2:

'Mr Wandsworth? Susie McBride, Harry Humphries' PA. You'll be pleased to know Harry was able to bring his Friday meeting forward so, if you would get someone to email me flight details etcetera for Friday plus an address as to where you'll be staying, I'll pass this all onto Harry.'

'Splendid Miss McBride but there's been a slight change of plan. Anticipating *Mr Humphries* would be able to make it I'm leaving for Genoa tomorrow which means I'll be able to meet him off his flight on Friday. I'll get all those details emailed to you within the next five to ten minutes.'

Mr Humphries? thought Susie, Well that's me put well and truly in my place!

'That sound's perfect Mr Wandsworth. I'll inform *Mr* Humphries and I look forward to receiving all details forthwith from your PA. Her name being …?'

'I don't have a PA Miss McBride. Any future dealings will be with a business partner, definitely a he as opposed to a she. In fact I have two partners, a Mr Paul and a Mr Nelson.'

'Oh,' said Susie, her mind racing. A gay *ménage a trios*! What bliss! 'And who will be contacting me, Mr Wandsworth? Mr Paul or Mr Nelson?'

'One or the other, Miss McBride.' There was a momentary pause before the man continued. 'I think that's about it. Please tell Mr Humphries I am delighted he can join me despite it all being so last minute and I'll look forward to seeing him at Genoa airport. Oh, and yes, as you will have gathered from what I've just said all those costs sent through are fine. Would you like a cheque sent round by hand today or shall I give this to Mr Humphries when we meet?'

'Sent round today would be perfect,' said Susie in her most clipped, business-like manner. 'That will be fifty per cent of the total excluding VAT. We'll only invoice you for the VAT when we require the final balance.'

'But of course. In fact, I've already drawn a cheque for the full amount of your charges including the dreaded value added tax.' There was another pause before Wandsworth spoke again. 'Within the hour then Miss McBride. I see you're based at Chelsea Harbour which is ideal, my London studio being in Notting Hill. Thank you for your help Miss McBride and good day to you.' There was a soft click followed by a quiet buzzing sound.

'And good day to you too, *Mr* Wandsworth,' said Suise looking at the receiver still in her hand before punching in Harry's mobile number. 'Harry, Willie Wanker Wordsworth just called. Wanker? Oh, I'll explain when I see you! Everything's arranged but you'll be meeting him out there in *Bella Italia* as he's flying out tomorrow.' She gave a laugh, 'And before you ask he's sending round a cheque made out for the full estimate *tout de suite.* How about that for keenness?'

'Sound's like our lucky week Suze. Maybe I should get stuck on the M1 more often!'

'Have you *seen* any pics of this Wandsworth guy?'

'No. Have you?'

'Several! Big ugly brute! Think the Incredible Hunk meets Pavarotti with a beard!'

'God! Talk about chalk and cheese!'

'Chalk and cheese?'

'TTT and WW! One's perfection while the other's a nightmare!'

'In other words, a wet dream and a scream! Now I *know* why I love working with you Harry – I beg your pardon – *Mr* Humphries!'

'Mr Humphries? Now what are you on about you silly cunt?'

'Hardly a silly one Harry *dear*! *Sublime* cunt is what most of the pussy-bumping herd calls little *moi*! What's that noise?'

'Me throwing up! Listen Suze, I've got to go. Missy Edwards is throwing a hissy over some bloody lintel that's been delivered and is too short!'

'I'll leave you to pacify the lovely Steve.' Susie gave a snort. 'He'd have an even bigger hissy fit if he'd heard himself referred to as Missy Edwards!'

'Only for your sacred ears, Suze angel fart! Only for your much pierced sacred shell-likes. Our big Steve sees himself more Sumo than simpering!'

'And a *hairy* Sumo at that! When do you think you'll be back?'

'By lunchtime easy. Tell you what Suze, see if Murray's free and if not, can he meet us later? If he can join us at the office around oneish that'd be great. It'll give us a chance to bring our East End whiz kid up to date. By this time next week I want our two new clients in every paper plus allotted magazine space. After we've had a glass of wine and a chat we can them amble over to the Design Cafe for a bite. My treat. After all what's a couple of quid when compared to Willie Wanker Wandsworth's so-called deposit!'

'The thought of any other deposit – apart from a cheque – from the likes of Mr Wandsworth makes me want to do what you were doing a few moments ago!'

'And what was that, Suze dear?' asked Harry innocently.

'Throwing up!' said Susie ending the call.

Murray Harbourd sat looking at Harry and Susie, his handsome face aglow. 'Tommy fucking Tyler *and* William bloody Wandsworth, both in the same day? Jesus team, that's fucking brilliant! OK! OK! (a regular quick-fire response from Murray when excited) I can see it! I can see it! Forget the Three Tenors, Murray Harbourd Associates is going to stun the shit out of everyone with *The Three Talents*! Designer, singer and painter! SDP! OK! OK! Terrif! Terrif!'

'I like it! I like it!' laughed Harry (Murray's sometimes repetition of words and phrases was catching). 'So M, it's now up to you!' He pointed to the near empty bottle of wine standing in the ice bucket on the low table in front of them. 'Shall we do one more Suze and then amble over to the Design Centre? So Murray, love, not that you don't always but this time *extra* surprise us!'

'I will! I will!' beamed Murray, his handsome face wreathed in smiles. 'Wow team, this is great! Great with a capital G! OK! OK! I *know* we've had names, celebrities whatever before, but this is big time!' Putting on his best East End gangster accent he growled through the corner of his mouth, 'Not only big time, me darlins'. Fuckin' *show time!*' Murray Harbourd, a dynamic twenty five year old cockney had started his own public relations company after a short spell working for a leading boxing promoter, another tough East Ender named Manny Durante. It was Manny who had suggested Murray 'go it alone' and giving the young man his blessing. 'There's more to you than the world of boxing, mate!' the old man had expostulated. 'So off you go and catch yourself a princess or two! As long as you remember your old mate Manny from time to time and invite me to one of them posh dos, then we'll be alright!'

The elderly promoter's parting gift had been the introduction to a multi-millionaire property developer about to invest in an imposing new luxury block of flats in London's answer to Manhattan, the mushrooming skyscraper area in London's docklands newly named Canary Wharf.

Lenny Freed, the developer, had taken an instant shine to the chunky, dark-haired handsome young man with his mischievous smile and dazzling blue eyes, promptly inviting him to Monte Carlo for the weekend where the two had fucked like rabid rabbits in between visiting the Casino and eating in extravagant restaurants.

A besotted Lenny had given the equally besotted Murray carte blanche in handling the promotion of the luxurious thirty story Garden of Freeden tower. As Murray would repeatedly say, 'Beginning with Lenny I've never looked back! He's always there or on it!'

Lenny, although married, continued to treat Murray as a prized mistress buying him a luxurious flat set on the exclusive Chelsea Embankment overlooking the Thames. It was through Lenny the ambitious Murray had met the much sought after Harry Humphries, Lenny's company having hired Harry Humphries Incorporated to design his dream project.

For Harry it was lust at first sight, the macho, chunky, slight rough East Ender being his ideal male fantasy. However Murray, his East End loyalty coming to the fore, had staved off the young designer's obvious advances by making it quite clear that he was Lenny's lover and nobody else's. Over the ensuing weeks of the two working together Harry's initial lust had turned to admiration with a firm friendship evolving and the two becoming virtually inseparable.

'What do you know about the Four Ts? That's what Suze and self have now dubbed him,' laughed Harry. 'And again, what do you know about the mysterious William Wandsworth – or William *Wanker* Wandsworth, another Suze-ism!'

'OK! OK!' Let's see! Let's see!' said Murray reaching for his refilled glass. 'Give me a few hours after lunch and then meet up again. Come along to the flat around eight – that's if you're free?'

'Jesus M! Of course I'll be free!' laughed Harry. 'With those two about to take us even further into orbit, who wouldn't be?'

'Suze?'

'I know its business but ...'

'Of course you must bring Big Bunti! Can't have you making quickies every five minutes to the loo for a frantic self-fingering, now can we?' sniggered Murray. 'Furthermore I'll get supper for four sent in.'

'As long as it's not a finger supper,' snorted Harry.

'You wish!' came Susie's quick riposte.

'I don't *like* fish fingers!' giggled Harry.

'OK! OK! You two!' cut in Murray with a grin. 'Just so nobody's offended I'll order in a Chinese.'

'Better watch out for those chopsticks then!' came Harry's choked reply. 'More than likely disappear up someone's chop phooey!'

'May I suggest we adjourn for that promised lunch, Harry dear?' said Susie primly.

CHELSEA EMBANKMENT:

'It's Indian!' cried Murray on opening the door to his sumptuous duplex flat. ('I want it Busby Berkley meets Harry Humphries on speed!' he had instructed Harry in their one and only meeting to discuss the interior).

'You poor ignorant queens have no idea as to what two dykes can do with a kebab!' shrieked Susie. 'Do they Bunti?' she shrieked again looking back at her grinning friend.

Bunti (known as Bulldozer in private by Harry and Murray) gave a deep guffaw before replying. 'Forget the kebab, see what we can do with chicken tikka when we really get going!'

'How fortuitous,' chortled Murray, 'for that's one of the dishes ordered!'

'Hey guys, this is meant to be a business meeting not a fucking sex show!' quipped Harry. 'I expect us to plan, ponder and *then* eat.'

'No way! No way!' said Murray, this time with a chuckle. 'We firstly drink – it's conducive to our planning – *then* we plan, eat, ponder and ponder some more, all in that order. Your hallowed PR guru has spoken.'

'Sounds good to me,' replied Harry following their host into the large art-deco styled entrance lobby with its illuminated and mirrored staircase leading up to the floor above. Glancing critically around the silver and black area Harry gave a satisfying grunt. 'Still looks bloody good M.'

'Bloody good? Bloody good? It looks fucking fabulous and all thanks to you, my love! Now, follow me! Follow me! I've champers on ice but please feel free to ask for anything else that tickles your oh so elegant fancies!'

'I'll have a rum and Coke please,' said Bunti in her gruff voice.

'I'll do the champagne,' said Susie.

'Me too,' said Harry.

'I'd like to begin as soon as possible,' said Murray having handed over the requisite drinks. 'No time for small talk I'm afraid, it's down to business right away.' He took a sip from his champagne flute. 'Lenny's calling by after some dinner he's had to attend. He's intrigued by Wandsworth and his *castello*. To quote Lenny, "I've always wanted to be king of the castle so why don't I just fuckin' well buy one and let you and young Harry have a field day! We'll turn it into one of the most luxurious complexes for country living that this green and pleasant land will ever see!"'

'That's the third,' said Susie.

'Third?' This from Harry.

'Third contract today,' Susie said with a delighted laugh. 'They do say all good things come in threes!'

'Which reminds me of something very odd, very odd and something I was going to keep until much, much later but now you mention it…'

'Don't tell me,' interrupted the young woman, 'William Wandsworth and his *menáge a trios*!'

'You *know* about them?' asked Murray, his face falling.

'In a roundabout way. Mr Wanky Wandsworth described them as his partners which, in this day and age could mean anything. However I gather Paul and Nelson must be gay which means so is our client.'

'Almost hot but not quite hot hot!' laughed Murray, delighted that he still held the trump card.

'Not quite hot hot? Put us out of our misery! Explain yourself Harbourd!'

'Well, you've seen Wandsworth, haven't you?' said Murray flipping open a folder lying on the low coffee table. 'If not, have a look. Massive hairy bloke isn't he? More Incredible Hulk than your run-of-the-mill artist.'

'Francis Bacon wasn't exactly a picture made in heaven either!' laughed Harry.

'Nor is this chap,' growled Bunti in her deep rumble. 'Looks positively Neanderthal if you ask me!'

'This gets better and better by the minute,' chuckled Murray, 'by the minute! My dears,' he added, grinning from ear to ear. 'While Mr Wandsworth may boast the attributes of the Incredible Hulk-cum-Neanderthal Man, Paul and Nelson Column, his partners, are not only siblings but dwarfs!'

'Dwarfs? You've got to be joking!' cried Harry, his eyes wide with disbelief.

'On my foreskin I joke not, joke not!' cried a gleeful Murray, his eyes twinkling with merriment at the three's response.

'Has our Murray *got* a foreskin to swear on?' guffawed Bunti.

'You could tie a knot in it!' chortled Harry.

'But this is so *cool*!' exclaimed Susie. 'Wanker Wandsworth aka Gulliver and his little Lilliputs aka Paul and Nelson! TTTT will have to do something *extraordinaire* to cap this!'

'Two dwarfs,' muttered Harry. 'Christ, the mind boggles!' He glanced down at the photograph before looking at a grinning Murray. 'Do you have a pic of the dwarfs?'

'No, but I did speak to someone close to Wandsworth, his agent in fact, and he told me about the gruesome twosome. Said I should warn you so they don't come as too much of a shock!'

'Charming!' quipped Harry. 'Tell me, is there anything else I should know before I meet this little lot on Friday?'

'You won't be meeting the Columns, they'll still be here. No, not in London; Wandsworth also has a studio in the country, a converted barn outside Petworth in Sussex. This is where the two Columns spend most of their time.'

'I've just twigged!' laughed Harry. 'Meet the two Columns, Paul and Nelson. Nelson's Column, geddit?'

'Sounds as if combined they'd certainly make a dildo with a difference!' said Bunti dryly and in her butchest voice, causing the other three to collapse into hoots of laughter.

CHAPTER 3:

'It's even more derelict than I remember,' muttered Harry looking around the cavernous, dilapidated building. 'What's your first reaction Alan?'

'The same as yours!' laughed the young architect running a stubby hand through his tousled mop of bright ginger hair. 'But the space is great. Your immediate ideas H? Anything typically Harry Humphries spring to mind?'

Harry stood staring at the void in front of him for a few minutes before answering. 'We gut the whole place; everything out. Then I suggest a new *floating* centralised island for the main reception and entertainment areas. This will be supported by a series of moulded steel columns each in the shape of a bass clef. All the other facilities, bedrooms, bathrooms and such will be situated here at ground level forming an outer rectangle of rooms all facing in to the supporting columns with an inner veranda-like effect. A compound surrounding a floating island as if it were.'

'Sounds brilliant, pure *Fantasy Island* if you catch my drift.' Alan gave an indulgent smile. 'How rich did you say this client is?'

'I didn't but he's very!' responded Harry with a grin. 'Now look, this is what I envisage.' Glancing round he spotted a lopsided table surrounded by several rickety chairs. 'Our office awaits! Let's sit down and rough out a few sketches before Tommy Tyler arrives.'

'This new client is *Tommy Tyler*?' gasped Alan. 'Tommy Tyler the ballad singer? The new Bublé to out Bublé Bublé?'

'Yes, didn't Susie tell you?' said Harry with a nonchalant grin.

'Of course she bloody well didn't!' cried Alan. 'You two are incorrigible! If it'd been the bloody Queen of England you'd still have kept me in the dark!'

'Oh Alan, I can assure you this is *definitely* a rival to the real one! And although our client queen has kept herself in the dark she's about to "come out" publicly. The O2 Arena to be exact and let's face it, you can't be more public than that!'

'Tommy Tyler "coming out" publicly? You mean he's *gay*?'

'Unless "coming out" means something else, Alana dear!'

'Good heavens! How sad I'm conjoined at the hip to my Jamie!' camped Alan.

'By the cock you mean!' sniggered Harry. 'So, let's quickly scribble down a few ideas before our minor royal appears.' Harry pointed to the holdall he'd been carrying. 'There's a thermos of coffee – black – and three mugs along with a hipflask of brandy should we find the place a tad chilly.'

'Strange you should say that, I'm suddenly feeling a distinct chill…!'

'Good morning Harry!'

Harry spun round in the direction of the voice.

'Ah, Tommy, punctual as ever! Tommy Tyler meet Alan, Alan Miller the company architect.'

'Hi Alan!' said Tommy giving the inanely grinning redheaded young man a dazzling smile.

Oh oh, thought Harry, another besotted fan and all in a matter of seconds! Talk about charisma! 'Coffee Tommy?' he asked.

'That would be great,' smiled the singer. He nodded towards the distant doorway. 'Bellings has a bottle on ice in the car so we can all have a celebratory drink later.' Sitting himself down cautiously on one of the spindly chairs he looked eagerly at the scattered sketches lying on the lopsided table top. 'Are those what I think they are?' he asked excitedly, 'And so soon?'

'Simply a few preliminary ideas Tommy to run past you.' Harry picked up his rough sketch of the proposed central island on its steel bass clef supports. 'Your bass section of your ballads always stands out,' he said, 'hence a music stand with a difference! Harry Humphries, designer supreme (here Tommy couldn't resist a small excited clapping of his hands), sees you enveloped in a twenty first century interpretation of art nouveau, swishes and curlicues with the suspended island floor being encased in a massive, sculpted wave taking up the space of this whole area. Do you know Hokusai's – the Japanese artist – woodcut *The Wave*?'

Tommy looked blank.

'Not to worry, we'll get a whole presentation together but I see your whole interior as a series of nouveau tendrils, a massive platform and lower surrounding *cubes* – the other rooms – all encompassed within a massive opaque about-to-break wave. What do you think?'

Harry looked across at a dumb-struck Tommy while ignoring Alan who was doing his best to keep a straight face.

'If it looks like anything you've made it sound like it'll be brilliant,' said Tommy in a hushed voice.

'Tommy Tyler, you've just said it; hit the nail bang on the head! Sounds inspire your music so your new home will *look* as its owner *sounds*! Mystical, moody and magical!'

'My,' breathed Tommy, his green eyes wide, 'All I can say is you go for it, Harry! Meanwhile I'll go and get Bellings to bring in that bottle and three goblets. I think champagne as opposed to coffee is definitely the call of the day!'

'So, what do think?' said Harry to Alan after their ecstatic client had finally left.

'Christ, isn't he a dish to end all dishes!' breathed Alan, a statement not a question.

'You made that little thought pretty obvious Alana, *dear,* but it's not Tommy Tyler I'm talking about! My *ideas* you vagina!'

'What? The bass clef meets art nouveau? Bloody brilliant as always Harry. I never thought of a bass clef as an art nouveau form but then, there's always a first time and you never fail to astound me the way you can *swirl* and *twirl* your words to convince some poor sod of your latest hallucination! But, when all is said and done I can only say again, bloody brilliant! No, I sit corrected, make that *fucking* bloody brilliant!'

'Thank you Alana dear, you sweet, devoted little leprechaun of architect, you!' camped Harry. 'Now, as there's still a smidgen of champagne left in that second bottle why don't we add a touch of Mr Flask to it.' Without hesitating Harry emptied their untouched coffee mugs onto the dusty floor before refilling these with the champagne along with the brandy. Leaning back against his creaking chair he gestured towards the vast surrounding space with his arm holding the coffee mug. 'Rather you than me, Al, my talk is cheap. Are you quite happy that you, me, us, the team can pull this off?'

'But of course maestro,' said Alan with a reassuring grin. 'Simply see it as a massive art nouveau and Japanese gang bang with William Morris, Charles Rennie Mackintosh along with Aubrey Beardsley all shacking up with the impassive, massive Mr Hokusai!'

'Jesus Alana,' chortled Harry, 'now you're talking!'

'How did it go?

'Need you ask Suze? I was a genius as always,' smirked Harry, 'and poor Alan has already swallowed his first Valium in anticipation of what he now has to do!'

'Poor baba Alan!'

'Poor baba Alan? Rich baba Alan, Suze dearest! I've agreed to give him a percentage of the design fee which is only fair seeing he's now got to interpret and *put down on paper* all my airy fairy *for* the fairy bullshit!'

Susie sat looking at Harry, a bemused smile on her face.

'What?' he asked.

''You, yes *you* Harry Humphries for you never cease to astound me. For all your impossible temperaments you can also be such an angel at times! That is *so* sweet of you H and it couldn't have come at a better time.'

'And why's that? Is our little Alana pregnant or something equally as shameful?'

'Almost! He and Jamie are seriously thinking of adopting.'

'Tell me you're joking?' Harry gave a rude snort. 'But then they're the sort of gay couple who would, wouldn't they? I mean, it's even more trendy nowadays for *gays* to adopt as it was a year or so ago when those publicity seeking pop and movie stars simply *had* to adopt a rainbow of vacuous-looking orphans.'

'Don't be so cynical.'

'But I *am* cynical, Suze, and that's why you love me!' Harry let out a snigger. 'Christ, next thing it'll be you and Bunti wanting a baba of your own!'

'Many a word, Harry dear, many a word.' Susie gave a mischievous giggle. 'We *have* discussed the very subject and who knows, Harry Humphries Esquire, we may even ask *you* to be the dada of our gorgeous-looking, genius child by donating some of your usually so liberally scattered seed!'

Harry, an expression of mock horror on his handsome face let out a camp shriek. 'What? *You* mixed up with *moi*? Or even worse, a combination of butch Bunti and the heavenly Harry? Now that is truly evil and very, very sick!'

'Oh, I don't know Harry, dear. I think you'd make a rather cute, miniature bull dyke!'

CHAPTER 4:

Mic Sandford glanced down the other end of the elegantly set dining table where Cynthia his wife sat chatting animatedly to Terence Carter, a potential client placed diplomatically on her right. As if feeling her husband's gaze Cynthia momentarily turned her exquisitely blonde coiffed head, giving Mic a subtle wink.

Atta girl, said Mic to himself, I knew sooner than later the old boy would be putty in you manipulative hands. Well done, Cyn. Turning to the matronly Mrs Carter seated on *his* right, he asked, 'And how is the house hunting going, Mrs Carter?'

'Oh Mic, Griselda, per-lease!' The large woman gave a girlish simper, her several chins trembling in the soft glow from the central candelabra. 'I must say I'm quite, quite exhausted. As Terry said to me this morning, you must slow down *Grizzle* old girl – the old darling calls me Grizzle which is something I *never* do! – the houses won't run away!'

'Oh,' said Mic, 'no, no I suppose they won't,' thinking, Grizzle? Wait until I tell Cyn this little gem!

'And I must say simply *love* your home,' Griselda Carter enthused, 'your lovely wife has such impeccable taste. I mean, *look at her husband*!' This bon mot resulting in a high pitched shriek, causing a startled Cynthia to look anxiously at Mic while Terence Carter gave his wife an indulgent smile.

'That's most generous of you, Griselda,' smiled Mic,' but I simply have to correct you on both comments. First, Cyn employed some high flying designer to create all this as she is always too busy with her agency – I should know, I'm still trying to recover from his final charges! – and secondly, she found *me* through a dating agency!'

Griselda looked aghast at her smiling, rugged, handsome silver-haired host, her tiny eyes bulging. 'A dating agency?' she gasped, a plump hand reaching for her impressive bosom. 'She *didn't*!'

Mic gave a laugh. 'Well, that's what she tells everybody. Apparently she asked for a George Clooney lookalike but ended up with The Ancient Mariner instead!'

'Oh, for a moment you were being serious you naughty, naughty man!' giggled Griselda, 'Now tell me truthfully, where did you two *really* meet and when?'

'Years ago at a party in Rome.'

What Mic did not go on to say was the party had been given by an acclaimed gay film producer where Mic had been the guest of his leading actor, a blond, extremely good-looking young Englishman named Howard Hanover and Mic's lover. Halfway through the evening Mic was introduced by Howard to his leading lady, Natalie Vine, an equally glamorous young English actress who had recently appeared in a highly successful historical television series on one of the more erudite channels. Cynthia Mason was also introduced, her role being that of Natalie's agent.

Later that night as Howard lay happily ensconced in Mic's broad arms he had sleepily murmured, 'Tell me, did you twig Nat and Cynthia were lovers?'

'Good heavens,' muttered Mic. 'And I thought I had reached the age and stage where nothing would surprise me. Well, well, you've just proved me wrong.'

It was inevitable that the four would be seen together over the next two weeks. Mic, his main purpose for visiting Rome being a combined business trip and spending a few precious days with Howard, found himself enchanted with the witty, elegant Cynthia. While Howard and Natalie were involved with filming during the day Mic found himself spending more and more time in Cynthia's delightful company, the two couples meeting up again each evening. The attraction was twofold with Cynthia delaying her return to her London office and arranging to fly back at the same time as Mic.

It was Cynthia who had suggested the marriage 'of convenience' which could only be of benefit to both partners. Howard and Natalie were delighted and were enthusiastic in their support. As Mic and Cynthia were to say to their two young lovers it was a marriage 'made in convenient heaven!'

The couple had duly bought the elegant house in Belgravia's Chester Square, a few houses away from the former Prime Minister, Margaret Thatcher.

'But that's *so* romantic,' gushed Griselda having listened avidly to Mic's highly sanitised version of his and Cynthia's whirlwind romance. 'But as I always say, love at first sight does happen. I mean, I took one look at Terry and immediately thought, "He's for me!"'

'Quite,' murmured Mic glancing down the long table at the bald, bloated, bug-eyed man talking to his wife. 'Quite,' he said again, this time slightly louder.

The following week the contract with Terence Carter was duly signed. 'All thanks to you, Cyn,' said Mic as he smilingly presented her with a sparkling Tiffany diamond brooch. 'In fact during his final meeting with myself and my directors I had to remind Terence not once, but twice, that we were there to discuss his affiliation with Sandford Holdings and *not* Cynthia Sandford!'

'Bless you, Mic,' said Cynthia leaning forward to give the big man a kiss on the cheek. 'You certainly know how to flatter a girl.' She gave her husband a mischievous smile. 'Oh dear, now I suppose we have to suffer a thank you dinner with just the four of us. The ghastly Griselda …'

'*Grizzle,* if you don't mind!'

'I stand corrected! *Grizzle* and the equally as ghastly Terence. We're fully committed for the next three weeks so there is no alternative but to use one of our "away nights" if that's alright with you, my darling?' (The 'away nights' being a referral to the evenings they spend with their respective lovers). 'Natalie's away in Ireland on location for a few days. She leaves tomorrow so I'm all yours, as they say!'

'May I suggest you arrange it with the dear Grizzle and I'll simply fit in with your plans. Howard, as you know, is quite easy about stepping aside as if it were when he knows its business involved for daddy Mic!'

'And quite rightly too seeing *sugar* daddy Mic has just given petulant toy boy a nice little playmate called Porsche!' Noting Mic's slight frown at her barbed jibe Cynthia quickly added, 'I'll go and call Griselda now, firstly to congratulate her and Terence on becoming part of our happy family and secondly, to organise our hot date! I'll call her from my sitting room. I won't be long.'

'Fine,' said Mic moving over the bar cupboard in the elegantly panelled study where he proceeded to mix a pitcher of martini. 'I do wish you'd stop having a go at Howard, Cyn,' he muttered. 'It's not his fault his last two films have bombed whereas Natalie just seems to go from strength to strength. For Christ's sake, the Porsche was only something to cheer him up. If you bring this up again I simply will have to say something as it is not at all fair. It's not Howie's fault he's having a bum run.'

Taking his martini glass he moved over to his favourite chair where he made himself comfortable before picking up the evening paper, neatly folded, from the small table alongside. He glanced up as Cynthia came back into the room. 'All fixed?'

'All very fixed!' Cynthia gave a slight grimace. 'May I have one of those lethal martinis I see you've made? I think I need it!'

Mic gave a smile. 'Oh dear, that bad, is it?' He stood up and made his way back over to the bar. 'One very large and very dry martini coming up.' Handing her the glass he added, 'Now Cyn darling, tell handsome hubby all.'

'Before I could even suggest dinner Griselda jumped the gun by inviting us for Thursday week to be exact.' Cynthia took a sip of her martini murmuring a soft 'delicious' before continuing. 'Not only are we going to be on parade at the Savoy, no less, but – are you ready for this – our lovely hostess has not only found but gone and bought a house… '

'Not the bloody one three doors away from us?'

'The very one.'

'Shit!'

'I thought you'd say something to that effect.' She gave a light laugh. 'And there's even more to it?'

'What? Oh no, don't even begin to tell me!'

'Yes, she's invited her designer and an associate for dinner as well.'

'And her designer – all due to my loud mouth – being *your* designer?'

'Yes, the very same. I should have thought something was afoot when she called the office and got his name from Stan. So my darling, at long last you will be meeting your *bête noire* the very fey and very gay Harry Humphries! Not your scene *at all*!'

'Ha! At long last I get to meet the man who almost broke the Bank of Sandford! What if I suddenly have an urgent desire to make a lunge at him with my butter knife between the first and second courses?'

'We're their guests, Mic darling, so you'll simply have to restrain yourself. Another time perhaps?' Cynthia gave a light laugh. 'Anyway, you do love to exaggerate darling. Poor Harry, he only went a teensy-weensy way over your suggested budget!'

'One hundred and twenty thousand pounds over anyone's budget is not "teensy-weensy" nor, as I see it, chicken feed!'

'There, you're getting all worked up again which you shouldn't as some of that extra costing did include a last minute gymnasium which was *your* suggestion, Mic, treasure.'

'It's still not chicken feed,' growled Mic but with a smile playing on his mouth.

'But then neither are we poor poultry farmers, are we hubby dearest?' Cynthia gave another laugh as she held out her empty glass to a now openly smiling Mic. 'With Sandford Holdings and Mason Enterprises we seem to have so many chickens laying nest eggs they can only be Faberge!'

'True, quite true, Cyn darling.' Mic gave a deep chuckle. 'To Thursday then,' he added raising his empty glass before reaching for Cynthia's and retreating back to the bar.

'And talking about nest eggs, Griselda has also asked if I have any *spare* time, would I go thought young Harry's schemes with her, a sort of shadow consultant as if it were.' Reaching for her refilled glass she gave a small giggle. 'She even suggested a fee.'

'A fee?'

'Yes, darling, a fee, which of course, being such a busy woman with my own agency to run I simply had to tell her no. Talk about not taking no for an answer, an insistent – and desperate – Griselda therefore simply doubled her quote!'

'And? Come on Cyn, the tension's almost killing me!'

'While my divine darling husband gives me diamonds I think it's now my turn to go and speak to either Algie Tomlinson or Jennifer Haydon again at the Tomlinson-Haydon Gallery about the William Wandsworth painting you fell in love at last week's preview.'

Mic gave out a low whistle. 'That much?' he said before adding with a grin, 'Ah, but what if it's already been sold?'

'Mic Sandford. One thing I've learned in my glorious years of being married to you is "he who hesitates is lost," so this clever woman put a reserve on the painting as soon as she saw her beloved's reaction.'

'You did?'

'I did!'

'And if you hadn't been offered a fee?'

'I would have still bought it and, just to let you know I refuse to be beholden to the likes of Griselda Carter or anyone of her ilk I refused to discuss a fee of any sorts. Said I'd look at her schemes simply as a friendly gesture. Besides, Griselda Carter wasn't prepared to be *that* generous!'

'You're a star.'

'And so are you.' Cynthia gave the smiling man an equally dazzling smile in return. 'To quote from one of our favourite DVDs, as Bette Davis *almost* says at the end of *Now Voyager,* "we may not have the moon but we each have our stars."' Unable to resist she added with a mischievous wink, 'Pun intended!'

CHAPTER 5:

So I'm to look out for a combination of the Incredible Hulk and a Neanderthal man, am I? Shouldn't be *too* difficult to spot, mused Harry as the airbus banked for its final descent into Genoa's Christopher Columbus International airport. Glancing through the plane's window his spirits soared as he took in the lush green hills surrounding the ancient maritime city followed by a first glimpse of the sparkling azure blue Mediterranean.

Reaching for his holdall from beneath the empty seat next to him and being first in line when the aircraft taxied to a halt, Harry was quick to disembark passing through both passport control and customs without any hitches before making his way confidently towards the crowded main concourse. Within seconds Harry caught sight of the famous painter, a giant, bulky, solitary figure standing well back from the meeters and greeters blocking the main arrivals gate.

'Jesus,' muttered Harry, 'forget the Incredible Hulk and Mr Neanderthal, the man's a fucking giant and furthermore, he's fucking gorgeous!'

'Harry Humphries!' shouted the big man, his deep bass voice reverberating around the busy area. Giving Harry a dazzling smile along with a sweeping wave, he shouted again, 'Welcome to Genoa!'

Taking a few massive strides towards Harry – a Harry stopped, literally, in his tracks – the giant stuck out a massive hairy hand and with a second devastating smile cried out heartily, 'William, William Wandsworth and all I can say it's a pleasure and an honour to meet you!'

'Err.... likewise, Mr Wandsworth,' stammered Harry, his hand feeling as if encased by a large, warm soft glove, 'a pleasure to meet you too!'

The big man broke into another beaming smile. 'May I suggest as we're going to be making beautiful babies together *we* make it William and Harry?' Giving a startled Harry a broad wink William added, 'And before you rush to catch the next flight back to London Harry, when I say "making babies" I really mean magical designs!' Giving a deep, rumbling belly laugh the big man reached out for Harry's holdall. 'Is this it?'

'Yes, a sketch pad, camera, a measuring tape and a change of clothes is all I'll be needing,' said Harry primly as he meekly handed over the Louis Vuitton bag, immediately chastising himself. Christ, don't sound such a prissy queen, Humphries. The guy obviously thinks you're shit hot so act the fucking part!

'The car is over there,' boomed William ploughing his way through the bustling crowd. 'Smooth flight?'

'Perfect,' gasped Harry almost running to keep up his host. 'Couldn't have been better.'

'Good!' came the strident reply. 'Meet Goneril,' said William gesturing towards a bright yellow, low slung Lamborghini Alar. 'I have a stable of such lovelies, Goneril's *numero uno* and she and I drove out here via Paris on Tuesday.' The big man gave another deep rumbling laugh. 'Next in favour to Goneril is Regan – she's a sprightly bright red Maserati Gran Turismo – followed by Cordelia, the only non-Italian member of the group being a one hundred per cent blue blooded German Mercedes coupé. Hop in!'

'You obviously see yourself as a bit of a King Lear then?' quipped Harry as he slipped down into the low leather seat.

'King Lear? Oh, and those dreadful scheming daughters? *Very* astute, Harry but *my* girls are complete daddy's girls meaning they all approve of his friends which must now include you!' William gave Harry another dazzling smile, his big teeth whiter than white between his thick, black bushy moustache and fulsome beard resting untidily against an equally hairy chest which sprouted in wild profusion from the top of his open necked shirt. 'I can see we're going to get on,' the big man added with a chuckle. 'Like I said, we're going to make beautiful babies Harry, you and I!' Giving Harry another broad wink he quickly strapped himself in – gesturing Harry to do the same – before firing up the powerful engine. Putting the motor into gear they roared out from the parking lot.

Harry sat clutching the dashboard, his mind in turmoil. In between glancing at the buildings flashing by he kept sneaking further looks at the larger-than-life artist sitting smiling alongside him, his brilliant blue eyes slightly narrowed as he concentrated on the traffic ahead. Christ, he's at *least* six foot six, if not more, built like a fucking tank and reeks, positively *reeks* of pure animal! Harry could not but help noticing a dark wet patch forming under William's right armpit which, along with a matching patch on his barrel-like chest, was slowly becoming bigger and bigger. Leaning slightly towards the big man and despite the breeze whipping in through William's open window, Harry was convinced he could even *smell* the man's animal-like musk.

Jesus, William, just *inhaling* you is giving me a hard-on! Who the fuck and what the fuck are you Wandsworth? I've *never* reacted to a man like this before! I bet you're hung like a fucking horse with balls like bloody grapefruits!

'I thought we'd go straight to the *castello,*' shouted William above the roar of the engine and breaking into Harry's reverie. Zigzagging his way expertly through the traffic he shouted again, 'It'll take us about half an hour once we're on the Autostrada. After I've shown you the place I thought we'd head on into Levanto for a late lunch. There's a great little *ristorante* I've discovered just off the main town square.' He gave another laugh. 'We're booked into Levanto's one and only attempt at a five star hotel so I hope you're happy with that!'

I'd be happier if I thought you we're going to be fucking me, thought Harry stifling a giggle, his hard-on pressing uncomfortably against his grey check trousers. Make beautiful babies with you William Wandsworth? I'm quite willing to die trying!

Having overtaken every other car on the Autostrada it seemed only minutes before William was slowing and changing down gear while indicating his turning off to the right. Due to the rush of the wind through William's open window and the roar of the engine conversation had been non-existent.

'Another ten minutes and we'll be there,' shouted William, his large, hairy hand leaving the gear stick for a moment as he patted Harry's knee. 'Great to have you here, Harry,' he boomed. 'You don't know how much I appreciate you changing your appointments to fit me in.'

Fit you in? I'd change every fucking one of my appointments to do just that, thought Harry.

'It's a fantastic road,' shouted Harry as the sleek car wove its way through the dense, overhanging trees, 'Absolutely stunning!'

'Wait until you see the *castello,*' laughed William, 'then you'll be completely stunned!'

Not as stunned as I'd be on seeing your stun gun, thought Harry wildly before reprimanding himself with a, Get a grip – ha, if only! – Humphries! He's a client, for Christ's sake and his penchant is for dwarfs! Not fey, erudite beauties like *vous*!

Changing down gear once more William slowed the Lamborghini to a rumbling snail's pace before turning into a deeply rutted lane. '*Castello Paradiso de Inspirazione,*' said the big man solemnly to the overhanging trees, 'you are about to meet Mr Harry Humphries who is now here with your new lord and master. Not only is Mr Humphries going to make you utterly and wonderfully beautiful, he's also going to make you look unique!'

Giving a startled Harry's knee another squeeze William accelerated causing the car to leap forward and make its way haphazardly down the narrow, disused track.

Not only God's gift to this salivating queen whose fantasies revolve around a macho, butch, massive bear but a gift who is also totally fucking mad! thought Harry wildly as the car bucked and slithered along. And I'm sorry for whoever else is waiting in the wings! Come hell or high water I'm the one who's going to be ending up in the role of William Wandsworth's leading lady!

'Behold!' cried William slamming on the brakes and throwing Harry forcibly against his seatbelt.

Harry sat staring at the building ahead of him, his heart racing. Jesus, what's happening to me? I've not only fallen head over high heels in love and lust with this macho man mountain, but now his castle as well! The place's a designer's wettest of wet dreams!

'Well, what do you think?' asked William, his deep voice anxious, as he looked at the young man leaning forward and staring out through the windscreen.

'Think?' said Harry, still staring, 'William I don't *have* to think,' he said softly, 'I know that with madam there' – he nodded towards the silent, brooding stone edifice – 'we're not only going to make beautiful babies but we're also going be a magnificent threesome!'

'You're not only beautiful and talented but also a mind reader,' responded William and before Harry realised what was happening the big man had unbuckled his own seatbelt and turning his large aromatic frame took hold of Harry in his brawny arms, simultaneously leaning downwards and kissing the startled young man resoundingly on his mouth.

Sitting back William gazed at Harry with a beatific smile. 'Not only do you *look* good, you taste marvellous! Now, let's go and introduce you to her ladyship. She can't *wait* to meet London's most sought after beautician of buildings.'

As if the most natural thing to do William took Harry firmly by the hand before leading them towards the vast, solid-looking door in the high stone wall.

'It's more of a mini-castle than a castle, castle,' explained William. 'An overgrown folly in fact, but I love it.'

Selecting a key from his key ring he deftly unlocked the shiny new padlock attached to a strong-looking new bolt. Giving a grunt William pushed strongly against the weathered wood with the door slowly creaking open. Following the big man Harry found himself standing in a small, rectangular courtyard surrounded on three sides by high stone walls with the main building in the form of a square tower facing them.

'This way,' said William reaching again for Harry's hand and moving over to the left. 'There's been a cave-in a few steps directly ahead and I wouldn't want you tumbling down into the dungeons, now would I?'

An hour later the two were seated under a large umbrella on the terrace outside William's new favourite restaurant.

'So, Harry, your honest opinion. Can you give me my magic castle?'

Harry looked directly into the gently smiling giant's anxious blue eyes. 'William, I can only offer you my best.'

'That's enough for me,' said William, his smile broadening. 'Now, where's that *vino*?'

'Can I ask you something, William?'

'Anything you wish, Harry.'

'Before flying out here I had a chance to look at various photographs of your converted barn and your lavish Notting Hill studio as featured in various magazine and newspaper articles (Susie having rapidly put together a résumé together for Harry about their prospective new client). Not only are you a genius of a painter, William, but you're pretty damn good at interior decorating as well.' Harry took a sip of his wine which had silently appeared. 'So why involve the likes of me?'

'Why the likes of you? Oh, that's easy Harry, very easy. Firstly, I've seen *your* work, a great deal of it and I can honestly say you're in a class of your own. There is nobody, but nobody in London – or anywhere else for that matter – who has that extra special touch, or flair, you are so specially blessed with.' This time it was William's turn to take a large sip of his wine while Harry sat looking at him, eyes wide.

'Secondly, not only have I been studying photographs of your *work* but I've also been studying photographs of *you!*' He took another sip as Harry sat silently staring at him. 'And why the likes of you and you in particular, Harry? Simple. Because, my divine young Harry Humphries I fell in love with you the first time I set eyes on you in some designer magazine.'

Harry, having just taken another mouthful of wine promptly choked.

After several hefty pats on his slender back from a solicitous William a still spluttering Harry sat mopping his eyes and grinning inanely at the big man.

'I didn't expect to cause *such* a reaction,' smiled William. 'You OK now?'

'Never better!' gasped Harry, 'Oh *William*!' he said chokingly, his voice a strangled squeak. '*You* fell in love seeing me in a magazine while *I* fell in love with you on seeing this unbelievable man waiting there to greet me at Genoa airport!'

William sat looking staring at Harry, a look of disbelief of his large, bearded, weather-beaten face.

'You did?'

'I did! I swear on my friend Murray's foreskin I did!'

'Friend Murray's foreskin?'

'It's an *in* office joke, William. I'll explain later.'

'I look forward to your explanation!' laughed William, his face wreathed in relieved smiles. 'Ah Mario,' he said smiling at a beaming, corpulent Italian making his way over to their table, 'Meet my friend Senor Humphries. He's come all the way from London to taste your cooking so what do you recommend today?'

'It's certainly a day for falling in love,' smiled Harry as Maria, Mario's smiling wife cleared away their empty plates.

'It is?' smiled William.

'Yes, it most certainly is,' said Harry letting out a small, satisfied sigh. He held up a slender hand, 'One,' he said, wiggling his little finger, 'I fell in love with my first view of Genoa. Two,' he wiggled his ring finger, 'I fell in love with my first view of a certain painter. Three,' he waggled his forefinger, 'I fell in love with my first view of Castle *Paradiso* and four, I've now fallen in love with Mario and Maria's restaurant!'

'And five? You've got *five* fingers on that elegant hand,' laughed a bemused William.

'Five? Oh number five is par of the course. With all this love in the air one cannot but help fall in love with that magical word *siesta*! I mean, what *else* is one expected to do after such a splendid lunch?'

'Have a *siesta*?' grinned William.

'As I've just said, number five,' giggled Harry, reaching for his third glass of after-lunch grappa. 'My *casa* or your *casa*?'

'Don't be so naive, young man!' snorted William. 'In anticipation of the gods answering my fervent prayers to something like this happening – I was seriously praying while we were roaring along the Autostrada, hence the lack of conversation! – I'd already taken the liberty of reserving the Hotel Splendido's one and only honeymoon suite!'

CHAPTER 6:

'How was *Bella Italia*?'

'*Molto*! *Molto*!' grinned Harry handing Susie a long, heavily wrapped tubular-shaped parcel. 'And before you ask, no, it's *not* a plaster cast of precious *moi*!' He gave another mischievous grin. 'Go on! Open it! Open it!'

'Christ! You sound just like maddening Murray!' said Susie giving an unladylike snort. ''OK! OK!' she camped, seeing Harry's impatient frown. 'I'm opening it! I'm opening it!'

Having done so she looked up at Harry before collapsing with shrieks of laughter back into her desk chair. 'You dirty bastard!' she managed to gasp, waving the giant, glistening, maroon-coloured salami sausage. 'Not even in my wildest of dreams …' she gasped again.

'That, my dear,' chortled Harry turning in a clumsy attempt at a pirouette. 'That,' he said again now facing the semi-hysterical Susie, 'is simply *not* what you think it is! Oh no, me dear, it's not a great salami lookalike dildo but, in fact, a more-than-accurate replica of William Wandsworth's mighty paintbrush!'

'You *didn't*?'

'Didn't what Susie precious hear?'

'Do *it* with William Wandsworth?'

'Please enlighten me, secretary supremo, which "do it" are you referring to for I can assure you in the vocabulary of gay high jink there are *endless* ways of "doing it!"'

'As they say, three's a crowd and if that salami is anything to go by it must have been pretty crowded!' Susie gave another uncontrollable giggle. 'So, I take it its full ream ahead with Castle Dracula and the two dwarfs?'

'By your well practised slipping of the tongue I trust you actually mean *dream* as opposed to *ream* or is that all part of your *scheme*, Miss Evil?'

'Oh, very droll, Mr Humphries, or – knowing part of this new *ménage* also involves dwarfs – perhaps I should have said *troll*?'

'And before you continue being more Roget than Mr R's own little book of words, Miss Sappho Susie, Mr Harry Humphries, designer *extraordinaire,* has been graciously – and no doubt lustily – invited down by the artist supreme to his country retreat this very weekend!"'

Susie gave Harry a look of disbelief. 'I can't wait for Murray to hear about your latest shenanigans; he'll have a field day!' She handed Harry a plastic folder containing several press cuttings. 'And these are only for starters; Saturday's and a few of the Sunday papers. Fairly amazing considering Murray has only had a few days in which to start the ball – or should that be balls? – rolling. Here, read this

One; *Harry Gets The Bacon* or better still, this one, *Tommy Tyler Gets The Midas Touch.* It's all there, Murray's being brilliant.'

'Good, very good,' smiled Harry eyeing the grinning girl. 'C'mon! Out with it! I know that McBride look!'

'Nothing really, I was just thinking up another could be Murray-ism regarding Willie Wanker. Something along the lines of *Harry Humphries and the Two Dwarfs* perhaps?'

'Very funny, Susie dear. Do try and seriously scald yourself when you finally get round to making that promised coffee!'

'So charming, my revered boss,' snickered Susie making her way to the kitchenette.

Still smiling Harry began idly sifting through his messages. However much he tried to focus on the small pieces of paper in front of him his mind kept flashing back to the past few days. After the initial shock of seeing William fully erect – his first thought being Christ! It's the size of a bloody giant pepper grinder! – Harry had been surprised by the gentleness and compassion shown by the massive, hirsute man. In between anxious murmurings of 'Tell me if I'm hurting you? Tell me and I'll stop,' Harry found himself deeply and ecstatically impaled, a sensation he was only too willing to experience time and time again. Not only was their passion repeatedly sated in the faded grandeur of the honeymoon suite but in the ruined *castello* itself where Harry insisted on being fucked in every room 'for inspiration.'

'Jesus, Harry,' whispered a sweating William kissing the young man gently on the throat as they lay entwined on a rug spread casually on the stone floor of the castle keep, a series of lighted candles placed haphazardly around them. 'If the soreness of my cock is anything to go by your inspiration must be even greater than that of all those Italian artists and architects put together!'

'Almost,' Harry murmured, pushing his nose deep against William's musky, sweat-drenched, dark, hairy chest. 'But I feel several more inspirational depths may still require, no, make that *many* more, if Harry Humphries Incorporated *and* inserted is to be truly *magnifico*!'

'Your coffee, sir!' said Susie breaking into his reverie. 'And Harry dearest, if you must sit there with such a blatant hard-on you could at least cover yourself with *today's Daily Mail*!'

'So observant and so witty!' laughed Harry, totally nonplussed by Susie's comment on the very apparent bulge in the front of his lightweight trousers. Taking the proffered mug he nodded towards the diary. 'Any further info on the Carter woman?'

'Nothing earth shattering apart from the fact she knows Cynthia Sandford – *adored* Mrs Sandford's house – quote, unquote, and now wants you, Harry dear, to give her something a teensy weensy – her words not mine – more show-bizzy! In fact, what is interesting is they've bought the Margolis place three or four houses up from the not so show-bizzy Sandfords.'

'Christ! That must have set them back a packet or two! I remember there being quite a furore some years back due to the Margolis lot excavating beneath the house so as to build a mega swimming pool plus cinema.'

'The very one. Anyway, the house in its present state is simply not acceptable to Mrs C and so your magic wand – oh dear, I hope it's not too exhausted! – is therefore desperately required to out-glitz both Mrs M and Mrs S!'

'How kind of you to have put their initials in that order!'

'M and S as opposed to S and M? But I did this deliberately, sweet Harry, so as to not get you requiring the need for the *Daily Mail* again!'

'My, we are sharp this morning! Last week it was the M1 and this week *la Bella Italia.* Obviously my dubious excursions work both ways, inspirational to you and to *moi*!' Harry took another sip of his cooling coffee and gave a grimace. 'Yuk! This is vile. Anything exciting in the fridge?'

'But of course! Fizz or vino?'

'Fizz I think, maybe with a *soupcon* of vitamin C?'

'Take it as done.'

'So when do I meet this Bollywood wannabe?' asked Harry having taken a sip of his Buck's Fizz.

'You're not only meeting her Harry, but if you deign to remember, the lovely Mrs C suggested a "getting to know you" dinner. True to form you did say you had a prior engagement with your PR to which her response was "how lovely" and suggested why not bring him along as well! To the surprise of all your humble underlings you agreed.'

'I did?'

'On your PR's foreskin!'

'Good heavens!' said Harry, looking genuinely bewildered. 'What on earth made me agree to that?'

'Two little words, boss dearest, two little words used by our Bollywood belle-to-be *before* the dinner invitation.'

'And they were?'

'*Carte blanche*!'

'I already *love* show-bizzy Mrs *Carte Blanche* Carter even though we've still to meet!'

CHAPTER 7:

'Gentlemen, we have a very special guest joining us this coming weekend; a very *special* person.'

'We do?' said Paul looking up from his cornflakes, the dripping spoon held halfway between his large, misshapen head and the nearly empty bowl.

'Indeed we do,' said William with a sardonic smirk. 'And furthermore I want the two of you on your best behaviour and to be extra nice to him.'

'Does that mean we have to fuck him?' wheezed Nelson, his mischievous jibe causing his brother to choke on his mouthful of cornflakes.

'That's very considerate of you but no thank you gentlemen. If anyone is doing any fucking round here it's yours truly.' William gave a deep chuckle. 'You two little sodomites will simply have to make do with each other as usual, or Rufus!'

'I'm tired of fucking Paul,' said Nelson in a petulant tone.

'And I'm tired of being fucked by Nelson!' snapped Paul.

'And we're both tired of fucking Rufus!' the two chanted in gravelly unison, their lewd, twisted smiles displaying each displaying a row of uneven, yellow-stained teeth.

William looked at the two distorted little figures glaring across at him from their high chairs.

'I'm sorry gentlemen but you have no choice. Either you behave yourselves or you'll be finding yourselves spending the remainder of the weekend in the cellar. The choice is yours.'

'No worry, I'll simply fuck Paulie instead and be done with it!' sighed Nelson.

'Boring!' chanted Paul, 'Boring, boring, *boring*!'

'Maybe we can both fuck Rufus and see if we can beat our last record of coming twenty times each over a weekend?' suggested Nelson rubbing his stirring, stubby, acorn-like erection, his cornflakes momentarily forgotten.

'As I've just said,' whined Paul. 'Boring, boring, *boring*!'

'So, what's it to be?' questioned William, a hint of impatience in his otherwise placid tones. 'Best behaviour and therefore part of the family? Or misbehaved and therefore treated as pariahs? In other words, banished to the cellar with only yourselves to play with apart from – to use Nelson's word of the moment – "boring" television and "boring" CDs.' William gave each dwarf a wry grin. 'It's up to you.'

'I'll be magnificently well-behaved,' grunted Paul.

'Me too,' growled Nelson, adding softly, 'Sorry, William.'

'Me too,' echoed Paul, 'And I'm sorry for teasing you, William. You can count on us.'

'Good,' smiled William, 'that's what I like to hear.' He lent back in the high-backed wooden chair. 'Well gentlemen, now you've both promised to be little angels instead of nasty little devils and as you've almost finished your cornflakes, I'll allow you your earlier-than-usual extra treat. Who'd like to be first?'

'Me! Me!' cried Paul.

William looked across at Nelson. 'Nelson?'

'OK by me,' growled Nelson. 'I *like* swallowing Paulie's seconds!'

'So Paulie, what's stopping you obliging both me and your brother then?' questioned William, a wry smile playing on his lips.

Scrambling down from his high chair Paul shuffled his way around the table on his tiny, broad bare feet – William's instructions being both dwarfs always breakfasted naked – to where William sat, his colourful silk dressing gown fallen open, his giant, flaccid cock with it's wrinkled sock-like foreskin hanging, reminiscent of a large pale fire hose, between his massive, hairy thighs.

Positioning himself between William's legs the dwarf, thanks to his height, simply took hold of William's cock between his stubby fingers and barely bending his oversized head deftly guided the giant bulbous cock between his fleshy lips.

'That's it, Paulie! That's it!' murmured William giving out a sigh of satisfaction as he leant further back into his chair. Eyes closed the sigh changed to a deep throated grunt of pleasure as Paul's rough, expert tongue, pushing back the heavy folds of his foreskin, began lasciviously rasping and expertly flickering up, on and around the exposed, swollen bulbous head. With his stumpy arms rapidly gathering momentum and his stubby hands moving piston-like up and down the shuddering shaft, it seemed only moments before Paul had driven William to a gasping, groaning frenzied climax.

His mouth full to bursting with William's hot jettisoned load Paul swung round to face a greedy Nelson who, without hesitating, clamped his own fleshy lips against his sibling's, greedily sucking and swallowing as Paul spat globule after globule of William's warm cum into his receptive gullet.

'Well done, gentlemen,' smiled William rubbing each of the grinning dwarfs' tousled heads. 'Now, chop, chop! Off you go and get showered and dressed. Like you, I've work to do. Join me in the studio at noon and, as you've promised to be on your best behaviour during the weekend, I'll allow you *two* William Specials before lunch!'

'Yippee!' cried Nelson giving a hop and a skip, his tiny, still erect cock bobbing like a small cork on his hairless body.

'Yippee!' crowed Paul in a grotesque parody of his brother before standing still, bowed legs apart, staring unblinkingly up at the artist, his stubby hands placed firmly on his crooked hips. 'Now William,' he said in his raspy voice, 'let's cut the crap! What's *really* up?'

'Yes, William,' growled Nelson striking a similar pose. 'Let's cut the crap. What *exactly* is going on?'

The little figures glanced knowingly at each other before looking up at William now lounging back in his chair, a dribble of cum glistening on the black hairs to one of his inner thighs.

'Oh,' said Nelson with a grimace, smacking his large, bulging forehead with a small, stumpy fist. 'Don't please tell us you've fallen in love!' A statement, not a question.

'Oh please, not *again*' groaned Paul, repeating Nelson's gesture. 'And don't tell us it's that designer we took a bet on?'

'No, gentlemen, I'm not exactly in love but it was quite a weekend!'

'And is this odious state of affairs reciprocal?' asked Nelson, his tone one of dismay.

'To quote an old proverb, I have a feeling that young Harry Humphries has fallen for your lord and master, *hook, line and sinker*!'

'Oh dear,' said Nelson, absentmindedly putting out a small finger and wiping the trickle of cum off William's thigh. Having taken a contemplative suck of the aforesaid finger he murmured again, 'Oh dear, dear, *dear*!'

'Yes, *very* oh dear, dear, dear!' echoed Paul. Looking over at Nelson he gave a lopsided smile. 'Here we go again, merry as can be, two little dwarfs about to wreak misery!'

'Don't even think of it!' said William with an evil grin. 'Best behaviour, remember? However, after your weekend of purdah I promise you on the next occasion … '

'Whoa! William! I somehow think this definitely calls for an after breakfast discussion! You've now got our gonads going and I don't think it fair to keep Paulie and self-waiting until noon to tell us what is going on!'

'You're quite right, my little friend, it's not fair. In fact the noon day talk is about a new general exhibition for which I've been asked to donate a painting or two.' He looked down at the two loyal stunted figures staring back up at him, their expressions troubled. 'OK my beauties, let's talk about Harry Humphries, a Harry Humphries whom I strongly believe will become a major problem but a problem we can easily deal with *after* the renovations to the *castello* are completed.'

'Must he *really* be involved?' This from Paul.

'Oh yes, gentlemen. It's all to do with the bigger picture, if you'll pardon the pun. So Paulie, I know I said a William special at noon but now's as good a time as any. I wasn't going to discuss Harry Humphries in detail until after the weekend but as we've now started talking about the young man, I may as well continue.' He looked at the two. 'Nelson, forget the William Special, what about that lethal so-called Ruskie concoction you make so well?'

'Oh,' said Nelson, his hooded eyes lighting up, 'you mean my special *Ivan the Terribles*?'

'If that's the name, yes! I know this is both your favourite tipple when I'm up in town so no doubt you've got all the ingredients stashed away somewhere?'

'I really can? At this time of the morning?'

'Why not? Besides, after what I'm about to tell you, you'll probably need one or two or maybe even more!'

'Three *Ivan the Terribles* coming up!' grinned Nelson. 'Paulie?'

Shuffling over to a row of low cupboards, Paul reached up bracing his arms on the edge of the worktop as Nelson clambered agilely onto his shoulders. Balancing on Paul's muscular shoulders Nelson reached into one of the upper cupboards, pulling out two bottles. Hopping back down onto the tiled floor he stretched up again, placing both bottles on the work surface.

Meanwhile Paul had made his way over to the large fridge where he procured a further bottle plus a tray of ice cubes, bringing these over to Nelson now busily mixing grappa and ouzo in a large jug, three martini glasses at the ready. Adding the iced vodka and cubes to the mixture he gave the liquid a firm whisking before filling the glasses. Solemnly handing his brother a glass, Paul – keeping one for himself – handed the third to William. Placing their glasses back onto the breakfast table, the two dwarfs scrambled back onto their high seats.

'So, what gives with this Harry soul?' asked Nelson having taken a long sip of his drink and smacking his glistening, fleshy lips with approval at the sharp-taste.

'Easy,' replied William. 'Take a look around you gentlemen and what do you see? A cleverly converted barn. Look around the Notting Hill studio and what do you see? A cleverly converted church. In Italy I will have a superb, uniquely designed castle but what I really want is a fitting memorial to Willliam Wandsworth; a memorial to *me*! Think Guggenheim in New York, *that's* what I want! Not a museum but a gallery bearing my name!

'By a gallery I don't mean some poxy place in the likes of Cork or Bond Streets but a major building dedicated entirely to me! Call it a mausoleum if you must but I am talking about a showpiece; a place along the lines of New York's New Museum of Modern Art – all those about-to-topple cubes! – or on the lines of Foster's The Sage Gallery in Gateshead, a shining tidal wave of steel. *That's* what I need for William Wandsworth to be remembered by!'

'Goodness,' murmured Nelson.

'Holy shit!' muttered Paul. (As he was to say in bed to Paul later that night as they lay cuddled together in bed in their own specially adapted quarters, 'Talk about delusions of grandeur, the big one's gone fucking mad!').

'But that doesn't answer my question,' parried Nelson. 'What has a squit-arse queeny designer like Harry Humphries got to do with all this? He's not a major architect by any means but an interior designer. Why the subterfuge?'

'And why the intrigue?' interrupted Paul.

'Harry Humphries – even though he may not be aware of it – is perhaps one of the most important and influential interior designers of the decade, his portfolio becoming more and more impressive by the day. I've seen how his PR guy is already using the name of Tommy Tyler along with mine.' William gave a reassuring smile. 'Don't worry your pretty heads about this and I couldn't help but laugh. Straight after lunch, having seeing the *castello* and agreeing the commission, Humphries couldn't wait to get on the phone to this Murray friend of his – though he did have the grace to let me fuck him first! – giving the go ahead for any possible PR apropos our contract.'

He gave a deep laugh, 'This titbit of information subsequently appearing in one of the Sundays under the rather trite headline, *Harry Gets The Bacon*! But I digress. Harry Humphries – although he doesn't know it yet – will be working hand in hand with my surprise architect and together they will create this sensational landmark; the icing on the cake as if it were. However this will also be Harry Humphries' swan song, his last work and final accolade. The ensuing publicity will be tremendous.'

'Swan song? Final accolade? Just *what* do you mean?'

'As I've said, it'll be an acclaimed tribute to his interior design and ingenuity but it will and must also be his last.'

'And what if this Harry Humphries – I must say I am beginning to find the name a tedious bit irritating – doesn't agree?'

'He doesn't have to. He'll be dead.'

'Oh, but of course, how silly of me,' said Nelson taking a long, thoughtful sip of his *Ivan The Terrible*. He glanced across at William's smug, bearded face, his small eyes glittering. 'Tell me something, William, apart from hideous Harry making his obliging exit so as if to double the ratings as if it were, plus this gallery to end all galleries becoming a so-called tomb and a monument to you, may I ask where all the money is coming from to finance such a venture?' Nelson took another sip, while gesturing Paul to refill their glasses. 'We know you're rich William but not that rich!'

'That's easy, little one, our old friend Prince Albert.'

'Prince Albert? Black Prince Albert, the – "I have a finger in every pie" – guy? I thought he was dead!' said Paul, giving William a curious look.

'A lot of people would like to think so!' laughed William. 'But he's keen keeping a very low profile since his court case, in which, I am happy to say, all those ridiculous, trumped up charges against him over those fraud allegations were dropped. No, Prince Albert is very much alive. In fact, if all goes to plan he'll be joining us here on Sunday evening.'

'I think I'd better make another jug of *Ivans*,' said Nelson clambering down from his chair.

'And what about Master Humphries?' questioned Paul.

'No need to worry about Mister Masthead Harry,' chuckled William. 'Slammer and Bees are coming to lunch on Sunday and I've already arranged for them to give our house guest a lift back to London with them in their helicopter. Something he is unaware of but no doubt will find preferable to another tedious train journey.'

'My, but you have been a busy boy, haven't you?' chortled Nelson, pouring himself a further refill. 'And where, may I ask, William, artist about-to-be-immortalised, do you plan to build this mausoleum – I mean gallery?'

'There's a property on Park Lane, a grotesque thirties eyesore which is about to come on to the market. I want this and once I've got it we simply demolish and rebuild.'

'And this Humphries is capable of doing all this?'

'No, not the initial architecture but he'll be working hand in hand with the architect. As I said a few minutes ago he's not fully aware of the arrangement but the prestige and the money will be too much to resist. I've been concentrating on the *castello* and only made a vague mention of the gallery saying – should it come off – he would be working on the interior but he would also be working to certain guidelines.'

'And this genius architect being?'

'The man responsible for the building known as *The Pillar of Light* near St. Pauls.'

'Ah yes, the architect who bills himself the *Archangel of Architecture* because all his buildings embrace the light!' mused Paul.

'The very one.'

'And planning permissions? I mean, per-lease, we're talking Park Lane here.'

'My dear Paulie if they can allow a fucking, phallic monstrosity like the Hilton Hotel together with the likes of that elephant turd on Hyde Park corner, the William Wandsworth Gallery will be a veritable soothing balm.'

'I can't wait to see Prince Albert again!' gurgled Nelson, giving a yellow-toothed grin. 'If Lazarus could rise up from the dead and remembering what Albert had rising up, hopefully we'll be able to add a new meaning to the term "dead boring!"'

'But of course! You two were holed up with Albert for a few days in the villa at St Tropez a few years ago weren't you? Err … before his unfortunate so-called demise.'

'Holed up alright! Why, randy Albert never stopped cornholing – his favourite word! – Paulie and me!'

'And it was Albert who suggested we should think about doing you-know-what!' snigged Nelson.

'So he did,' said William breaking into an amused smile. He looked affectionately at the two grinning little figures. 'Have you ever thought about it? Considered doing it?'

'Oh yes, many, many times,' said Paul, nodding his large emphatically. 'Many, many times.'

'And your conclusion or decision?'

'We'd really like to do it if you wouldn't mind, William?'

'Mind? Why would I mind? I think it'd be great fun for all of us!' William let out a deep guffaw. 'Poor Rufus! He'll get one hell of a shock!'

'Where is he, by the way?' asked Paul.

'He went into town with Skids to get some extra provisions for the weekend and pick up a few extra cases of wine.' (Skid Mark or Skids being the three's private name for Mark Elliot, the general factotum and handy man, full nickname Skid Mark Idiot because of his limited intelligence and preference for not wearing underpants resulting in some rather noticeable, dubious stains on his well-worn jeans).

'Do you think Skid Mark's secretly fucking Rufus?' sniggered Nelson.

'I doubt it,' laughed William. 'Skid Mark's idea of wild sex is Mrs Idiot, a prime example of a walking missionary position if you can work that one out! So no,' he added with an even deeper laugh, 'I can't see our Skids fucking a pug!'

CHAPTER 8:

'Whereabouts are we dining?' asked Murray as they pulled into the small forecourt of the Savoy.

'The River Room,' said Harry, adding a murmured 'Good evening' to the top-hatted doorman opening the door to the taxi. He glanced at his watch. 'We're few minutes early so why not a drink in the American Bar before we face the lions' den?'

'I trust this is worth it,' grumbled Murray as they made their way up the wide staircase to the bar.

'It'll be worth it,' grinned Harry. 'Oh Murray, Murray, ye of little faith! You'll love Cynthia Sandford, she's every gay's dream; elegant, simpatico and very, very funny. I haven't met hubby but if she's anything to go by, he must be OK. As for out hosts, Mr and Mrs Terence Carter? We'll simply have to wait and see.' He paused for a moment at the entry to the bar before hissing from the side of his mouth, 'There, on our right, Cynthia Sandford and a rather striking gent whom I can only assume is the mysterious Mr Sandford. I'd better go over and say hello. I'll join you at the bar.'

Putting on his most dazzling smile Harry swanned across to where the couple were sitting, their heads close together in what appeared to be a light-hearted, animated conversation, two champagne flutes on the small table in front of them.

'Cynthia!' cooed Harry, 'Sneaking a quickie before dinner, I see!'

Cynthia looked up, her face breaking into a warm smile. 'Harry! Trust you to catch us in flagrante delicto and *before* dinner!' Giving a light laugh she turned to her bemused companion. 'Mic darling, at long last you meet Harry Humphries, the Svengali responsible for Chester Square.'

'Harry,' said Mic looking up at the smirking young man, 'After what Cynthia's told me about you I was beginning to believe such a magician couldn't exist in human form!' Drawing himself to his full six foot four height, the smiling man thrust out a large tanned, perfectly manicured hand.

While shaking hands Harry eyed Mic appraisingly. Handsome bugger, he thought, straight out of a GQ advert for the more mature man. The complete antithesis to my William! While William is all towering, tangy testosterone you, Mic Sandford, are Mr Smooth and Mr Suave personified.

'Likewise, Mr Sandford,' Harry murmured quickly withdrawing his slender hand from Mic's cool, firm grasp.

'Make that Mic, Harry,' laughed the big man. 'I already feel we know each other, Cyn having never stopped talking about you.'

'Would you and your friend care to join us?' suggested Cynthia nodding to where Murray was waiting patiently alongside the bar. 'I know we're all dining with the Carters so we may as well be fully prepared!'

'Oh, it's going to be like that, is it?' commented Harry with a mischievous grin as he beckoned Murray to come over. 'Wicked, wicked Cynthia, no wonder Mic calls you *Cyn*! What *have* you done?'

He gave a small, arch giggle. 'I was given to understand you were still blissfully happy with what HH Incorporated designed for you or is this some sort of latent revenge? A getting-your-own back so to speak? Ah Murray, meet Cynthia and Mic Sandford. This is Murray, Murray Harbourd our PR guru.'

'Murray Harbourd? But of course!' beamed Cynthia, 'The other man with the magic touch!' She gave a tinkling laugh before adding, 'Mic and I are having a glass of champagne but perhaps you young men would prefer something else?'

'I'd like a vodkatini, please' said Murray glancing up at the hovering waiter, 'with a slice of lime.'

'Make that two,' said Harry settling himself down on the banquette next to Cynthia while Murray placed himself in a chair alongside Mic.

'Tell me a bit more about Griselda Carter, please Cynthia. A quick résumé before we join our hosts.'

'Griselda will be putty in your hands, Harry dear!' laughed Cynthia. 'Think Zsa Zsa Gabor playing Shirley Temple and you've pretty much got the picture!'

'God!' said Harry with a grin.

God being exactly what Mic was also thinking, not about his wife's remark but about Harry. Feeling as if he's been struck my a mega bolt of lightning he went on mentally to say, Putty in your hands, Harry? Christ, in your hands I'd be having the biggest hard-on of the twenty first century! You're not only staggeringly handsome and a turn on, young man, you're dangerously beautiful!

Murray, instantly aware of Mic's reaction to Harry glanced warily at his friend giggling with Cynthia and obviously oblivious of the impression he'd just made. Turning to a dazed-looking Mic he added loudly, 'Sandford Holdings? I hear you're now adding textile manufacturing to your portfolio,' the comment breaking into Mic's reverie. 'Congratulations on your deal with Mumbata Textiles. Quite coup if I may say so.'

'How very well-informed you are, Murray,' said Mic with a false laugh, gratefully grabbing at the lifeline offered by the gently smiling young man, 'I can wager you a bet some of my own directors aren't even aware of *that* latest development.'

'Ah, but Mic I keep an eye out on everything and everyone,' laughed Murray, taking a sip of his vodkatini.

'Obviously,' smiled Mic, staring thoughtfully at the chunky, well-groomed young man for a few seconds, adding, 'Here's my card with a private business number. I'd appreciate you giving me a call in the morning. I've some thoughts on the Mumbata deal which I'd like to run past you. Dependant of course, on whether this is something you would be interested in discussing further?'

'Why, I'd be delighted to, Mic!' cried Murray, his face lighting up. 'Shall we say ten o'clock?'

'I'm sure ten would be fine, Murray,' responded Mic, smiling at the young man's enthusiasm. 'However, please call me around eight thirty on that number just to make sure.' He gave another laugh. 'Marjorie, my wet nurse, minder, jail keeper of a secretary is the only one with the keys to my schedules so if *she* says I can see you at ten, I'll look forward to seeing you then!' He glanced across to where Harry and Cynthia were still giggling away like a pair of naughty schoolgirls. 'Come on you two,' he said, 'I hate breaking into what ever you're discussing but it's time to gird our loins and face the Carters!'

'They're *that* grim?' cried Harry, giving Mic a coquettish grin.

Jesus Christ! Harry, thought Murray. There's no need to be so fucking madcap Maisie!

Christ, thought Mic. Oh Howard, dear Howard, despite all your makings up and promises I dread to say it but I think you may have just made your final exit.

'Terry! They're here!' shrieked Griselda rising up from where she and Terence had been sitting in the small reception area adjacent to the restaurant.

'My God, is that a levitating Christmas tree I see before me?' hissed Harry to Cynthia resulting in a sharp nudge in the ribs and a strangulated 'Stop it!' from the giggling woman.

'Cynthia! Mic!' Griselda, uttering another high-pitched shriek thrust herself forward to greet the guests, a beaming Terence hovering behind her. With exaggerated cries of 'Mwah! Mwah!' the large, ebullient woman vaguely kissed the two on their proffered cheeks before turning to a smiling Harry and Murray.

'And nobody, but *nobody* could be so naive as to *not* recognise *Harry Humphries!*' she chortled. 'I'm Griselda Carter and this is my hubby, Terry!' Still smiling broadly she turned to Murray. 'And you, of course, you oh so devilishly handsome young man, you, you are Murray Harbourd, the man who turns nothings into somethings and nobodies into somebodies! Boys! Call me Griselda and Terry is Terry! Now, may I suggest we go straight into dinner? Oh Cynthia, this is going to be *such* fun! Harry, your arm please!'

Like a stately galleon Griselda, in a full-length voluminous creation of emerald chiffon, enhanced by a pair of emerald and diamond pendant earrings (later referred to by Harry as a pair of 'fucking, dangling Faberge eggs!'), matching necklace, brooch, ring and several bracelets, sailed triumphantly into the lavish dining room, her arm firmly gripping the sleeve of Harry's brightly coloured bargello-patterned velvet jacket.

'So what did you think?' asked Harry as he and Murray sat sipping a late nightcap in their favourite Balans restaurant bar on Soho's 'gay alley,' Old Compton Street.

'More importantly, what did *you* think?' said Murray, completely flummoxed by Harry's apparent non-awareness of Mic's continous stares across the dinner table.

'I'm in love with Grizzle – don't laugh, M, that's *exactly* what I'm to call her! – and Terry is a doll, even though a bit of an odd-looking one!'

'*Doll*-ar, you mean!' laughed Murray. 'Lots and lots of lovely doll-ars, Euros, pounds – you name it, he's got it! I checked him out as soon as Suze told me who our hosts were.'

'Whatever! Anyway, Grizzle is going to be fun, fabulous and spend a fucking fortune! Christ, one of those bracelets alone must be worth a queen's ransom.'

'Talking of which?'

'Yes, I'm all ears even though I haven't got Grizzles' earrings – yet!'

'Not you, you idiot! The other queen at dinner, Mic Sandord! Jesus, if ever I saw someone pierced by Cupid's little poisonous dart it was Mr Sandford tonight!'

'Mic Sandford's not gay!'

'And the Queen of England is really a man! C'mon H, the guy's as gay as a Gay Pride parade! Still waters run deep and let me tell you my friend, Mic Sandford is deep, very deep!'

'Well tough shit because Harry Humphries is spoken for! In fact Harry Humphries has never, ever been so in love before, now and forever!'

'Ah yes, the wondrous Wandsworth. Susie told me briefly about your sluttish cavorting in *Bella Italia*!' Murray gave a mischievous giggle. 'Honestly H, you're already successful enough without having to *prostitute* that much used, abused and exhausted frame to seal a deal!'

'Ha! Look whose talking! Talk about the pot calling the kettle pink! If Sandford *is* gay as you so vehemently tell me, why oh why then was he giving *you* the eye and whispering sweet nothings into your shell-like as well as *giving you his card*? So don't talk to little *moi* about prostituting oneself to get a deal!'

'I think it's time for two more Amarettos,' said Murray gesturing towards the barman. 'For your information Harold, my sweet, Mic Sandford and I have a bona fide business deal to discuss whereas, if he could have had his wicked way this evening, he'd have much preferred discussing a *boner fiddle* deal with you!'

'So, can I help if I'm so devastatingly alluring?' camped Harry,

'Rhymes with whoring!' came Murray's quick riposte.

'Well, compared to William Wandsworth, Sandford's simply boring!' Harry snapped back.

'Two artists together? Two artists together and all that artistic temperament?' laughed Murray picking up his fresh Amaretto. 'I can just see it now, the two of you living in castellated conflict rather like those other two old artist perves, Gauguin and and Van Gogh. It wouldn't surprise me if, in a year or two I heard you'd cut off your ear in a fit of queeny pique – Faberge earring et al! – and posted it to your artist lover!' He gave another laugh. 'Or being a tad *less* flamboyant, your cock!'

'Not in a million years,' said Harry smugly. 'This is for keeps.' He let out a snigger.

'What?'

'You saying me cutting off my cock, that's what.'

'Wouldn't cost much postage-wise,' giggled Murray. 'You'd simply place in a small jiffy bag and stamp it, that's all! No special delivery as it'd easily fit through any post flap!'

'Very funny, Murray Harbourd,' sniped back Harry. 'However,' he continued, a smug expression forming on his face, 'If it was to be the other way round, *William's cock* would require a whole FEDEX van and *at least* two weightlifters to deliver the parcel!'

'You're joking? Tell me you're joking?'

'MH,' said Harry letting out a theatrical, exasperated sigh. 'How long have we known each other? Three, four years? Well, in all our devoted time together the one thing I have never, *ever* joked about is the size of someone's cock!'

'So it's *forever* William and *farewell* Sandford?'

'Farewell Sandford? Why, Mr Harbourd,' camped Harry going into his Scarlet O'Hara mode, 'I nevah, evah sai-yed *Hello* Sandford!'

'I wouldn't bet on it,' murmured Murray, staring reflectively into his drink. 'I wouldn't be on it at all.'

'Oh no?' Draining his glass Harry gestured for another two Amarettos. 'Rest assured, dearest, you're now looking at the future Mrs William Wandsworth, queen of the Castle – or *castello* – and queen of all she surveys!' Giving Murray a supercilious look Harry couldn't resist the final barbed dig. '*Mary*!'

Unfazed Murray relied calmly, 'That's exactly what another Mary said.'

'Another Mary?'

'Yep, Mary Queen of Scots, before she lost her head.'

'She didn't *lose* her head, well not in my way!' Harry gave a definitely drunken snort. 'Although she may have attempted to *give* head in *my* way!' With another snort he added, 'Anyway, the silly bitch was simply executed.'

'OK! OK! But having her head chopped off was a definite way of *losing* it I would have thought!' sniggered Murray.

By this time the two young men were obviously drunk, Harry more so than Murray, and beginning to slur his words.

'OK, OK! Shame thing!' slurred Harry falling into Murray's repetitive routine.

'Shame thing? From the moment you're sitting on your throne – oh, pardon me, that should have been as soon as you're sitting on *your* fuck hole – beware fickle wandering *Willy* doesn't find another!'

'Another fuck hole?' Harry have Murray a look of haughty disdain. 'Jealousy is sush a very sad thing amongst the lonely and forlorn. So is envy.' Tut-tutting Harry swallowed his newly replenished drink before turning blearily to smirking friend. 'An' for all your poisonous predishuns and wishing me ill you may nowsh buy me anusha Amaretto.'

'Anusha Amaretto?' grinned Harry imitating Harry. 'I'll buy yoush a whole fucking farewelsh bottle!'

CHAPTER 9:

'Ah, you must be Mr Harbourd. Mr Mic will only be a few minutes.' The plump, grey-haired motherly-looking woman dressed in a dark navy suit with a dazzling white blouse gave Murray a warm smile as she rose from her desk, gesturing towards a seating area comprising of a sofa and two comfortable-looking armchairs. 'I'm so sorry, I had to change the time of your meeting to twelve noon,' she continued, 'but, typical of Mr Mic, he had quite forgotten a longstanding meeting with one our retiring sales reps, something he simply had to do.'

She gave Murray another warm smile. 'May I get you something to drink? Coffee? A soft drink?' Still smiling she added, 'I can even offer you a cup of proper tea if you'd prefer as I've just made myself a fresh pot.'

'A cup of tea would be great,' said Murray having already downed several cups of strong black coffee, his head still throbbing from the after effects of the previous night's endless Amarettos.

'Milk or lemon?'

'Lemon, please.'

'I won't be a moment,' said the woman, 'meanwhile Mr Mic asked to let you have this while you wait.' She handed Murray a slim black folder. 'I'm Mrs Wells, Marjorie Wells but everybody calls me Marge apart from Mr Mic.' Giving a nod towards a large, closed panelled door which Murray assumed must be Mic's office, she added with an even bigger smile, '*He* refers to me as Argy or Argy-Bargy, depending on what he wants!'

'Oh,' said Murray, 'Err … thank you err… Marge. In the meantime I'll have a look at this.' With a vague wave of the folder he made his way over to the seating area.

'Argy Bargy?' Murray muttered with a grin, 'What's Mic on about? She more everyone's favourite aunt as opposed to a minder or jail keeper!'

Seating himself in one of the wide armchairs Murray opened the folder. Taking out the several printed sheets he laid these out in a row on the small coffee table in front of him. While some of the sheets contained nothing but printed information regarding Mumbata Textiles, others showed photographs of majestic, colourful jewel-like fabrics, the likes of which Murray had never seen before. But these are fantastic, he thought, and I can honestly say I've never seen such incredible designs and colours mixed and matched so brilliantly. Talk about unique. For a moment his thinking was interrupted by Marge placing a small silver tray carrying a cup of tea, a small plate with slices of lemon plus a silver bowl of sugar cubes along with a pair of delicate silver tongs, onto one of the small side tables (Murray having left no clear space on the coffee table).

'Thank you Marge,' murmured Murray, barely glancing up from the page he was reading. Absentmindedly reaching for the cup he took a small sip before setting it down again, his mind totally mesmerised by the sheets in front of him.

'Murray! You made it!' said the warm, rich baritone. 'Sorry to have kept you waiting but I see Argy's been mothering you!'

'Good morning, Mic!' smiled Murray rising to his feet while eyeing the big man appreciatively. Good looking bugger, he thought again taking in the immaculate light grey suit, the dazzling white shirt all sartorially set off by a gold and terracotta patterned Gucci tie with complimentary pocket handkerchief. Even better bloody looking second time round!

Chunky, hunky and very butch, thought Mic. Shorter than I remember though. Hmm, I wonder if he and Harry are lovers?

'Argy,' said Mic turning to the comfy woman now back behind her desk, her eyes concentrating on one of two computers. Marge looked up at the mention of her nickname, a small smile playing on her lips. 'Yes, Mr Mic?'

'As its gone noon I'm sure Mr Harbourd would prefer something more substantial than Earl Grey! Am I not right, Murray?'

''Well, while the tea was delicious,' – he gave Marge one of his most charming grins – 'I wouldn't say no to something a bit more fortifying.' Looking again at Mic he gave a hollow laugh. 'Harry and I simply could not resist dropping into a favourite haunt of ours with one nightcap ending up in several nightcaps too many!'

'I'm sure one of Argy's White Bears will do wonders for your err… affliction?' Mic gave a deep, rumbling laugh. 'May we have two of your lethal potions, please Argy?'

'But of course Mr Mic. I'll bring them through.'

'Murray?' said Mic gesturing to the open door of his office.

Following the big man Murray found himself inside a large, airy office overlooking a verdant green St James's Park.

'Fabulous room, Mic,' he said, 'and what a fantastic view over the park.' He gave the panelled room a quick look of approval. 'Don't tell me,' he added, taking a few steps forward and placing himself in front of a large, abstract canvas, 'you actually *own* a Helen Steele? But this is brilliant!'

'You know her work?' questioned Mic, his admiration for the young man's astuteness and general awareness growing by the minute. 'I must say Murray, I am most impressed.' He gave a chuckle. 'Last night you took me completely by surprise knowing about my company and its recent affiliation with Mumbata Textiles. Now you walk into my office and not only do you immediately home in onto my favourite paintings but you recognise the artist! Incredible!'

Before Murray could answer Marge bustled in carrying a tray holding two silver goblets, a silver flask and an ice bucket containing an already-open bottle of Veuve Cliquot Black Label champagne.

'Two White Bears already poured and champagne and iced vodka should you require a refill,' she beamed. She looked at Mic. 'Do you wish me to do anything about lunch, Mr Mic?' Giving Murray a quick glance she added, 'Your next appointment isn't until four.'

'Lunch? I hadn't really thought about it, other things on my mind,' murmured Mic. He looked at Murray. 'Unless you're free Murray and would care to join me?'

'Like you Mic, my next meeting is also at four, with Harry actually at his studio up by Chelsea Harbour. I have stacks of time and lunch sounds great!'

'Do you like oysters?'

'One of my passions!'

'A table for two at Wilton's at one o'clock, please Argy.' Mic gave Murray a warm smile. 'What we start to discuss here we can continue over a dozen of Whitstable's finest.'

Having handed Mic and Murray a chilled, moisture-beaded goblet each Marge made her exit softly closing the door behind her.

'Mumbata Textiles and Sandford Holdings,' said Mic sitting himself down on one of the chairs surrounding a small oval boardroom table positioned at one end of the spacious office and gesturing to a chair opposite. 'Mumbata Textiles,' he repeated, staring directly at the young man. 'I must explain Murray textiles are a totally new field for us.' He gave a small smile. 'I couldn't help but notice you were so engrossed in the folder you appeared oblivious to me ushering out my earlier visitor!'

Murray gave a nod. 'Quite a track record.'

'Good,' said Mic, his smile growing. 'As you say, quite a track record. The sky's the limit with what they produce and what they *could* produce. Let me explain further. While I see this as a new interest for Sandford Industries it is really more of a pet project for myself. Call me selfish but the rest of the business is so cut and dried and we have our fingers in so many pies, so to speak, and all managed by a handpicked team all personally groomed by yours truly here.' Mic took a long sip from his goblet before adding somewhat ruefully, 'At times I simply feel I'm sitting here twiddling my thumbs while everyone else is buzzing about like workers in a hive.'

'Hardly!' laughed Murray thinking, You said it mate! The Queen Bee in *his* hive, but saying, 'At the end of the day there is only *one* Mic Sandford!'

'Thank you, but the one Mic Sandford, as you've just said, feels now's the time to have a bit of fun. Oh, please for one minute think I don't enjoy being head of a company which I've so painstakingly built up over the years but I need a break, a complete new challenge as if it were.' He took another prolonged sip. 'One of these new challenges is to launch a revolutionary range of new fabrics, fabrics the richness and likes of which the design world has not seen for some time. Oh I know there are endless, hallowed names around attached to endless existing fabric houses, but why not a *new* name with a *new,* as never-seen-before, spectacular promotion?' Mic paused, giving a seemingly impassive Murray an anxious look.

'And you want Harry Humphries Incorporated to be part of this?' said Murray, thinking, Christ, this guy doesn't waste anytime when it comes to getting something he wants.

'What made you say that?' said Mic, a startled expression on his handsome, craggy face.

'Mic, it's obvious. Harry designed your house; you *know* his work and furthermore it couldn't have been more fortuitous you meeting Harry last night, plus the fact he's about to redesign the house of someone who just happens to be – apart from Mumbata Textiles – the latest addition to the ever-growing Sandford portfolio!' Murray gave a light laugh. 'Am I right in saying meeting Harry planted the seed (Fuck! Did I have to use *that* phraseology?) as to what you could actually *do* with Mumbata? I was quick to note the company already has a worldwide distribution but with an exclusive, new Harry Humphries range it could be final the gilding of the lily – or lotus blossom – as if it were.'

'That makes it three,' said Mic, 'three things you've stunned me with, young Murray. Knowing about Mumbata, knowing about Helen Steele and now putting two and two together regarding Harry Humphries Incorporated. Amazing intuition; absolutely amazing.' Taking hold of Murray's empty goblet he poured in a generous portion of vodka topped up with champagne. 'What I'd like you to do Murray is get together a proposal for us to present to Harry. I'm prepared to give you a free rein on this. It will, of course, involve the three of us paying a visit to the factory in India; Calcutta to be exact.'

He took a sip of his drink. 'If you agree to what I am proposing, I'd like Murray Harbourd Associates to handle the whole promotion from the very start. We can even take a separate showroom within that fabulous Chelsea Design Centre itself. A Harry Humphries Textiles sort of thing. What do you say?'

'And you're prepared to do all of this for *Harry*?' questioned a stunned Murray.

'All for Harry? What exactly do you mean by that remark?' snapped back Mic, his face flushing. 'It's me as well as Sandford Holdings I'm talking about!'

Murray stared unwaveringly at the red-faced man. 'Mic,' he said softly, 'if we're going to be working together – which I most certainly hope we are – can we start with a clean slate, please? I saw your reaction on meeting Harry last night – no, please let me go on – and I'm sure he'll be more than delighted to take you up on your offer. In fact, he'll grab at it! However, I do know him almost better than I know myself. He'll be brilliant as a business partner, or associate, but no more.'

Completely stunned by Murray's frankness Mic simply sat staring back at the still gently smiling young man before saying in an icy tone, 'Anything else Murray? Anything else I should perhaps know?'

'Yes Mic, something else you should definitely *know*! Harry's about to embark on a disastrous love affair; an affair that can only end in tears. However, H is besotted – apparently they both are – but I can't see any of Harry's relationships ever bearing the mantle "long term." Particularly when two such volatile personalities are involved.'

'Harry volatile?'

'Harry volatile? Mic, dear Mic, his temperamental blow ups would put an erupting volcano to shame!'

'And this other man?' whispered Mic, his face now pale.

'A fellow artist, so to speak, also known for his temperamental tantrums!'

'Well at least I know it can't be the lovely Helen Steele,' said Mic letting out a hollow laugh. Giving Murray a furtive look, he asked softly, 'Was my reaction to Harry that obvious?'

'Not to a straight man,' smiled Murray, adding softly, 'I know you're gay, Mic.'

'Yes, I am,' said Mic without any show of defiance. 'As you said Murray, a clean slate. Although happily married I also have an on, off relationship and have had so for some years.'

'Howard Hanover, the actor,' said Murray, causing Mic to visibly start.

'Christ Murray Harbourd! Is there *anything* you don't know?'

'Put it this way, Mic. I make it my business to know and after Argy, I mean Marge, gave me the later time for our meeting I put this to good use and did some sleuthing. I also know about your wife and Natalie Vine.'

'Jesus Christ!' exploded Mic. 'Enough! How the *hell* could you possibly know about that?'

'Easy,' said Murray with a soothing smile. 'Nat's a great friend. I've known about the mysterious Cynthia for some time but it was only when I mentioned you to Natalie in one of our daily phone catch-ups earlier this morning I got the whole story; hence knowing about Howard.'

'You *know* Natalie? But this is incredible!'

'Not only do I know her Mic, we've also got a lunch date scheduled for next week when she's back from Ireland. She's presently working on a film over there.'

'Good God,' muttered Mic. He pointed at Murray's goblet. 'I'm definitely having a refill! What about you?'

'Please.'

Mic gave a smile. 'Well, it certainly seems to be my day for being continually stunned by Mr Murray Harbourd; astrologer, voodooist and witchdoctor supreme! So, you may as well stun me once more before we go to lunch, please tell me the name of this mysterious artist who just happens to have stolen Harry's heart.'

'Does the name William Wandsworth ring any bells?'

'William Wandsworth?' exclaimed Mic his expression one of growing confusion. 'Yes, it most certainly does. Why?'

'Oh dear,' said Murray, a mischievous grin appearing on his handsome face. 'Obviously the name rings quite a few bells! Perhaps it's your turn to stun *me,* Mic!'

'William Wandsworth – or one of his paintings – is being delivered to the house this very afternoon. By tonight William Wandsworth will be waiting to greet me from the very noticeable position above the fireplace in my study!'

'Harry – or perhaps that should that be Houston – we have a problem!' grinned Murray bouncing into Harry's studio.

'And good afternoon to you too, fair Murray!' came Harry's smiling reply. He looked up from the display table where he was concentrating on assembling a selection of fabric cuttings in readiness for fixing them onto a presentation board. 'Don' tell me Mic the Slick made a pass at you and you simply *had* to succumb?'

'More than that! Much more than that! Mic the Slick – as I told you – not only has the hots for your delicate, well-worn body but he wants to possess you, body *and* soul!'

'Oh? And how has Murray Harbourd, he who can out-oracle the Oracle at Delphi, come to such an earth shattering – and totally ridiculous – assumption?'

'He not only told me, *dear,* but he's determined to woo and win you over and is quite prepared to pay a queen's ransom in his efforts to do so!'

'A *queen's* ransom you say?' Harry gave his friend a camp look, raising an eyebrow and pursing his lips. 'Hadn't you better explain,' he added before turning his attention back to the fabric board. Placing two pieces side by side Harry gave the layout a final scrutiny before muttering, 'Bloody marvellous, Humphries, bloody fucking marvellous!' Turning again to Murray he gave a mischievous smile. 'Right, oh ye bearer of ill-tidings, you were saying something about how the divine HH is about to be vilely abused and spiritually possessed! Let's go back into my orifice and you can tell me all about it.' Harry glanced down at his watch. 'Just after four! La! How time flies when one's being a creative genius. I take it you've had lunch?'

'Wilton's in Jermyn Street. With your nemesis!'

'*Nemesis*? Tut tut, sir! I think – for once – the Oracle at Delphi is talking undiluted shit!' Harry shook his head in mock disdain, his blond locks tumbling down across his forehead. 'And while my misguided PR continues to live the louche life this poor about-to-be both mentally and physically raped soul has been slaving away all day and, apart from Italy's finest, hasn't had a morsel – no snide comment, per-lease! – pass his lips.'

Walking past Susie's empty desk he gave a brief nod. 'Furthermore, madam and her madam are seeing some quack or visiting some dubious clinic with regard to having a *child*, would you believe? Hence more neglected *moi.'*

'Poor neglected *moi*?' said Harry making his way into the kitchenette. 'I very much doubt it!' There was a momentary pause before he called out. 'Smoked salmon sandwiches, chicken sandwiches and a whole Key Lime pie here in the fridge? Yes, I can see Susie in all the excitement of having her ovaries interfered with has quite overlooked her master's needs!'

'Isn't she a *doll*!' cooed Harry, coming up to behind Murray and giving him a light kiss on the neck. 'Maybe I *will* donate some of my sacred sperm towards her daddy wank!'

'Christ! A combination of you and Susie! Talk about a double drag infant!' Murray turned to look at his friend. 'You are joking, of course?'

'Oh, I don't know … could be rather fun to become a daddy without actually having to perform the disgusting deed!'

'Jesus Humphries, at times …' leaving his sentence unfinished Murray placed the three cling film covered plates on the worktop before reaching back into the fridge for a bottle of Pinot Grigio. 'C'mon, I'm sure after you-know-who you can manage a mere three! I'll bring the wine and a couple of glasses and whilst you sit and guzzle in your abode I shall reveal all!'

'He wants to do all this for the sake of glamorous, irresistible *moi*?' camped Harry a few moments later. 'Even though the poor man will never, ever, have the extra glorious sensation of romancing the lovely Harry Humphries from behind?'

'Don't kid yourself, dearest; he's not only planning romancing you from behind, he's planning to *completely* and utterly romance you, full stop! No holds barred and certainly it's to be a case of "on your bike, William Wandsworth!"'

'La! The power of infatuation!' cried Harry, 'but how *weak* compared to the power of *love*!' He took a sip of wine. 'Oh, for God's sake M, don't stand there smirking at this much desired persona! Plonk yourself down on your much desired, delicious butt – who *are* you fucking at the moment out of interest? – so that you may continue to entertain me even more with these inane and insane fantasies of Mr – "you can look but you can't touch!" – Sandford.'

Murray sat staring at Harry with a bemused expression before saying, 'Forgetting the fantasies for a second perhaps you would deign to tell me what you think, Miss Temptress supreme? Not only are you about to become the belle of Italy but, if you play your cards right, also the star of India!'

'Although you may inadvertently be making your lovely business associate *sound* like some downmarket, cheap curry joint, he forgives you and therefore says as they do in Calcutta – or so I'm told – "velly bloody good show, Mr Mullay! Let's bloody vell go for it!"'

'And Willaim Wandsworth?' Murray glanced down at his watch, murmuring, 'Ah yes, the clash of the Titans should be taking place in approximately an hour's time.'

'Clash of the Titans? Now what are you on about, oh odious oracle?'

'Mic Sandford and William Wandsworth, together, in a very clandestine meeting this very evening!'

'Pull the other one!'

'Not quite person to person, Harry sweetness! More person to painting.'

'Now I *am* confused.'

'Don't be. The lovely Cynthia has just bought macho Mic a William Wandsworth painting, one the unknowing man has been coveting for a time! It's probably being *hung* in his study at home as we speak!'

'But that's bizarre!'

'Not as bizarre as the sordid little drama you're about to be starring in if you take the two of these on, Juliet! Shylock Sandford's *also* going to be demanding his pound of flesh and probably sooner than later! Seriously H, I wouldn't lead the guy on, if I were you. Best to say no; nip the contract in the bud before it turns into an ugly blossom.'

'How can a blossom ever be ugly?' camped Harry.

'Think of the *Venus Fly Trap* for one! A lovely blossom as you say – rather like yourself – but nasty, very nasty!'

'Well, I'm not a fly trap … '

'Oh no?' Murray let out a yelp, 'Bloody fly *and* zipper trap if you ask me!'

'I repeat, I am *not* a fly trap – nor any other sort of trap for that matter,' said Harry with a sniff. 'Simply a heavenly flower.'

'That's what worries me.'

'What?'

'The "heavenly" bit!'

'Very funny, Murray dear!' Harry gave a mischievous giggle. 'I can't *wait* to tell William about his rival when we meet on Saturday.'

'Harry, being seriously serious for a second; don't. Don't mention Mic Sandford and the Mumbata deal. For once in your technicoloured life, listen to your friend. Sandford's deal is mega, with more money to be made than you and I have ever dreamed of. Keep the whole matter under your hairnet until things are up and running and then – but only then – perhaps all can be divulged. But until I give you the green light, the go ahead, promise me you'll keep your mouth shut!'

'Surely you mean my *Venus* mouth trap?' asked Harry with a grin. 'But that's so very, very cruel! How on earth will I be expected to blow William if my luscious lips are sealed?'

'Silly cunt!' laughed Murray. 'You know exactly what I mean!'

'On your foreskin I promise!' smiled Harry. He sat for a moment, sipping his wine while staring thoughtfully at his friend before saying softly, 'Now Murray Harbourd, my friend, enough about me; it's time to talk about *you*!' He shook his blond head in mock despair. 'Yes, you, and what are we going to do about *you*! Here I am, feted and desired by so many while you, like poor Cinders, remain sitting all on your solitary by the hearth!'

'No, dear, *you're* Cinderella with two potentially dangerous *suitors* as opposed to two ugly step-sisters. Mark my words!'

'Well, if I'm to be Cinderella it'll be a Cinderella with a difference in that I don't *need* a Prince Charming!' Harry gave a light laugh in an attempt to defuse the slight frisson in the air. 'Maybe I'll let *you* have my *third* would-be Prince Charming!'

'Thanks a lot!' laughed Murray. 'However you seem to have overlooked the fact I already *have* a devoted fairy godmother by the name of Lenny Freed loving and looking after me!' He gave another laugh. 'But out of sheer curiosity – and I know you're just dying to tell me! – if I may be so ignorant as to ask, just who is this mysterious princeling of yours?'

Widening his lightly out-lined blue eyes Harry, in his best Scarlet O'Hara voice girlishly cried, 'Why, Mistah Murray! I know the veray man' an' I do declare I'ma seein' him next week for ah meetin'!'

'Oh yes, Miss O'Horror,' replied Murray with a grin. 'And who may this answer to Wrecked Butler be?'

'Why, Mistah Murray, the cutest lil' honey pot you evah will see!'

'Oh?'

'Yais, Mistah Murray! I'ma talkin' about the boy wonder of all time. Mastah Tommy Tyler!'

'Harry dear, I appreciate last week I said I'd be working on the Three Talents; a designer, a singer and a painter and, if it's still in the running, Sandford Holdings which will again come under the designer label, but I have never, nor will I ever, mix business with pleasure – not even for a one night stand – unlike *some* I know! So you can forget any attempt to throw Tommy Tyler into my arms, or vice versa! He's a client. End of story'

'Wanna bet?'

'I don't bet,' smiled Murray.

'I'm scheduled to see Tommy next week along with Alan to go through some preliminary plans. We'll be meeting at the new property.' Harry gave a light laugh. 'Poor Alan's been holed up on the site for the past few days having even set up a makeshift office there, as if it were, and I've invited Tommy to lunch afterwards. As the company's PR I feel it very necessary for you to be there and meet the guy.'

'Is that an order, *boss*?'

'No, merely a suggestion, Murray dear! After all you'll have to meet the second of your three talents sooner or later.'

'And this is when?'

'Next Thursday.'

'Christ, everything seems to be revolving around a fucking Thurdsay.'

'*Thursday's Child Has Far To Go,*' simpered Harry, quoting from the children's nursery rhyme.

'Do shut up, partner dear!' Murray checked his mobile before punching in the details. 'And where is this Cupid's luncheon taking place?'

'The Ivy, where else?'

'Hmm, knowing you Harry Humphries, it may very well end up the Poison Ivy.'

'Then you'll have no alterative dearest but to scratch the itching!'

CHAPTER 10:

'What time's your fuck bag due in at Petworth?' sniggered Paul.

'Please, stunted one, he's not my fuck bag, he's my *luck* bag,' laughed William, patting Rufus, the pug, dozing fitfully on his massive lap. 'Noon, Skids is collecting him and, if I'm not mistaken, I heard Skids leaving a few minutes ago.'

'That should make the poor man turn tail and take the next train back to London!' chortled Nelson. 'Christ, imagine stepping down onto the platform and seeing *that*?'

'Perhaps this Harry creature will not see him and *step* on him instead!' cackled Paul. 'What a welcome; a massive dump of shit on your shoe!'

'Enough!' chided William, trying to keep a straight face. 'Remember, you're on your best behaviour otherwise it's the cellar for you until Harry leaves. Besides, there is method in my madness, in my sending Skids. You *did* say wanted a "weekend with a difference" didn't you? Well, perhaps if I feel you really deserve it, you most probably will!'

'We already *lurve* your thrust and parry Harry even though we've still to meet him, don't we Paulie?' said Nelson, winking at his sibling.

'Of course we do,' sniggered Paul. '*Lurve* him to bits!'

'Talking of which …?' questioned William.

'Wednesday,' said Nelson.

'Is it going to hurt?' questioned Paul.

'There is no gain without pain,' remarked William in his best, philosophical manner.

Harry, holding a holdall – and muttering 'talk about déjà vu' – stepped down off the train onto the platform of the small country station. Expecting to see William he completely ignored the solitary, sinewy tramp-like figure standing alongside the exit.

'Mr Humphries?' questioned the man in a low, rasping voice. 'Mark Elliot, Mr Wandsworth's estate manager.'

'Oh,' said Harry looking aghast at the tall grubby man dressed in an old torn, badly stained tweed jacket and a pair of filthy, very worn jeans, his thin, sallow face framed by a few locks of lank, greasy strands of hair poking out from beneath an equally stained cloth cap. 'Oh.' He said again, his handsome face wrinkling in distaste on catching a sudden strong whiff of shit.

'Can I take you bag, sir?' rasped Elliot reaching out with a large grubby hand to take the holdall.

'Err … thank you,' murmured Harry glancing around the pristine platform for the source of the ever-strengthening stench.

'The car's outside,' snivelled Elliot, wiping his runny nose on the back of his huge hand before taking an extra deep sniff. 'Mr William sends his apologies for not meeting you himself, sir,' he added, 'but there's been an emergency.'

'Oh?' said Harry following the shambling man over towards a gleaming, dark green Range Rover, 'How very inconvenient.' Hmm, he thought, not exactly one of the other three devious daughters but I suppose I really can't complain. Climbing up onto the high passenger seat (he had given a grimace on seeing Elliot open the front passenger door for him and not one at the back) Harry was quick to change his mind. Jesus, it's this bloody man stinking the place out! Nothing else! Without hesitating Harry pressed the button to fully lower the side window.

'Your seat belt, sir' said Elliot turning to Harry.

And his breath? Christ William, if this is your idea of a joke it's well and truly backfired – or back farted – take your pick!

By the time the Range Rover finally drew to a halt in front of the massive red-painted barn it was taking Harry all of his willpower not to throw up, the foetid stench inside the vehicle now unbearable. Not waiting for Elliot to fully stop Harry pushed open the door, gagging and gasping as he staggered out onto the gravelled forecourt. Taking several deep, grateful gulps of fresh air he glared towards the giant approaching figure.

'Harry! You made it! Welcome to the Barnyard!' boomed William, uncannily reminiscent to the greeting in Genoa. 'Pleasant journey?'

'Jesus, William!' snapped Harry. 'Barnyard being the operative word! What the *fuck* do you mean by sending that giant stinking *cesspit* to collect me? In fact, what I'd like you to immediately do – no, I *insist* you do – is ring for a fucking taxi! I take it there is such a thing as a taxi service operating in this fucking, foetid fucking area?' He paused, taking another deep breath of fresh air before furiously continuing. 'I'm telling you now, William bloody Wandsworth,' he gasped, glaring at William who stood standing looking stunned by his wild-eyed tirade, 'I have no intention, no intention *whatsoever,* staying here a moment longer than I have to! I've never been so bloody insulted in my whole fucking life!'

'Harry, Harry, calm down,' said William soothingly. 'Look, I'm sorry and I apologise. If Mark has somehow offended you ...'

'*Offended me*? The fucking, stinking bastard has almost *gassed* me! That poor excuse of humanity, that ... that ... why, that rancid, fucking cunt would have put anything in bloody Auschwitz to shame! No William, there's no excuse! I want a taxi, please. Now!'

'Harry, dear Harry, it's me, William, you lover, and I'm sorry. What more can I say? Please forgive me as I do so want this weekend to be special...'

'Oh, it's special alright,' snarled Harry. 'Only in *your* case "special" is spelt s-h-i-t!'

'I do think you're overreacting ... ' began William, hi composure beginning to crumble.

'*Overreacting*?' screamed Harry, 'You don't know what me overeating is! Jesus Christ,' he muttered his eyes caught by a sudden movement in the open doorway behind William. 'Oh Jesus,' he muttered again.

Turning to where Elliot had left his holdall alongside the Range Rover before slinking out of sight, Harry quickly snatched up the small Louis Vuitton bag. 'Fuck you, Wandsworth!' he spat. 'Or better still, go fuck those two grotesque troglodytes gawking behind you! I've heard it's something else you do besides turning out that shit – yes, shit certainly seems to be the *real* William Wansworth's forte – you call art! Oh no! No raised fists, William!' cried Harry, unflinching at the big man's sudden movement. 'For I can assure you, if you so much as even *touch* me *ever bloody again,* you'll have the biggest lawsuit against you imaginable and I will make sure you and you puny talents are completely and utterly destroyed.'

Glaring up at the heavily breathing, wild-eyed giant, Harry couldn't resist adding in his campest tone and manner, 'How many miles to London, *Prick*?' before turning on his heel and storming back down the driveway.

'What do we do now?' asked Paul shuffling up to William and reaching out for his still-clenched hand.

'Leave the little bastard for a while. He'll soon simmer down.' William patted the dwarf gently on his misshapen head. 'Then I'll simply go and fetch him and make it up to him like he's never experienced "making up" before!'

'And us? He was very, very nasty about us?'

'Later Paulie, later; let me deal with Miss Hysteria Humphries first.'

Bastard! Filthy, fucking, dirty bastard! Harry fumed, striding furiously down the narrow country road. Filthy, fucking freak! Wiping his teary eyes with the back of his free hand he said out loud, 'Murray, you were right. Fuck it, Murray! You're *always* right and I, as usual, was fucking wrong! Oh well, *c'est la vie*! One door closes – particularly one to a shit house! – while another opens. So Murray, it's *Hello, Mr Sandford* after all! Oh shit!'

Harry having stopped midstride, stood listening. 'Fuck!The cunt commeth,' he muttered on hearing the sound of an approaching motor. 'That's a sports car for sure. Well, fuck you *Lear*-y!' With a quick leap Harry plunged into the dense undergrowth flanking the road. Crouching behind a clump of thick foliage he peered cautiously through the branches as a grim-faced William roared past in a gleaming red Maserati, his eyes fixed solidly on the narrow road ahead.

For the first time in his life Harry found himself genuinely afraid. Jesus, Humphries! he thought. Just what have you, or worse, could have gotten yourself into? Reaching for his mobile he punched in Murray's number. 'Answer, M,' he muttered 'For God's sake answer … '

A rustling sound behind him caused Harry to swing round, his eyes wide in genuine terror.

'Are you alright, young man?' asked a concerned voice coming from behind some nearby bushes.

'Err … no. Who are you?' asked Harry in a quavering voice, cowering from the dark, approaching figure but relaxing when a panting spaniel bounded up to him and started licking him furiously on one of his clenched fists.

'Well certainly not the person or persons you're so obviously avoiding,' said the speaker coming into full view, adding 'Borgi! Leave the gentleman alone!'

'Oh err … Borgi can lick away,' said Harry smiling with relief and patting the slobbering dog on the head. He gave the man smiling down at him a wan smile. 'I'm just so pleased it's him and you.'

'I'm a local and Borgi and self were just having our usual short break,' said the burly man. 'I own the pub you may or may not have seen about a mile up the road from here.' He gave Harry an anxious look. 'Do you think you could stand up now? You look scared to death crouching down there.'

'Sorry,' said Harry pulling himself to his feet. Stepping forward he held out his hand. 'Harry, Harry Humphries.'

'Dave, Dave Mosten.

'Mr Mosten, if you will kindly escort me to your pub and let me ring for a taxi, I'll be eternally grateful.'

'A taxi to fetch and take you back to Petworth I presume? To the station?'

'No. To London.'

'London? I'll have to warn you Mr Humphries, the cost – as opposed to the train – will be exorbitant.'

'Exorbitant? Oh no, Mr Mosten! Let me assure you my life's worth much more to me than the cost of any taxi fare to London!'

Mosten gave Harry a long, quizzical look. 'Something has really scared the hell out of you, hasn't it, young Harry?' adding, 'Well, relax. With the fearsome Borgi and me you're quite safe.' Leading the way back to the road the big man glanced back at Harry. 'Anything else I should know?'

'Yes,' said Harry, 'if a red Maserati happens to come along I'm back in the bushes and you haven't seen me!'

'Ah,' said Mosten. 'Wandsworth up to his old tricks again. No wonder you're in such a state! C'mon then, Harry. Let's get you to the pub and get you on your way to London. I'll give Gerry Marsden, the owner of the mini-cab company in our village a call and make all the arrangements while you sit and have a much-needed drink with Janet, my other half.'

'And then what happened?' questioned Murray, his face agog.

'Dave the rave Mosten, my knight in shining armour, escorted me back to his pub but not, may I add, without incident!'

'What do you mean? What do you mean "without incident"?'

'In that fucking Wandsworth had to reappear, didn't he? Roaring up the road, his face – or what you could see of it behind that filthy fungal growth – almost as black with fury as his beard. Screeching to a halt he bellowed out at Dave, asking if he'd seen a stranger walking along the road to which Dave played gloriously dumb saying, apart from William, not another living soul!'

'And where were you?'

'Doing what that filthy handyman Elliot seems to never stop doing! But only in theory so to speak!'

'Shitting yourself?'

'Mentally, not physically, behind a clump of bushes!'

'And this wondrous Dave, his comment "Wandsworth up to his old tricks again." Did he ever get a chance to explain that?'

'Only to the extent of saying William was a bit of an enigma, didn't fraternize with anyone locally but kept to himself and his household of freaks; no doubt referring to the dwarfs and the likes of Elliot.' Harry gave a grim smile. 'The dwarfs … Jesus, although I only caught a glimpse of one, Disney you're forgiven!'

'And the so-called driver?'

'You mean Elliot, aka the shit heap? Christ knows where he fits in! Another thing; Dave mentioned frequent helicopter flights. Wandsworth has never mentioned anything about a helicopter.'

'What I find confusing,' said Murray, toying with the stem of his wine glass (Harry, having finally got hold of Murray had the taxi driver drop him off at Murray's flat), 'is why Wandsworth should have sent that creature to meet you off the train? Surely he must have anticipated your reaction, though perhaps not so dramatically?'

'Tell me about it! I've been trying to work that one out all the way back to bloody London!' sniffed Harry. 'All I kept saying to myself was, why, why, why?'

'Look on the bright side, the bright side, Harry dear! At least you got a trip to Italy, a substantial fee up front and – from what you tell me – endless sensational fucks out of it!' said Murray, unable to hide a slight snigger. Taking another long sip of wine he looked again at Harry, his handsome face now sombre. 'Seriously Harry mate, consider yourself lucky. Christ only knows what could have happened to you down there.'

'Thanks M, I appreciate our concern, I really do.' Harry gave a wry smile. 'Jesus, I certainly know how to make a real cunt of myself at times, don't I?'

'Only at times?' laughed Murray. 'Don't make me bust a gut! C'mon, drink up and I'll take you out to dinner. My treat.'

'I don't think I fancy a MacDonald's!' said Harry giving a wan smile.

'Nah! Not MacDonald's tonight. Let's push the boat out!' grinned Murray. He gave a theatrical shrug saying in an exaggerated Yiddisher accent, 'So vhat, my boy, if you've just lost zee business a major contract! Fancy somewhere Italian?' he added innocently.

'Something Italian? You must be fucking joking, dear!'

Murray gave a mischievous smile. 'For what we are about to receive may I suggest we go Indian? We may as well start getting used to curry and more curry!'

'You've got it totally wrong, dear.'

'I have?' said Harry, a look of genuine alarm crossing his face. 'Not more bad news I trust?'

'Not at all. It's simply your choice of words. Shouldn't we start getting used to *currency* and more *currency* as *well* as the curries?'

At the Barnyard the scene could not have been more dissimilar.

'Fucking, traitorous, pathetic, insignificant little shit!' William roared, hurling a further of bottle of wine across the spacious kitchen where it shattered and splattered with a great crash against wall. Panting, he glared at the two silent little figures watching him, their malformed faces expressionless.

'Right,' said William. 'Right,' he said again. Leaning forward, his hands on his thighs he inhaled deeply. 'So, gentlemen,' he growled eyeing Paul and Nelson, 'my plan backfired which mean's we're now back to square one. Shit! Shit! Shit!'

'Just what was your plan? The whole point of that debacle involving Skids?' grunted Paul softly.

'Simplicity itself,' said William, drawing himself to his full height. 'I truly believed Harry Humphries was so screwed up in his fucking head that he would have happily agreed to my portrait of him, a portrait I was planning to surprise him with and get started on this weekend.'

'How screwed up? Just what do you mean, William?'

'When someone, on being asked, *is* happily prepared to shit on you! *That* sort of screwed up.'

'You asked Harry Humphries to *shit* on you?'

'I did.'

'And what happened?'

'He said he'd have to think about it!' William gave a wry laugh. 'He said he'd heard about "it" but never been asked to "do it" before!'

'Not like us, eh Paulie?' chuckled Nelson.

'So what happened next?' asked Nelson, ignoring Paul's lascivious grin.

'An audition as if it were! One night I'd fucked him so often – three or four times, he couldn't get enough – there came the moment when I finally pulled myself out of him resulting in Humphries unable to control a massive fart combining a mixture of my cum and his shit spraying out all over me! He found it hilarious!'

'He did?'

'Most definitely. He said I looked like a massive shit-covered bear!'

'Which in a way you were,' giggled Nelson.

'It was then I came up with the idea and put it to him.'

'And that was?'

'I paint a full size nude portrait of him positioned like Rodin's *The Thinker*. Only he wouldn't be nude, nude, but covered in shit, the portrait being called *The Dumper.*'

'Per-lease!' This from Paul.

'And he agreed?'

'I don't think he took me seriously at the time but secretly I had a strong feeling he would eventually go for it. Deep down he seemed quite turned on by the suggestion.' William gave the two dwarfs a smile. 'Obviously you two would have been called in to help provide the extra body makeup!'

'But that still doesn't answer my question,' said Paul in his usual grunting tones. 'Why send Skids to meet him?'

'Simply because I strongly believed Skid's presence would have a stimulating effect, an effect somehow reminiscent of Pavlov and his dogs; stir up recent memories; memories of all that shit over me, his amusement etcetera. Make him begin to salivate as if it were!' said William, his heavy moustache twitching as he began to laugh.

'Holy shit, William!' cackled Nelson. 'If that isn't about the biggest load of ...'

'*Shit*!' bellowed William and Paul in unison.

'*I don't know what is*?' chorused the three collapsing with laughter.

The following morning William telephoned Harry.

'Harry, its William. No, please, *please* don't hang up. I'm sorry, so very, very sorry but if you'd allow me to explain.'

A very hungover Harry slammed down the phone.

CHAPTER 11:

'Tommy, good morning!' Harry gave the young pop idol a welcoming smile. 'May I introduce you to Alan, my architect and the twenty first century's incarnation of Frank Lloyd Wright!'

'Hi Alan,' said Tommy giving an overawed Alan a gentle handshake. 'Harry tells me you've been a double genius apropos what you're going to be showing me today!'

'He did?' said Alan shooting a smiling Harry a curious glance.

'He most certainly did. In fact, he even went on to say the unique wave you've created for me, for my new home, outdoes any of the rave waves, those seas of waving arms, ever seen at Glastonbury or the O2!'

'Oh,' said Alan, this time giving Harry a startled look. 'Oh,' he said again before breaking into a shy smile, 'Wow, Harry! You've never said anything like that about any of my work before!'

'Can't have anyone else in the company with another swollen head,' laughed Harry, eyeing Tommy for any reaction to the double entendre. 'Have to keep you under control, Alan dear!'

Giving another light laugh accompanied by a theatrical toss of his contrived hairstyle for the day (Harry having gone for the peekaboo for the occasion, a long sweep of blond hair falling languidly across his left eye), he gestured towards the temporary display table, drawing board, plus a further table surrounded by four plastic folding chairs, all set up in the one corner of the vast space.

'The Tommy Tyler Creation Centre,' he camped, 'courtesy of Harry Humphries Incorporated. Over there, please note a counter unit with relevant percolator and kettle, de rigueur red and navy blue cups – like the chairs please – plus a small, well stocked fridge. You will be pleased to know Tommy the small cupboard next to the fridge contains both wine glasses and champagne flutes!'

'Now that's what I call supremely civilised,' said Tommy sitting down, 'And Harry it hadn't escaped my notice you have two red and two blue chairs *plus* coordinated coffee cups!'

'But of course,' said Harry bestowing a gracious of smile upon the bemused young man, 'Only the *best* for our special guest!' He sat himself next to Tommy while Alan stood facing them, several rolls of plans and four brass paper weights – each in the shape of a chunky cock and a pair of balls – ready next to them.

'Right Alan; lights, camera, action!' camped Harry.

For the next hour Alan led Tommy through the preliminary plans with well-balanced interjections from Harry who would then elaborate on Alan's details discussing the relevant accompanying sketched perspective. A silent Tommy sat enthralled, his initial cup of coffee forgotten.

'And this,' said Harry, 'will be the overall impression your visitors will get as they step out of the top of cylindrical entry from the housing the circular, steel staircase and onto the metallic bridge leading to the reception platform.'

With a flourish he lifted the thick, black card cover to the last and largest display board. Tommy, his eyes wide, sat gazing for several minutes at the details elaborate perspective in front of him before finally emitting a long, deep sigh.

Looking across at Alan, Harry gave the architect a brief wink as Tommy continued to stare at the presentation, his eyes taking in time and time again the open reception and entertainment platform encompassed by a giant metallic wave, a giant replica of the six steel bass clef-inspired supports carrying the platform. Surrounding the central sculptural piece were a series of smaller, similar waves housing the guest suites, dining room and kitchen plus a miniature recording studio and office. Finally Tommy turned to Harry saying in a small incredulous whisper, 'Is this really going to be all mine? Will it really look like this?'

Harry and Alan smiled back at the young pop star, nodding in unison.

'It's not only the most amazing, beautiful concept of anything I have ever seen, it's complete and utter magic. Unique!' breathed Tommy, adding simply, 'Thank you Harry, thank you Alan, thank you both so much. I love it.'

'And thank *you,* Bobby,' smiled Harry, 'Thank you for being a dream client and giving us an uninterrupted free run with the best of our ideas.' He gave another smile. 'I think a little celebratory drink would not go amiss, don't you think?'

'Aha!' said Tommy with chuckle. 'You beat me to it but I think it's definitely my turn to show my appreciation.' Taking his mobile from the pocket of his leather jacket he punched in a number. 'Bellings, we're ready,' he said into the phone. He gave Harry and Alan another dazzling smile. 'I just *knew* what I would be shown today would be good but I never imagined … well, how could I?' he said, giving a light self-deprecating laugh. 'After all, why else would I come to a pair of geniuses like you two and boy, am I glad, so very, very glad I did!' He gave another laugh. 'Hence the champagne sitting and waiting in readiness in the car… ah, and here it is!'

'Dual purpose there,' Harry whispered across to Alan as Tommy went over to meet the chauffeur. 'We could have been celebrating a wake!'

Bellings, having poured and served the three goblets of the sparkling wine, tactfully withdrew at Tommy's discreet, 'Thank you, Bellings, we'll help ourselves but perhaps that second bottle in perhaps, say, fifteen minutes?'

'Very good, sir,' said man, giving a nod and making a silent exit.

'Now,' said Tommy having taken several deep sips, 'an apology. I know you've very kindly invited me to lunch but would you be very offended if I suggested a change in plan?'

'Of course not,' smiled Harry thinking, Sweetheart, for the amount you're about to be fucking spending with Harry Humphries Inc you can suggest any changes you wish!

'In fact,' continued Tommy, 'I've taken the liberty of asking an actress friend and her manager to join us – she's been away on location for her latest film and only got back last night. I want Nat and Greg – he's a top notch producer – to meet, you because there's talk of a new mini-series and, as I said to Nat, why not Harry Humphries for the interior sets – if you'd be interested, that is?'

'Your Nat wouldn't be Natalie Vine, by any chance?' asked Harry.

'The one and only! Do you know her?'

'No, not know her but I certainly know *of* her. Murray, Murray Harbourd, our PR – Christ! He's meant to be meeting us for lunch! – is a great friend of hers.'

'Murray? Nat's Murray is your PR? What a coincidence! Nat never stops talking about him but I had no idea he was your guy! But isn't this great?'

Not my guy, Tommy dear, our PR, said Harry to himself while giving a tight smile. 'So, what *is* your alternative plan for lunch, Tommy?' He glanced at his watch. 'Murray was meeting us at the Ivy so I'd better let him know where we're going to be instead. That's if it's OK for him to join us?'

'But of course. Lunch is at my most favourite hidey-hole in London.' Tommy gave a small laugh. 'Contrary to rumour it's not fun always being gawked at, hence me avoiding places like the Ivy and the Wolseley. Where I'm taking you the only people gawking at me, us, will be our reflections!'

'I'm confused,' laughed Harry. 'Enlighten me so that I can ring the mighty Murray, pronto!'

'The mirrored room at Flemings in Mayfair. It's not only private but the sexiest dining room in London!'

At Tommy's suggestion they left Alan's 4X4 parked outside the old candle factory, the plans and presentation boards safely stored aboard and the vehicle securely locked. Once organised the three young men settled themselves comfortably in the back of the Bentley.

Harry, unable to get hold of Murray had left a message on his mobile, also calling Susie asking her to keep trying Murray's number or, if not successful, to leave a message – when cancelling their reservation – asking Murray to call her.

'Tell us again, Tommy, about this "sexiest dining room in Mayfair"' said Harry, taking a sip of his champagne as the luxurious car made its way smoothly across Battersea Bridge towards Chelsea.

'Aha!' said Tommy. 'Just wait and see! Now it's my turn to surprise you!'

Twenty minutes later Bellings drew the Bentley to a stop outside a neat portico gracing the entrance to one of Mayfair's most exclusive, boutique-style hotels.

'Flemings? But of course! When you mentioned the name I simply didn't put two and two together.' cried Harry. He gave Tommy a broad grin. 'Tommy Tyler, this *is* a surprise. Fleming's is one of my most favourite hidden secrets! It's their champagne bar I covet but I never realised they had a hidden, sexy, mirrored dining room!'

'Well you do now,' said Tommy with a pleased smile. 'And it's great!' Stepping out of the car he was greeted by a loud cry of 'Tommy!'

'Nat!' Tommy turned to greet a tall, elegant auburn-haired young woman hurrying along the pavement followed by a plump, bustling Danny De Vito lookalike.

'Natalie Vine, meet the fabulous Harry Humphries and his genius sidekick, Alan! Harry and Alan meet Natalie and of course, you sir, must be Greg!'

'Greg, I am!' spluttered the little man in between trying to catch his breath. 'Greg by name and gregarious by nature! And I recognise you, Tommy Tyler! Put it there, super star!'

Harry glanced towards Alan who was too star struck by meeting Natalie to even notice Greg's corny self-introduction to their client.

'Afternoon Paul,' said Tommy to the handsome doorman standing smiling from the open doorway.

'Afternoon Mr Tyler, Miss Vine,' said Paul standing aside to let Tommy and his guests through into the spectacular marbled lobby but not appearing to recognise Harry.

'Oh Paul,' added Tommy, 'there'll be another gentleman joining us, a Mr Murray Harbourd. Can you get someone to show him down, please.'

'Murray's joining us?' cried Natalie. 'But that's divine! In fact, he and I are meeting for lunch tomorrow!'

'I've been watching you in *Tomorrow's Way,* Miss Vine,' gibbered Alan as they made their way across the lobby, oblivious to the startled stares of a few hotel guests. 'Jamie, my partner and I have just bought the whole series on DVD. It's fab!'

'Why, thank you Alan,' smiled Natalie, 'and please, it's Nat or Natalie, but my friends call me Nat, so why don't you?'

'Gosh, err… thanks, Nat,' said Alan, blushing furiously. Giving another inane grin he added, 'Fuck! I can't wait to tell Johnny not only did I lunch with Tommy Tyler but, better still, I also had lunch with Natalie Vine!'

'I wouldn't let Tommy hear you saying that,' said Natalie sotto voce, adding with a mischievous grin, 'otherwise he'd have – to almost quote you, Alan – a "fucking" fit!'

'Star fucker!' Harry hissed at Alan as they made their way down the wide marble steps to the lower floor.

'Yes, I know,' breathed an ecstatic Alan, adding, 'Oh, Harry Humphries, how I *love* working with you!'

Murray's surprise on seeing Natalie could not have been greater. 'Nat!' he cried, 'what on earth are *you* doing here?'

'Don't look so shocked, Mur,' said the elegant young woman with a playful smile. 'You're not the only dashing Lothario in London town allowed to entertain the lovely Natalie!'

'What do you think?' questioned Tommy gesturing at the sumptuous red, ivory and mirror panelled room.

'Absolutely fantastic,' said Harry. 'Those full height, elongated diamond-shaped mirrors are quite brilliant!'

'Hence the reason for Tommy always insisting on coming here,' said Natalie mischievously.

'Oh, and what would that reason be, Miss Vine?' camped Tommy.

'Now that sounds almost like the cue for a song, or rhyme of sorts,' laughed Natalie, 'In fact, knowing you Tommy, I'm surprised you *haven't* turned it into a song.'

'And if I did, Natalie dear, perhaps you'd deign to give me a hint as what this would be?'

Giving a light laugh followed by a mischievous grin Natalie – tossing back her shoulder length hair – announced in a camp voice reminiscent of Carol Channing, 'With apologies to *another* wicked queen, the queen from Snow White, Natalie Vine's very impromptu *Tribute to Tommy*!'

Taking a deep breath and improvising both the words and the tune as she went along, Natalie began to sing,

'*Mirror, mirror on the wall,*
Who is the fairest of us all?
Is it Natalie? We know she's divine,
Or Gregarious Greg, with shows sublime!
Or Harry, Alan, Murray, perhaps all three?
No, it's Tommy Tyler crying me, me, me!'

'Cow!' cried Tommy, his face beaming with delight.

'Atta girl!' guffawed Greg.

'Bravo!' called Harry.

'Bril!' smiled Murray proudly.

'Oh Jamie pet I think I've just fallen in love with a *girl*!' giggled Alan.

CHAPTER 12:

'Harry Humphries Incorporated,' cooed Susie into the phone, a sudden look of irritation on her face as she recognising the caller. 'Good morning Mr Wandsworth and no, I'm sorry, Mr Humphries is not in, in fact he dictated a letter to you yesterday which went in last night's post. You should be receiving this today. The contents? Oh, Mr Wandsworth, I am only Mr Humphries' secretary, not his PA – that's Mr Murray Harbourd – and therefore I am not at liberty to disclose the contents as written. Excuse me? What was that you said, Mr Wandsworth? Would you please say it again? Oh, "fuck off you bitch!" Why, *thank* you Mr Wandsworth, you are so kind!' Susie slammed down the phone, glaring up at a grinning Harry.

'Did he really say "fuck off, you bitch?"'

'Unless my shell-likes deceive me.'

'Sorry about that, Suze.'

'Not to worry, boss dear. He could have called me worse, much, much worse.'

'Oh? And what could that possibly be?'

'Miss!'

'Silly cunt!' snorted Harry making his way towards his office. 'Have those samples from Bernard Thorp come in?' he called over his shoulder. 'They were promised for yesterday.'

'Margaret rang a few minutes ago to say they're being dropped in by Bernard himself no later than eleven this morning.'

'Perfect, seeing I'm planning on a Griselda Carter day today. I'll also need to see Alana later. How's he coming along with Tommy's quotes?'

'He's on site again this morning with various heavenly bodies but plans to be back here by four, latest.'

'Good, and Nick?' (Nick being Nick Reynolds, another assistant designer).

'He's seeing Johno about those sample boards for Tommy and then joining Alan on the Tyler site.'

'Great, so that's all melding together nicely. Just as well seeing Wandsworth is now a "no go!"'

'Ah, but *that* castle in the air is about to be replaced by another and one certainly more on terra firma.' Susie gave a light laugh. 'As you always say, bossikins dear, as one door closes, another opens etcetera etcetera.'

'Meaning?' Harry stood looking at Susie, a bemused expression on his face, Griselda Carter momentarily forgotten.

'Remember Larry Freed casually mentioning his own magic castle at Murray's the other evening?'

Harry gave a brief nod. 'Go on.'

'Murray called earlier – where have you been by the way? It's well after your rise and shine time? – Lenny's been sent details of a property, some castle in Wales of all places. The property overlooks the sea and Lenny needs you and Murray to have a look at this, to quote our macho man, *tout de suite*!'

'So, exactly like silly Cinders going to the ball, handsome Humphries gets to the castle after all!' camped Harry. 'And by the way, the reason I wasn't here at my usual dawn crack was because, if you had deigned to check, I was having a fitting for my new Ascot number with the lovely Mr Parker.'

'Never a dull moment,' laughed Susie, 'and why another Ascot number? How many tail coats *do* you need?'

'As many as until I get a winner,' giggled Harry. 'Preferably *with* a furlong's length as opposed to "by a furlong!"'

'Sooo disgusting, my employer!' Susie gave another glance at the papers on her desk, 'I'll leave it to you and Murray to sort out a time for your camping trip to Wales. Meanwhile, off you go and concentrate on lovely Mrs *Carte Blanch* Carter. I'll bring you through a coffee and then get started on typing these reams of estimates for Tommy T. The buggers now seem to be coming in non-stop. Shit! If that's that bloody Wandsworth …' Susie snatched up the phone. 'Harry Humphries Incorporated,' she said with her usual coo.

'Mr Humphries' secretary?' questioned a calm, female voice.

'Yes, 'tis she, Susie McBride. How may I help you?'

'My name's Marjorie Wells,' said the voice, 'Mr Mic Sandford's personal secretary. I understand Mr Murray Harbourd has already briefed Mr Humphries with regard to a possible new business venture?' Not giving Susie a moment to reply, Marjorie continued, 'If convenient, I would like to arrange a meeting between the three gentlemen, preferably next week and, better still, on the Wednesday, Wednesday the twenty sixth at noon. Furthermore, Mr Sandford would be delighted if Mr Humphries and Mr Harbourd join him afterwards for lunch.'

Talk about going straight for the jugular, thought Susie, before replying in her most efficient manner, 'Yes, I do believe Mr Humphries is aware of such a venture, Miss Wells...'

'Mrs Wells,' the voice cut in, 'but please call me Marge as I have a very strong feeling we are about to be having a great many more conversations in the not too immediate future!'

'Thank you Marge, and I'm Susie. Could you hold on a moment, please, while I check the diary.' Putting Marjorie on hold Susie glanced up at Harry leaning against the doorway to his office. 'It's the curry queen's ayah with a royal command!' She gave a giggle. 'Though with her brisk attitude she's definitely more of a Madame Defarge than ayah Marge! You, dear Harry, along with the magical Murray have been summoned for an audience with the curry queen at Sandford palace next week.'

70:

'Aha! The time has come as the wise old oracle predicted! Time for this artistic lamb to be lead to the slaughter! Agree, even if one is not free – we can always change any other lowly subject – to whatever date the royal curry house demands. I will face my execution with my usual panache!''

'Idiot,' grinned Susie, flicking through the diary. 'Oh Harry, dear Harry, aren't we a busy, busy little bee? Now, quiet please whilst I finish with Madame D!' She clicked back onto Marjorie. 'Sorry to have kept you waiting, Marge, but I had to take another call.' She gave a light laugh. 'And how very fortuitous seeing Wednesday *is* the only day next week Mr Humphries is free both at twelve o'clock and for lunch.'

'Mr Sandford will be delighted. And please don't worry about Mr Harbourd, I'll call him myself. *Immediately.* Hopefully, appreciating the importance of this initial get together, he too will possibly change any previous appointment. If not, I'm sure Mr Humphries and Mr Sandford will still find a great deal to discuss.'

Susie gave Harry a startled look. Covering the mouthpiece she made a cutting motion across her throat. 'Quite so, err ... Marge,' she said smiling weakly at the phone, adding, 'and as you say, no doubt this will be the start of many.'

'I hope so Susie,' said Marjorie with a light laugh. 'And do give my regards to Mr Humphries, even if I have still yet to meet him.' The phone clicked off.

'She *couldn't* have heard our conversation?' gasped Susie, staring aghast at an equally stunned looking Harry. 'Oh *shit*!' she added, 'Oh bloody super shit!

I didn't put Marge Defarge on hold, I put her through to speaker phone in your office. She must have heard every effing word!'

'I wouldn't worry your pretty cropped head to much about Marge Defarge as you so aptly dubbed her,' said Harry, a grin on his face, 'and in the light of Madame Defarge and chopping off heads, what on earth is this with you and your *cropped* head? What with the new hairstyle? Talk about looking like a dyke coconut!'

'Dyke what? Jesus Harry, at times…'

'Yes, but what times!' cried Harry stepping up to Susie's desk. 'Sandford Holdings, Suze the cooze! Sandford bloody rich holdings! Our aged oracle once again proves not only has he the power to get blood from a stone – or in the case of Sandford, from a beetle nut! – he also gets to show yet again he is *always right*. Well done Murray! Well done!' He gave the smiling girl another grin. 'Or as our PR surpremo would say good, bloody good, bloody, bloody good!'

'More likely bloody *Bolly* good!' shrieked Susie.

'You're so right,' cried Harry moving nimbly round the desk. Grabbing Susie by her hands he led her into the middle of the office where he began prancing around in a circle, Susie following suit.

'*Bloody Bolly Good*!' cried Harry.

'*Bloody Bolly Good*!' cried Susie.

'*Bloody Bolly Good*! *Bloody Bolly Good*!' the two sang in unison, as they pranced and danced.

'I assume from the appalling, spoof *Slumdog Millionaire thé danset* taking place in front of me Sandford Holdings has come through?' said Murray's amused voice from the main door. 'Vell, jolly good show! Jolly good show! And like you, I to say velly, velly bloody bolly good!'

THE BARNYARD, THE SAME MORNING:

'That the post?' growled William pausing, paintbrush in hand, as Paul shuffled into his studio, a sheaf of papers in his stumpy hand.

'It is indeed,' said Paul reaching up and handing the bundle to William.

'Good,' said William muttering, 'Not at fucking liberty to disclose the contents. Stupid bitch!' Seizing upon a cream vellum envelope, the initials HH Inc heavily embossed in black alongside the lower right hand corner, he angrily ripped it open, pulling out a neatly folded A4 page and a piece of paper the size of a cheque.

Having skimmed over the brief, typed print William allowed himself a small pause before bellowing, 'You arrogant little prick! Not compatible? I'll give you not fucking compatible!' Glaring down at the impassive-faced dwarf the almost apoplectic man added in a low, strangulated whisper, 'Paulie, I need you and Nelson to find out all, and by all I mean *everything* there is to know about this little turd Humphries! I need to know who his friends are – his closest friend especially – and furthermore I need the names of his present clients. I already know of Tyler, but there are obviously more equally as rich and prestigious.' Glaring abstractedly back down at the letter he muttered chillingly, 'Oh Harry Humphries, how you're going to rue the day you walked away from me back down that drive!'

Crumpling the offensive letter and cheque into a tight wad William threw it into a nearby waste bin and, as if nothing untoward had taken place to interrupt his concentration, simply picked up his paintbrush, calmly adding a bright daub of colour to the large canvas on the easel in front of him.

Several hours later – William having retired for his usual afternoon 'power nap' – Paul and Nelson quietly entered his studio. Shuffling his way over to the waste bin Paul quickly retrieved the crumpled wad, the two leaving as quietly as they had arrived.

'What's it say? What's it say?' questioned Nelson impatiently, the two having retreated to their own quarters.

'No need to flutter so, Nelson,' admonished Paul. 'Remember, patience is a virtue …'

'Fuck patience! Just tell me what it fuckin' well says?'

'Dear Mr Humphries,' Paul read out. '*Due to the unfortunate incident which took place at your country residence last Saturday, August 23rd, I feel it best in the circumstances not to accept your proposed Design Commission.*

I therefore enclose a cheque to cover all monies paid to Harry Humphries Incorporated by your goodself.

In addition to the total reimbursement of the agreed Consultation Fee I have also included costs for my airfares plus fifty percent of any hotel expenses incurred by my stay at the Hotel Splendido, Levanto, Italy (my secretary having duly contacted the aforesaid hotel for the relevant information).

Yours sincerely, Harry Humphries.

'Oh dear,' said Nelson.

'Oh dear, dear,' sighed Paul. 'I certainly wouldn't like to be in Harry Humphries' shoes, would you?'

'Definitely not,' said Nelson. 'Nor any of his poor friends' or clients' shoes for that matter.'

'So Sherlock, are you ready?'

'Never more so, my dear Watson! Let the hell-raising and hideous havoc begin!'

'Err …Sherlock?

'My dear Watson?'

'This cheque, it's made out to Wandsworth Art, the business account for which our signatures are also valid,' said Paul softly.

'So?'

'So, if the amount went back in and out again rather like a yo-yo, he'd never know! As far as he's concerned the money's been spent, anyway!'

'What a clever little person you are, brother dear! This needs a celebration! Err… shall we find Rufus?'

'Why not, and then do each other! After all, from tomorrow it'll be the last time we will be able to fuck the little bugger!'

'Yippee!' cried Nelson, doing a little dance and singing, 'Heigh ho! Heigh ho! A fuckin' we will go!'

Going to the door Paul turned the strategically low-placed handle, pulling the door open. Looking out into the courtyard he gave a piercing whistle before calling, 'Rufus! Rufus! Here boy! Your daddies have some sweeties for you! Rufus! Rufus! Here boy!'

Within a few minutes the bug-eyed, fat black pug was being tightly held in Nelson's stumpy arms as Paul, a wild look in his bulging eyes, his plump little acorn-like cock an angry, orange blur, furiously fucked the yowling dog.

LONDON:

'I need a break,' whined Howard, his handsome face petulant, as he looked at Mic lying propped up against the pillows in the large bed.

'Break?' questioned Mic, giving the young man a sardonic smile. 'Break from *what* exactly, Howie? You've just spent the last two months doing nothing apart from spending an inordinate amount of time either in expensive restaurants or travelling to the likes of Venice, Amsterdam or Paris for so-called weekend breaks.' He gave a dry laugh. 'And I should know, seeing you've been signing bills willy-nilly at our usual restaurants without so much as a by-your-leave, plus arranged your five star, all inclusive trips through Stephen Maldon, the gay travel agent; again on my account.'

'Because, unlike you, my dear Mic, I like to enjoy myself!'

'Is that so?'

'Yes, Mic. It is very much so!' Howard let out a theatrical sigh. 'Poor Mic, have you taken a really long good look at yourself lately? Well, perhaps you shouldn't! You may be shocked by what you find.'

'Howie, dear Howie, please don't start up again.' Mic stretched out his hand. 'Come back to bed. Please... I've missed you because of our cancelled meetings ...'

'You cancelled one!' cried Howard, his dark eyes flashing angrily.

'OK, I cancelled one but it was a business deal which' – Mic paused, knowing he would regret what he was about to say – 'which,' he repeated, 'you, of all people, should appreciate seeing these keep funding your extremely selfish and extravagant lifestyle, a lifestyle which seems to expand rather than diminish during your ever increasing and prolonged periods of so-called "resting!"'

'Are you suggesting I'm nothing more than a talentless whore?' hissed Howard grabbing hold of his formidable cock. 'Are you suggesting you're paying for this?' Opening his hand, he let his cock swing free before thumping the left hand side of his muscular chest, 'And this, my heart?' Giving a deep, prolonged sigh he added in a dramatic whisper, 'When all the time I, poor fool, thought you loved me for *me*.'

'Oh, for *fuck's* sake!' roared Mic, causing Howard to jump back with a camp shriek. 'Not those tired old lines again! Jesus Christ, no wonder you're still bloody "resting" if that's the best you can come up with!' Having pulled himself from the rumpled, sweaty bed, the stained sheets still pungent from their earlier energetic fucking, Mic, his powerful, hirsute body gleaming in the light of the bedside lamp, stood glowering at the sulking young man.

Pointing at his own chest Mic said softly, 'This person, Howard, this person, me, Mic Sandford, has had enough. This,' he said, pointing at his own thick, heavy, rope-like cock, 'has also had enough. Oh yes,' he added, 'go on, now give me the hurt look. Oh yes, I *have* just fucked you twice and yes, and as always while fucking you I tell you I love you, that I've never known such orgasms before; but has it never occurred to you, Howard dearest, that *unlike you* I may, in fact, be a bloody good actor?'

Reaching for his clothes Mic started to get dressed, his eyes never leaving the ashen-faced young man. 'So, Howard Hanover – dreadful name by the way, Howard Hanover – let's just say you taken your final bow on this very over-extended run.' Mic pulled on his jacket, adding, 'Why not *rest* a little longer? You've got the Porsche and the rent for this place is paid until June of next year.' He gave a tight smile. 'As a farewell gesture – I prefer calling it this as opposed to severance pay – I will deposit ten thousand pounds into your bank account tomorrow – I *do* have the details – and again, as from tomorrow no more credit at our regular restaurants and no more travel arrangements booked through Stephen.'

Mic glanced down at his watch. 'Good heavens, is that the time?' Reaching inside his jacket he took out a set of keys. 'The keys to the house; I won't be needing them any longer.' Giving the stunned young man a grimace of a smile the big man strode purposefully from the bedroom and into the small entrance hall before letting himself out of the tiny house and into the picturesque, cobbled Mews.

Mic kept walking briskly until he reached his car where he momentarily slumped against the bonnet. 'Oh shit,' he murmured, 'talk about burning one's boats, but enough is enough ... or is it?' With a soft sigh he climbed into the driver's seat of the Jaguar saloon. Turning on the ignition he slowly edged the motor out of the parking bay before accelerating down the silent street.

Back inside the Mews house, Howard, still naked but with a large tumbler of neat vodka and ice clutched in his hand, sat staring into a large wall mirror facing the neat conversation area of two sofas set at right angles to a low table. 'Silly queen,' he muttered to his handsome reflection, 'silly fucking old queen, he doesn't mean it, he never does. He'll be back for he *knows* he'll never find another me, another arse like mine, plus the fact – resting or not – I am still a *very* recognisable star!' He took another large mouthful of vodka before loudly assuring his reflection in a slurred voice, 'Ish not ash if we haven't gone through thish thene many, many timesh before…'

An hour later a very drunken Howard – having swallowed three more tumblers of neat vodka – tearfully admitted to the blurred reflection that the 'many times before' had never included a personal attack on his acting talents nor the cancellation of any accounts and certainly *not* the return of the keys to the house.

Mic, lying in his own bed, was thinking similar thoughts. 'Oh Howie, you silly idiot. Why, oh why do you have to goad me so? Can't you see everything you seem to be doing recently is simply being destructive as opposed to constructive?'

He gave a yawn, his big hand moving inadvertently down to his thick, long flaccid cock. After several more yawns Mic began stroking himself, his cock starting to harden. Grasping hold of the rigid shaft he began wanking himself off. With his hand moving faster his mind started to focus, not on Howard but on the image of Harry, Harry laughing, his blond hair shining and his eyes twinkling as Mic had looked on admiringly across the dinner table at the Savoy those few nights back.

'Harry!' Oh Harry!' Giving a loud cry Mic jettisoned copious globules of warm cum onto his hairy stomach and clenched hand, muttering a softer 'Harry' followed by another and another before falling into a dreamless sleep, a small smile on his lips.

CHAPTER 13:

'Before Nelson and this brilliant second sleuth produce your requested list,' said a smug-looking Paul looking across at William while stretching over the breakfast table to hand him a plastic folder, 'It strikes us both you've probably not had a chance to look at these. They were left on your desk a few days ago.'

'No, I've had a lot on my mind,' said William, his voice irritable. 'Why, what are they?'

'Press cuttings.' Paul gave a small grimace. 'Our Mr Humphries' PR, manager, whatever, seems to have jumped the gun somewhat. It's all to do with him, you and the castle plus working at the same time for Tommy Tyler. Hence these rather trite captions, and I quote, *Harry Gets The Bacon* – a crack at you and those endless comparisons to Francis B – along with *Tommy Tyler Gets The Midas Touch.* Here again your name is mentioned along with vague assumptions as to the ridiculous amounts you two are supposedly spending with the avaricious Mr Harry Humphries.'

'Bloody PRs,' growled William. 'As I always say, who, with any genuine talent, really needs them?' He stared at Paul. 'This Tommy Tyler, who and what is he exactly?'

'Who is Tommy Tyler? William Wandsworth may you be forgiven! Why Tommy Tyler's the hottest thing on the current pop scene. He's gorgeous and there also rumours pretty little Tommy is also gay!'

William gave the dwarf a crafty look. 'So why are we waiting?'

'What do you mean?'

'It'll obviously take you some time to get all the information I've asked for but, unwittingly you've already struck gold, my clever little one by handing me this Tommy Tyler on a plate – or should that be palette?' William gave a small smile. 'As soon as you two have finished breakfast, Mr Tyler takes priority over anyone else. I need to know all about him and, more to the point, what exactly Humphries is doing for him.' He looked at the two solemn faces studying him. 'As soon as possible, little sleuths, which means by the time we meet again in my study at noon.'

'Noon it shall be, William, but do remember Nelson and little self are due to go up to London this afternoon for our, err... enhancements.'

'Christ! I forgot!' William looked apologetically at the little man, 'Paulie, I know I promised you both...'

'Don't worry your shaggy head about it, William,' said the dwarf. He gave a twisted, yellow-toothed smile. 'Let's put it this way, Harry Humphries comes first – we both saw his reaction to us when he arrived here the other day – so Nelson and I can wait another day or even a week or two if necessary.'

'Thank you,' said William giving the two siblings a warm smile. 'And I promise you *this* William will make sure it's an extra special occasion when the two of you first *come* with your *new* willies!'

'All you need to know about Tommy Tyler,' said Paul several hours later as the three sat around the coffee table in front of the fireplace in William's study.

'Do you have a contact number? His address?'

'Not per se, everything has to go via his agent who is also his manager.'

'Good, I need a letter to go off to Tyler today, so Nelson, got a pen and paper?'

Nelson lifted a notepad and biro from off the table. 'Like the battery in our giant-size vibrator, I'm ever-ready!' he quipped.

THREE DAYS LATER

'Interesting letter in today's post, Tommy Tom,' said Mac Guthrie, Tommy's agent and manager, an immaculately groomed albeit bearded and with a moustache, burly, no-nonsense Scotsman known in the music business as 'Big Mac,' not only because of his physical size but particularly for his formidable manoeuvrings on his client's behalf in both the field of music and public relations. 'And could be very good for you, too.'

'What's it say,' questioned Tommy looking up from a copy of *Entertainment Weekly* from where he lay sprawled on a sofa in Mac's office.

'William Wandsworth – *the* painter of the moment – is offering to paint your portrait, free, *gratis* and for nothing.'

'So?'

'Simply William Wandsworth, my dear Tommy Tom, is about the hottest name in the art world today,' smiled Mac, looking adoringly across at his young protégé. 'Not only has he been billed as the new Francis Bacon but there's also a rumour he's planning to build his own very personal gallery here In London, but to date it's only a rumour.'

'Ah yes, I knew I'd heard the name somewhere before. I think Harry, that's our Harry Humphries, is about to work on some old castle for him.'

'So Murray Harbourd claims,' smiled Mac, adding, 'Glad to see you occasionally read some of your press cuttings, my dear.'

'Ha! Ha!' said Tommy, playfully throwing his magazine across at Mac. 'The letter, Mr Guthrie, the letter. What does this Francis Hambone say?'

'And ha ha, to you too, my lovely! Now shut up and listen.
Dear Tommy Tyler,

Firstly, my congratulations on being voted Pop Personality of the year two years running and secondly, your continued place as No 1 in the current charts – six weeks to be exact.

My purpose in writing is to ask you to sit for a portrait, one to be part of an exhibition "Illustrious Illuminati," I am planning for next year.

Should you be interested please be kind enough to ask your agent to contact my agent, Mr Paul Column, at the above address.

Yours sincerely, signed, *William Wandsworth."*

Mac looked up at Tommy. 'Though not William Wandsworth in full, simply a rather strange signature of what looks to be a W, a dot and another W, an A and an N. That's it, WAN. How very bizarre, makes himself sound almost oriental. Me William Wan!'

'You could be wong,' giggled Tommy. 'Perhaps he's trying to be William the *won* and only!'

'At times I simply cannot understand why I adore you, put up with and, what's even more odd, love you, terrible Tommy Tyler,' laughed Mac, 'but then I suppose, being a mad Scot, it fathoms!' He gave Tommy an indulgent smile, tapping the letter with his hairy forefinger. 'Seriously, Tommy Tom, this is quite an accolade.'

'You think I should do it?'

'Without a doubt! And when I spread the word that William Wandsworth is painting you, it'll simply snowball. However, I need to spend a bit of time working out a watertight deal before we see our artist friend.' Mac gave a grin. 'While Mr Wandsworth may be willing to offer his services for free he's not getting Tommy Tyler for nothing! I can see us using this portrait as a major franchising exercise; postcards, posters, Tee shirts, maybe even for a new album cover. The prospects are limitless. Meanwhile, let me call this Column fellow and set up an appointment.' Mac opened the large, leather-bound diary in front of him. 'We don't want to sound too keen so I'll arrange a get together in about six weeks' time. By that stage I'll have worked out a contract. If Wandsworth agrees, fine, if not so be it and silly Mr Wandsworth. After all, there is only one Tommy Tyler whereas there will always be another wannabe Francis Bacon!'

'Am I that unique, Big Mac?'

'To your fans? Most definitely. For me? Well, there's a wee rumour…!' Mac gave Tommy a lascivious wink. 'If he agrees to our terms I suggest you do your first sitting on your return from your German tour.'

'I know he's offered, and you mention the franchising resulting from the painting and so on, but maybe there should also be a fee?'

'Never look a gift horse in the mouth, Tommy, my boy! Have I ever let you down? We'll make a killing out of the franchising alone added to which I will be demanding a massive commission on the eventual sale of the portrait. I'm talking of at least forty percent here. At the moment William Wandsworths are going for five figures. From the sounds of it, with this exhibition of outstanding personalities, personalities as opposed to dumb fly-by-night celebrities, I'm already seeing seven.'

'Make the call!'

'I thought you'd say that!' grinned Mac. 'Let me set up this meeting and then I'll Google Mr Wandsworth and print off a few of his paintings for you.' The big Scotsman gave a deep, rumbling laugh. 'I don't want to startle that pretty head of years but some of Mr Wandsworth paintings are rather nasty for the unenlightened.'

'Nasty? Why a portrait of me, then?' cried Tommy in feigned alarm. 'You're meant to be my manager, my PR person and taking care of me!' Clutching his throat he added with a camp cry, 'You're supposed to promote me as "Tommy Tyler, all things bright and beautiful," *not* "Tommy Tyler, all things blight and buggered!"'

'Really? Is that so, wee Tommy Tom?'

'OK,' laughed Tommy, 'forget the buggered bit – that's between you and me! –but think blighted!'

Mac smiled across at the grinning young man. 'God, I love you, Tommy Tom.'

'And I love you too, Mac, that's why I said forget the buggered bit as well as saying that's strictly between you and me!'

'I must say I prefer it when it's *in* between you and me,' chuckled Mac starting to dial a number taken from the letter heading. He held up his hand, cutting off any riposte from Tommy, 'Mr Paul Column, please. Mac Guthrie, Tommy Tyler's manager and PR calling.' After a brief exchange of words he replaced the receiver. 'That was easy. Mr Column couldn't have been more affable. It's arranged we meet exactly six weeks from today.'

'Sorry, I wasn't really listening,' said Tommy glancing up from his magazine. 'You know I leave everything to you.'

'I told Column we'd meet at your favourite Flemings. I'll book a suite for the meeting and arrange for lunch in what you claim as London's sexiest dining room. Now, move your wee butt over here while I Google Mr Wandsworth for you.'

'Heavens!' cried Tommy, peering over Mac's broad shoulder, 'He's could almost be your twin!' The young man gave a laugh. 'I say "almost" because, whereas you're definitely Mr GQ, Mr W is more Wild Man of Borneo!' Tommy gave Mac a light kiss on his neatly combed head. 'Just as well I'm not planning on adding my rendition of the Troggs' *Wild Thing* to my repertoire otherwise it could easily end up being William Wandsworth!'

''Unfaithful tart!'

'Not as yet! Not as yet!' laughed Tommy. 'Unless things change dramatically in six weeks time I'm still your whammy and *very* jammy tart!'

'So you are and I wouldn't say no to a little nibble of my jammy, whammy tart right now!'

WEDNESDAY

'How do I look?' camped Harry as Murray walked into his office.

'Velley bloody what the fuck!' said Murray, bursting into laughter. 'Susie,' he called back over his shoulder, 'have you seen this?'

'Unfortunately I have,' came the quick reply, 'Not so bolly bloody good, is it? More velley, velley bolly bloody balls-up if you ask me!'

'Harry, oh Harry,' chortled Murray, 'While you certainly make a truly lovely Cunt of Calcutta, do you think you could possibly drag down a bit? In case you may have forgotten in that addled – or should that be curried? – brain of yours, we're due in Arlington Street within thirty minutes. I've got a taxi waiting and, according to our morose driver, the traffic's bloody.'

'But you haven't answered my question,' said Harry, pouting. 'How do I *look*?'

'I've just told you, "velley bloody what the fuck" is how you look,' snorted Murray. 'Didn't your ayah ever tell you maharanees do *not* wear a sari over a blazer and trousers, it's somehow not quite right? And as for that bright red blob in the middle of your fair forehead, what – out of my most ardent curiosity – is it meant to be? To me it looks exactly like some very accurate assassin's bullet hole!'

'Who on earth – apart from William Wandsworth – would wish to assassinate *moi*?' simpered Harry, striking a Bollywood pose, his hands clasped demurely and pointing upwards to his chin. 'And while you may *in*-accurately call me the Cunt of Calcutta, I am in fact the mysterious, beautiful Maharanee of Muchi-whore!'

'For fuck's sake, Harry!' cried Murray, gasping for breath, 'Enough's enough! We've got a serious meeting to get to so, off with your sari, sweetmeats, and get your Punjabi butt in gear!'

'So you *don't* approve of me getting into the feelie goody moody of making muchee, muchee money with Mumbata monstrosities,' said Harry sulkily. 'Up you chapatti then is all I can say, and see if I care!' Unwrapping the length of silk wound around him Harry bundled it onto the top of his desk before reaching into a desk drawer for a box of tissues. Pulling out several he spat lightly on the wad before briskly wiping the daubed lipstick mark from his forehead. 'And to put you in the picture, for the informed the dot's called a tilaka and *not* a bullet hole as by the misinformed! My lovely, now destroyed tilaka, being all thanks to the equally lovely Misssy Susie Floosie!'

'Enough! Enough!' cried a laughing Murray grabbing Harry by the arm and dragging him from his office past a giggling Susie. 'We're getting the *tilaka* out of here! See you later, Susie!' he called, pausing momentarily in the open doorway. 'And next time please do what I suggested, slip a bloody Valium into his coffee before any meetings involving our golden pensions!'

'I slipped in two!' shrieked Susie to the departing figures. 'On my hymen, I swear it!'

'Like your bloody boss, you're a fantasist!' called Murray, his voice muffled by the closing of the studio door.

'Mr Harbourd, how very nice to see you again,' said Marge giving Murray a warm smile as he and Harry were shown into her office. 'And Mr Humphries,' – she gave light laugh – 'I recognise you from your photographs! However I must say they do not do you justice!'

'How very kind of you to say so,' smiled Harry at his most charming, adding with a mischievous grin, 'At least you were tactful enough *not* to say you recognised me by my voice.'

To both the young men's delight Marge let out a peal of laughter, 'Touché, Mr Humphries! Now, if you gentlemen would kindly follow me.'

'Harry! Murray! How good to see you both again!'

'Sorry we're a few minutes late, Mic,' said Murray, 'but the traffic …'

'Not to worry, you're here now.' Mic gestured towards the conversation area. 'Please take a seat. Care for a quick aperitif before lunch?' he added nervously. 'I thought it would be more comfortable if we sat and talked somewhere less formal than my office so Marge has made an earlier reservation at the Ritz. Much easier to err … thrash out matters round a luncheon table, don't you think?'

Jesus, thought Murray, cool it Mic. Anyone would think you were meeting a delegation from the Dark Continent as opposed to your muse but, in a way, I suppose Harry is far more terrifying! 'An aperitif sounds great, thank you, *Mic,*' he said firmly, a slight frown creasing his forehead as Mic kept staring fixedly at a coquettishly smiling Harry. 'Err … anything *wrong,* Mic?' he questioned.

'No, nothing's wrong but I've just noticed the mark on Harry's forehead. It looks as if he's had a nasty knock or a bump! Are you alright Harry?'

'Absolutely fine, Mic,' camped Harry. 'It's only lipstick.'

'Lipstick?'

'Yes; blame Susie my secretary! She's very kissy, touch, feely whenever I leave the office. The dear girl always has to give me a good luck kiss before I leave for an important meeting. She has to make do with my *forehead* as my cupid bows are taboo!'

Murray, unable to control himself, let out an explosive snort.

'I trust she keeps a good supply of lipsticks in her drawers,' said Mic dryly, resulting in a bemused look from Harry at the possible double entendre. 'Now, that aperitif; I'm a martini man myself or, as before Murray, and perhaps you too, Harry, a glass of champagne instead?'

'Champagne for me please, Mic,' smiled Harry.

'I'll do the same, thanks,' said Murray.

'No problem,' smiled Mic. Making his way to his desk he pressed a button for the intercom. 'As you thought, Marge, champagne for our visitors.' Giving the two seated figures a broad smile he couldn't resist adding, 'Marge anticipates everything! Not only is she a wonderful secretary she can also adapt to the role of bartender or ayah without any fuss.'

'Shit!' cried Harry, starting to laugh.

'Considering what's on the agenda to be discussed over lunch, Harry, perhaps "shit" should be "curry!" chuckled Mic, quickly adding, 'And before we make our way up the road I want you to know, gentlemen, how thrilled I am at the prospect of working with the both of you. Ah, Marge, thank you.'

He smiled up as the woman came in with a tray holding two champagne flutes and a martini glass. Waiting until Marge had left he then continued. 'As Murray will have explained to you, Harry, this is to be my pet project, my own private venture as if it were and a mere subsidiary to the main Sandford Holdings.' Mic held up a leather folder he'd picked up from his desk before sitting down and facing the two. 'I have here a draft contract along with a general business proposal, the one complimenting the other. I've been over the whole deal with my personal lawyer and accountant.' He handed the folder to Harry. 'I would like you and Murray to study this – perhaps with your own lawyer – in your own good time. Anything you are not happy with, please do not hesitate to inform me, us.'

Mic took another sip of his drink before giving Harry a tentative smile. 'Basically, as the young Yves St Laurent did with the House of Dior, you Harry – if you are agreeable of course – take over the complete design side of Mumbata

Textiles. I've already earmarked two adjoining showrooms for you at the Design Centre, Chelsea Harbour – the existing occupants, an American company, are downsizing and only too happy to do a quick deal in order to offload the premises.

'There is also a second provisional contract confirming Murray Harbourd Associates as sole representative for all future promotions and publicity for what will be – again, subject to your both agreements, Harry *and* Murray – Humphries Mumbata Worldwide.' Mic drained his martini while eyeing the two silent figures sitting staring back at him. 'Well,' he added nervously, 'How does that strike you? Err… Harry? Murray?'

'I'm somewhat overwhelmed, to be quite honest,' whispered Harry. 'I mean, what you're offering me, us, Mic, is mega.' He gave a slight shrug of his narrow shoulders. 'Why, it's almost too good to be true.'

'No, dear Harry, not too good to be true but a golden opportunity for all of us, an opportunity too good to be missed,' said Mic, his eyes shining, his voice back to its usual confidence.

'A chance of a life time,' muttered Murray. 'A chance of a life time.'

'Of course there will be a substantial salary and expenses, plus a commission on all sales for you Harry with Murray on an equally substantial retention fee plus introductory commission for any new contracts. However, business is business and the proposed contract is to be reviewed after a three year period.' Mic gave the two a reassuring smile. 'But as I see it, these will be three years of absolute triumph and the contract, instead of being reviewable, simply renewable.' Mic gave Harry a piercing stare. 'There's also a bail out clause, Harry, which gives you the right to call it a day if you find yourself not happy with the way matters *do* turn, or are turning out.' There was a slight, uncomfortable pause while Mic drained his glass. 'Now, may I suggest you finish your drinks – you've hardly touched them – and then we'll go and have a spot of lunch and take this further.' He gave a forced laugh. 'Although, I feel we've already discussed in detail what was to be discussed!' Standing, he added, 'After lunch, Hector my driver will take you wherever you wish to go. I take it you did come here by cab?'

The two nodded dumbly.

'Good. Hector will have with him two portfolios – Murray has already seen one – for you both to study.' He gave them another smile. 'Between the two of you I would like to see a melding of Harry Humphries meets India as if it were. I want the *feel* of Harry Humphries!'

(As Murray was to later say to Harry, 'Christ! When he said the *feel* of Harry Humphries, I nearly pissed myself laughing!' This followed by a moment of feigned disbelief. 'Nearly?' camped Harry. 'How could you *not* but notice the stain on the sofa when *I* stood up?')

Lunch over, Mic shook hands with Harry and Murray as they stood on the steps at the side entrance to the hotel, Hector, Mic's driver and car discreetly parked by the kerb.

'As I said, take your time over your decision, Harry,' said Mic smiling gently at the bemused young man. Turning to an equally bemused Murray he added, 'I rely on you to use all your powers of persuasion in getting Harry to initially agree to all we've discussed, Murray, whether subtle or not! Give Marge a call when you're ready to meet up with me again. As I said, if it's full steam ahead I'll need a full week of both your times to travel with me to India, so please bear that in mind as well.' He gave out an unexpected chuckle. 'Griselda Carter will not be best pleased when she hears I'm about to spirit away her favourite young man of the moment!'

'But don't you see, Mic?' cried Harry, his face lighting up. 'If Murray and I can spin it, Griselda Carter will be the first extravaganza, the *exposé extraordinaire,* the flagship as if it were of Humphries Mumbata Worldwide. And in her case Mic, let me assure you, all that glisters will be velley velley gold!'

'So what do you think?' asked Harry as one of the fleet of dark blue Sandford Holdings Bentleys glided its way down Piccadilly towards Knightsbridge.

'Is there any need to think?' laughed Murray taking a sip of champagne from a silver-plated goblet, the iced champagne having been duly offered before the start of their journey by the attentive Hector, there being a well-stocked bar in the back of the luxurious car. He squeezed Harry's knee. 'Forget any other arrangements, we'll go through the portfolios at mine this evening, then again tomorrow and, if necessary, again the day after! I need to go through those contracts with a fine pin – I may even get Henry along to take a look.' Henry being Henry Wilkins, the company solicitor.

Murray glanced sideways at his friend. 'I must say, talk about baiting the bloody hook with caviar as opposed to a mere worm! Sandford, come what may, is determined to pull you in!'

'Hush, Harbourd! Even partitions have ears,' said Harry with a grin, nodding at the silent Hector sitting up front in the driver's seat and separated from them by the glass divider.

As if taking Harry's observation to heart, Murray added sotto voce, 'Seriously, H, what *are* you going to do with Sandford? I ask you this because I'm not joking. There's got to be a day of reckoning and I have a gut feeling that day is going to be sooner, much, much sooner than later.'

'What am I going to do? Before we commit ourselves I think it vital Mr "I want to give you the world," Sandford and yours truly have a very necessary tête-á-tête!'

'And if he demands his err … pound of your virginal, hallowed "no entry" entry as opposed to his mere pound of your puny protrubrance?' said Murray with a giggle.

'Then I'll simply have no alternative but to lie back – or on my flat front – and think of curry-ency and more curry-ency!'

'Tart!'

'Not a tart, Murray dearest, but a delicious and very rich Indian sweetmeat and it's not as if *you* won't be getting an equally delicious bite!'

CHAPTER 14:

'Good morning, Marge, Harry Humphries. Is Mr Sandford free to take my call?'

'Good morning, Mr Humphries. Unfortunately Mr Sandford is out of the office until tomorrow. May I take a message?'

'Err… no thank you, Marge, it's not important. However, I do know Murray, Mr Harbourd, will be calling you later to arrange another meeting.' Harry smiled conspiratorially into the receiver. 'My call was more err… of a personal nature.'

'I see,' muttered Marge before saying briskly, 'I look forward to Mr Harbourd's call.' There was a slight pause. 'Are you quite sure you don't wish me to leave *any* message for Mr Sandford?'

'No, not at all. Thank you again, Marge. It can wait until *we three meet again*,' he added camply, quoting one of the witches from Macbeth. 'Goodbye.' Harry put down the phone while looking across at Murray. 'What?' he asked, the whole conversation having been put on speaker.

'*Till we three meet again*!' snorted Murray. 'More bitch than witch if you ask me!' He gave a grin. 'I give it half an hour, top whack, before Sandford calls you back. I bet you your last rupee Sandford's given Marge strict instructions to let him know the moment should *you* call. I'm sure the love struck Mic is not all that interested in a call from me.'

'You really are such an old slut, Harbourd, determined – and sod the consequences – to sell this innocent designer to the highest bidder!'

'But of course! Like the so-called innocent designer I too am a greedy little fuck when mucho money just happens to be involved!' Murray's grin widened as the main line rang. 'Wanna bet?' he asked.

Seconds later Susie came through on the intercom. 'Bolly bloody good for you, Harry. Shall I put him through?'

'Please Suze,' said Harry, unable to suppress his giggles, 'And it would be appreciated if you would, in future, show our patron saint of rupees some respect!' He picked up the extension waiting for Suzie to transfer the call. Giving Murray the thumbs up, he cried gaily into the phone, 'Mic! This *is* a surprise. I've just been speaking to Marge who told me you were not *available* until tomorrow.'

'Cunt!' hissed Murray at Harry's emphasis on the word 'available.'

'Oh, I see, you just happened to call in and Marge said I'd rung. How fortuitous. No, my reason for calling was nothing to do with our about-to-be business deal – Murray's arranging another meeting regarding all that with Marge, he'll be calling her sometime today – but really about us. You and me.' Harry gave a coquettish laugh into the receiver while ignoring Murray's mawkish expression. 'I've been thinking… as we're about to become partners in crime as if it were (another giggle) perhaps a little get together? Just the two of us? What do you think?' Covering the receiver Harry hissed across at Murray now sticking his fingers in his mouth and making a retching sound, 'For fuck's sake, M!' before saying, 'This evening? Oh, forgive me Mic but you've taken me completely by surprise on that one.' He gave Murray now simulating a blow job, a quick wink. 'Sadly this evening's a no no but how about a drink on Friday? Dinner? Why not? *Scalini's*? I adore *Scalini's*. Tell you what, Mic, why don't you come and have a drink *chez moi* – the flat's in Lexham Gardens – and then we can walk round from there? It's no more than a five minute stroll.'

'In heels!' hissed Murray, his face puce.

'Seven would be great,' trilled Harry pointing a revolver-like thumb and fingers towards Murray. 'Let me give you the address and phone number.' Having repeated the details twice Harry – after a cheery 'See you on Friday then. Look forward to it!' – hung up.

'Oh what a tangled web we weave,' chortled Murray.

'When first we practice to deceive!' chanted Harry, picking up on the quote from Walter Scott.

'I wonder if he'll want to fuck you *before* or *after* the pasta?' said Murray, giving out an explosive snort.

'Oh my God!' cried Harry, holding his hands to his face in a parody of Edvard Munch's *The Scream*.

'Now what?' sniggered Murray. 'Having second thoughts about your sacrificial debut?'

'Yes and no but may I just remind you of what happened the *last* time I over-indulged in a bit of pasta passion!'

'Silly tart!'

'It's alright for you to sit there and laugh, Murray Harbourd. You're not the one about to be on the receiving end!'

'Aha! But what if, Harry dearest, *he* wants to be on the receiving end? Did you ever think of that?'

'Oh, my *God*!' squawked Harry again as he frantically tapped into the intercom. 'Suze! Suze! Can you come in here *immediately*!'

'Where's the fire?' gasped Susie, instantly appearing.

'No fire, but a favour!' cried Harry, his hands still held to his face. 'A *big* favour! I desperately need – no, make that I *demand* – you do as I ask!'

'Jesus Murray, now what's he up to?' groaned Susie, giving Murray a pained look.

'God only knows,' grinned Murray. 'Good question Susie! Yes, what exactly are you up to, Harry my sweet?'

'If I'm to do what you've just suggested I'll need to borrow a vibrator, won't I? And who else would I ask for a loan of the biggest vibrator available but my lovely, loyal, lezzie secretary!'

As a giggling Susie had returned to her office Murray looked across at his friend. 'You do realise, don't you H, you're totally, fucking raving?'

'That's why you adore me!' laughed Harry. 'But back to business. As we've now agreed it's full steam ahead with Humphries Mumbata Worldwide when do you suggest we see our err… sponsor?'

'I was rather planning on getting the deal signed and sealed *before* you and he got together.' Murray gave a frown. 'What if Friday's a total cock-up – if you'll excuse the expression – and you, or he, decide you can't abide the thought of being involved with each other, business or otherwise?'

'A thought that struck me as soon as I agreed to Friday's meeting, so this is where *you* now come in, riding to the rescue!'

'Me?'

'Yes, Murray dear, you! When you call Marge later to arrange next week's meet may I suggest – in other words I *insist* you say – whilst I, no make that we, had been planning on seeing Mic this coming Friday there's be an unexpected development and the two of are having to travel to Wales on Friday morning. Therefore, as we do need to see Mic ASAP and will be back Monday evening, can we possibly see him, at any time to suit, Tuesday or Wednesday, whenever.'

'Jesus, you really are a sly puss, aren't you?' said Murray, shaking his head in admiration at Harry's blatant duplicity. 'Christ, am I glad, so very, very glad I'm not your lover!'

'You don't know what you're missing!'

'Ah, and you've just, inadvertently, explained the very reason for my cheerful disposition!'

An earlier message from Mic was found to be waiting for Harry on the answering machine when he returned to his flat later that evening following an impromptu dinner with Murray and Lenny.

'Harry, Mic Sandford. I've just been going through my messages. Marge now informs me you and Murray will be in Wales as from Friday. I'm somewhat confused as I thought we'd arranged to meet. Can you please give me a call at home this evening. I'll leave both my private number and my mobile.' Having repeated both numbers the anxious-sounding man had hung up.

Harry glanced at his watch. 'Hmm, I don't think you'd appreciate a call at a quarter to one in the morning, Mic *dear,* however keen,' he muttered, slowly taking off his jacket and loosening his tie. Making his way over to a large French armoire which served as a bar, Harry poured himself a large Courvoisier brandy. 'As they say, Mic, absence makes the heart grow fonder and, if one's lucky, your cock even longer!' Giving a giggle he took a large sip before turning on a late night music station and collapsing onto a nearby sofa. Picking up the Evening Standard he was about to open the paper when the phone rang.

Expecting the caller to be Murray – they inevitably rang each other after an evening out together – Harry casually picked up the phone saying, 'Good evening, Roving Rimmers Rampant, your arse is our command. Assorted tongues available.'

'Harry Humphries?' said a strange, echoing voice.

'Err... yes,' spluttered Harry into his brandy, sitting bolt upright. 'Murray?'

'Harry Humphries?' said the strange voice again.

'Murray! Cut the shit! You scared the living daylights out of me for a moment. Murray?' Harry listened for a moment to the eerie sound of only static on the line. 'Who *is* this?' he demanded.

'Harry Humphries?' repeated the voice, sounding even more sinister this time.

'Look, whoever you are, fuck off!' cried Harry, slamming the receiver down.

Staring at the silent instrument he was about to pick it up to call Murray when it rang again. Slowly lifting the receiver Harry held it to his ear, determined not to say a word.

'Harry Humphries,' said the eerie voice, 'if that is Harry Humphries, there's no need to be so rude.' The caller clicked off.

'Sod you for starters!' said Harry, switching the phone on to silent mode. Half an hour later, having had a relaxing shower, Harry climbed into bed. Switching off the bedside lamp he was gently drifting off to sleep when he heard a voice calling softly from the dimly street below. 'Harry Humphries?' called the voice. 'Harry Humphries?'

With a cry Harry leapt from the bed and dashed across to the large window overlooking the silent street and gardens. Glancing down at the pavement, three floors below, he saw nothing apart from an empty pavement and a few parked cars along the kerbing and across the street by the shadowy, leafy square.

'What the fuck,' he muttered. 'Just how much wine and brandy did I have this evening?' Giving a dismissive shrug Harry slowly clambered back into bed and within moments was sound asleep.

Across the street two, small silent figures stood staring up at the impressive duplex flat where they had been patiently watching as the lights in various rooms were turned off, the room they assumed to be Harry's bedroom, being the last.

'Shall we press the intercom buzzer?' suggested Paul to Nelson, nodding towards the elegant ground floor portico housing the main door to the luxury block of flats, the brass name plate glowing softly in the light from a pair of wall sconces.

'Another time,' whispered Nelson having taken a miniature, voice-distorting mouth organ from his fleshy lips. 'After all, we've only just begun.'

'One last thing…' said Paul looking at his brother. 'Being ever-ready do you, by any chance, have any jiffy bags or envelopes in your shoulder bag?'

'But of course,' said Nelson, his misshapen face breaking into a mischievous grin. 'Can you do the honours?'

'With a bit of effort there shouldn't be a problem,' snickered Paul. 'Here, let's move behind this car.'

While Nelson rummaged inside his shoulder bag, Paul carefully pulled down his new, extra-large trousers followed by his new, equally large underpants, the trousers having been suitably cinched in at the waist by a thick leather belt. Squatting on his stumpy, bowed but muscular legs the dwarf, his face reddening with the effort, began pushing down and squeezing on his bowels. 'Quick,' he grunted as Nelson, just in time, managed to catch the oozing, soft brown turd inside the proffered bag.

Allowing Nelson to vigorously wipe his arse with a stubby finger, Paul watched admiringly as Nelson lasciviously licked and sucked it. 'Nice Nellie?' he asked.

'Always, Paulie, 'grinned Nelson. 'Yummy, yum, yum! Your turn next time.'

'But you can never shit on command,' giggled Paul. Reaching for the packet he quickly stuck the ends together and, taking a felt tip pen from the always prepared Nelson, neatly printed in bold, black letters, *HARRY HUMPHRIES – PERSONAL & CONFIDENTIAL.*

Minutes later the two little figures made their ways stealthily along the street soon leaving the elegant garden square to where Skids was patiently waiting, the package having been dropped through the main letter box serving the block of flats.

A sleepy Harry, a mug of coffee in his hand, glanced in surprise at the neat package lying on the carpet by the front door alongside the morning papers.

'Too early for the post' he muttered, 'Sid must have dropped this through the letter box along with the papers. (Sid being the elderly porter usually on early morning duty).

Harry read the heavy black print. 'Personal and confidential?' He gave the package a gentle squeeze. 'Feels like a fabric sample of such. Interesting, but who…?' Taking the thick, padded envelope through to the kitchen he rummaged through the knife drawer for a small kitchen knife, deftly cutting open the sealed end and emptying the contents onto the breakfast bar.

'Shit!' Harry cried as the foul potent smell from the brown lump hit him. 'What the fuck…? Jesus!' he gagged before vomiting up his coffee into the kitchen sink.

CHAPTER 15:

THE BARNYARD:

'You gentlemen were late getting back last night; Skids tells me it was well after two this morning before you arrived home.'

'Two thirty to be exact,' said Paul with a smirk.

'From both your expressions there's no need in me asking how the *first* even went.' William gave a broad smile. 'Just look at you both, like a pair of very puffed up fucking pouter pigeons!' He gave the grinning dwarfs a mischievous wink. 'Is William allowed to take a look?'

With smug smiles Paul and Nelson loosened the thick, wide belts holding up their extra-large trousers, both pairs ballooning out obscenely over their crotches.

'*Voila*!' cried Paul proudly displaying a grotesquely distended, salami-like cock and enormous pair of swollen balls, each the size of a small grapefruit.

'Jesus!' exclaimed William. 'Talk about game, set and match! But this is incredible!'

'Me! Look at me!' cried Nelson in turn, cupping his hugely exaggerated cock and balls in his stubby hands. 'I'm even bigger than Paulie!'

'And now we've bought our own sets to make ourselves even bigger!' laughed Nelson. 'Aldo, having first done it for us, then showed us how we can do it at home.' He gave a snigger. 'Even Skids wants to have a try!'

William, making a clucking sound, shook his head, a big smile gleaming between his thick, untidy beard and unruly moustache. 'When you told me about Aldo and how you wanted saline injections into your balls plus your willies pumped up, I didn't think you were really serious. But just look at you and yet you're now saying you still would like to make yourselves even *bigger*?'

'Yes!' said the two in unison, looking exactly a precocious Tweedle Dum and Tweedle Dee.

'And,' added Nelson, his gravelly voice rising to a high, excited rasp, 'Next time we travel up to London Aldo's going to organise for us one of those things your friend's called.'

'One of those things my friend's called?' said William, a baffled expression on his face. 'Explain, mighty midgets! You've lost me there.'

'*A Prince Albert*!' the two cried excitedly together.

'We're going to have the heads of our cocks pierced and a silver ring inserted!' explained Paul.

'It's called a Prince Albert like our black friend who was here the other week,' added Nelson, determined not to be outsmarted by his brother.

'Not any silver ring,' laughed William. 'No sirree! But two *wedding* rings! With the both of you looking so delicious I have no choice but to marry you today!'

'Marry us?'

'Not quite marry you, little ones, but we are together until death do us part, as if it were. So, when you *do* decide to have your piercings, your Prince Albert's – a very different Prince Albert to my Prince Albert I have to say! – the rings can only be a couple of those silver bracelets from Tiffany's, the ones with the small ball which screws on to the end! Don't look so surprised, my lovelies! With those giant, bulbous cock heads no ordinary ring would ever fit, only a miniature bracelet will suffice!' William gave another laugh. 'May I have a feel?'

Taking hold of both dwarfs' bloated cocks and balls, Paul's in his left hand and Nelson's in his right one, William gently squeezed both sets. 'Magic,' he said with a deep sigh, 'Pure magic! Like holding a pair of velvet clad cannon balls! But, little ones, with your new giant willies you now have a problem, you'll never be able to fuck each other and certainly not poor Rufus ever again!'

'We thought of that,' said Paul giving out a matching sigh.

'But,' cut in Nelson. 'We can still wank each other off! It's the first thing we did when we got home last night.'

'Which is something I'd like you both to do for me in a few minutes,' smiled William. 'The two of you shooting out of those big new willies should be quite sight!' He gave another smile. 'And as for finding someone or something else to fuck, leave that one to me!' Looking down at the two smirking faces he asked, 'And the scary phone calls? How did they go?'

'Oh, we did more than simply telephone,' giggled Nelson. 'You tell, Paulie!'

A few moments later William's loud bellows of laughter could be heard reverberating throughout the whole converted barn.

HH INC:

'Someone dropped a jiffy bag filled with shit *through your letter box*?' repeated Murray, his voice incredulous.

'No, not someone, Sid the porter did! Poor bugger found it pushed through the main reception door when he came on duty and, being a good lad, dropped it in with the papers.' Harry glanced at Murray. 'It must have been in the early hours for it certainly wasn't there when I came in… But of course! The phone calls and the voice in the street!'

'Phone calls? Voice in the street? What are you on about?'

Quickly Harry explained the mysterious phone calls and the later two from the street below. 'At first I thought the voice from outside was nothing more than a figment of my imagination – after all I was pretty pissed! – but now I'm positive… well, the bag of shit proves it, doesn't it? Proves the outside calls were also genuine.'

'But who on earth…?' pondered Murray. He looked at Harry, a small smile playing on his lips. 'Let's face it, Harry. With you the list could be endless!' He gave a light laugh in an attempt to relieve the tension. 'Take Aaron the plumber for example. He wasn't best pleased when you gave him that bollocking in front of his workmen, calling him not only a lying shit and a piss poor plumber but the final straw being your comment about his eyes.'

'His eyes? What the fuck would his eyes have to do with his plumbing *in*-capabilities?'

'Nothing really, apart from you saying they were obviously brown due to him *being* full of shit!' Murray gave a laugh. 'Oops! Sorry, the S word again!'

'I actually *said* all that to poor Aaron?'

'You most certainly did! Hence Alan having to get in another plumber *tout de suite* to complete the Young's contract.'

'Oh dear,' said Harry, not at all contrite. 'I wondered why I hadn't seen the Adonis-like Aaron on any of our sites recently.' He gave a snigger. 'Anyone else I should perhaps consider?'

'Can you spare the whole day?'

'Touché Harbourd! But back to reality and the cold, cold light of *today*. Let's have a look at these pics Lenny had sent over.' Spreading the coloured prints fan-like on one of the display units in the main studio Harry gave them a cursory glance before saying, 'Jesus, Murray! I know Lenny's a fucking old queen but it's hardly Carnavon castle, is it?'

SANDFORD HOLDINGS:

'Mic, its Howie! Howard!' said the voice sobbing gently. 'Can we please, please meet?'

'Oh, Howie,' said Mic exasperatedly. 'You're making this so difficult for both of us!' He took a deep breath. 'And no, Howie, I don't think it's a good idea at all!'

'There's someone else, isn't there?' came the harsh, accusatory reply, the earlier sobs forgotten. 'I knew it, I just *knew* it! There *is* someone else!'

Mic, staring at the phone thought for a second before taking the plunge. Why not? he thought to himself. Why bloody not? 'Yes, Howard,' he said, 'now you've brought up the matter, there most certainly is.'

'There *is*?' Howard's usual tenor came out in a piercing shriek. 'How can there possibly be? Who is it? Who could possibly replace Howard Hanover?'

'A charming, talented and extremely successful young man, that's who!' snarled Mic.

'That doesn't answer the bloody fucking question!' screeched Howard, even louder. 'Who is he? Who is he?'

'Harry Humphries,' whispered Mic thinking, There, I've done it! I've now committed myself totally to you, come what may, Harry, you dear, darling young man!

'*Harry Humphries*?' screamed Howard. 'That fucking, phony designer? The queen who utterly destroyed your fucking house? Please tell me you're joking Mic, otherwise you're sick, very, very sick and you need help!' There was a long, dramatic pause before Howard managed to finally hiss, 'If that is the case, thank *God* I got out when I did!' prior to slamming down the phone.

HH INC:

'You're to be at Battersea Heliport at eight o'clock sharp,' said Susie. 'Lenny Freed's chopper – you should be so unlucky! –will be ready and waiting to fly you off to wildest Wales. The journey will take approximately an hour and ten minutes.'

'An hour and ten minutes?'

'I don't know if that's a note of amazement I hear or angst but imagine several hours on a dreary train or, worse, sitting in endless traffic jams.'

'It's amazement, Suze. I'm not always unimpressed!'

'And Harry dear, there are helicopters and helicopters! I'm sure Auntie Lenny's little flying machine will be quite comfortable and knowing you and Murray, he'll have made sure it's well stocked with a case or two or even three!'

'So astute, my Suze! What else?'

'The Donaghues. You're there for dinner tonight, a thank you dinner in your honour. Black tie, in the private room at Annabel's so even you can't gripe about that!' (Annabel's being London's most exclusive, private night club next to Mayfair's romantic Berkeley Square).

'I *like* the Donaghues!'

'So you should after all the money they spent with you redoing that monstrosity of a plantation house on Barbados!'

'Ah yes, now you've said Barbados, it's all coming back to me! The house where – as a joke – I suggested sisal carpet throughout, but sisal carpeting hand painted to look as if you were walking on carpets of exotic flowers!' Harry gave a camp shriek. 'Remember my hysterical phone call to you when they took my flip remark seriously?'

'Lucky for you the idea was not so improbable after all.'

'And thanks to you, Suze, for *knowing where to ask*!'

'No, thanks to Colleen and Bob Bery of Bery Designs. Only Colleen could have risen to the challenge which saw the lovely lady and her team painstakingly hand painting flower after flower for several weeks on site until you had your bloody fields of flowers! According to Colleen they never even had a moment to have a dip in the sea!'

'Ah, but all true artists have to suffer for their art ....' murmured Harry, striking a pained pose against the door jamb and adding mischievously, 'I take it the macho M hasn't been invited?'

'No, you two Siamese twins are being separated for once.'

''Fuck off, wench!'

'And up your well-worn flue, you!' carolled Susie. 'Now, in case it's escaped your notice, you have at least six calls to make and then Alan wants to see you about some problem with Tommy's bass clefs! So, maestro dear, will you please deal with what you have to deal with while I attend to my own workload which would make even the most devout workaholic blanch!'

A few minutes later Susie buzzed through to Harry. 'Bossikins dearest, there's a rather strange, semi-hysterical man on the line claiming to be Howard Hanover, the actor. If he is the genuine article, he's a dream. And no, he won't leave a message, doesn't want to make an appointment but he *does* want to speak to you!'

'Howard Hanover? I've heard the name before. Wasn't he in that hit mini-series a few years back, the one set in Medieval England or some such shit?'

'The very one. Shall I put the hysterical Howard through?'

'Why not? Perhaps he's thinking of creating his own medieval monstrosity for his twilight years.'

'Harry Humphries?'

Harry froze.

'Harry Humphries?' said the voice again.

'Err... Mr Hanover?' said Harry, thinking wildly, Is it or isn't it the voice from the other night?

'Humphries? A word of warning you cunt! Leave Mic Sandford alone!' There was a sharp click as the line went dead.

'Suze!' yelled Harry. 'Can you try and get hold of that number Hanover's just called us on?'

Susie appeared a few moments later. 'The number was blocked. Jesus Harry! You look as if you've just seen a ghost!'

'Not a ghost Suze, but now I know the identity of my night caller and bearer of unpleasant gifts! A very upset Mr Howard Hanover!'

'But why him?' questioned Susie.

'If you promise to be bad, very, very bad for the rest of the day I may just tell you,' said Harry with a forced smile. He gave a small, hollow laugh. 'After that shattering denouement I don't suppose a little libation…?'

'You do surprise me! Red or white?'

'Oh, definitely red seeing blood is about to be spilled! Meanwhile, let me call Murray.' Harry picked up the phone. 'M. Harry. I've just found out the identity of the bastard responsible for those calls and the packet of shit! Are you ready for this? Howard Hanover, the actor!'

'You mean Sandford's lover?'

'You know him?'

No, but Natalie does.' Murray's voice rose sharply. 'What do you mean? Hanover's the culprit?'

'He's just rung me, his opening line being exactly the same as the caller a few nights back. Not only that, he *sounded* identical! Furthermore, he told me to leave Sandford alone!'

'But why should he be doing all this and what does he mean by "leave Sandford alone?" You've only met the bloody man twice and always in company!'

'Exactly. Unless Sandford's gone and said something to him about the irresistible *moi*!'

'Jesus, Harry! Stop arsing about! I was just about to call Marge to confirm next Thursday – Sandford can't see us until then but I seriously think you should give him a call and explain what has just happened.'

'You do?'

Yes, I do, Harry my love. I mean, if this Hanover guy is to start threatening you – which, in a way, he already has – either Sandford tells him to back off or else you tell Sandford that, if this continues, you've no option but to get the police to intervene.'

'Isn't that a bit harsh?'

'No, Harry, not at all. Once again listen to your old tried and true mate!' There was a slight pause before Murray added softly, 'Natalie's always said Howard's a bit of a loose cannon. Furthermore he's overly possessive of Sandford and insanely jealous. Not the best of combinations! Tread lightly, my friend. Forget *hell hath no fury as a woman scorned,* think of a manic, jealous queen hell bent on revenge instead!'

'I'll call Mic on his mobile right away.'

'You do that and let me know what he says. Otherwise tell me in the morning as we fly a la Busby Berkeley down to wildest Wales as opposed to Rio!'

'Off the phone then, chop, chop! And I'll make the call.'

'Whoa! Hold on a sec! Look Harry, before you do or say anything rash – remember we have a lot at stake – I'm seeing Nat this evening at some promotion bash to do with her latest TV series. Maybe I should have a discreet word with her about Howard, see if she knows anything? Suss out the landscape as if it were?'

'No Murray, let me deal with it and there's no need to involve the lovely Natalie. Look, let's definitely try to speak later if we can, before we meet up in the morning. I'm ringing off and calling Sandford *now*!'

Harry put down the phone. Taking Mic's card from his wallet he dialled the relevant number.

'Mic, Harry Humphries.'

'Harry! What a delightful surprise! Please tell me you're calling to say you can make tomorrow evening after all?'

'No, Mic. I'm calling to tell you your lover, Howard Hanover, has just rung me at my office, called me a cunt and told me – in no uncertain terms – to leave you alone.' Harry took a deep breath, his heart racing. 'Firstly, I have no idea as to what he's on about and why he should have called me and secondly, I do not – and I repeat – do *not* appreciate your fucking lover ringing me at one in the morning, being abusive and, furthermore having a packet of his own shit *shoved through my letter box*!'

Before the startled man could respond Harry cut off the call.

'Your wine, sir?' said Susie staring at a scowling Harry. 'Oh dear, no, please don't tell me, our rupees just have or are about to be severely ruffled?'

'More than bloody ruffled Suze.' Harry gave the concerned young woman a wan smile. 'Made bloody redundant more likely.' He took a sip of wine before giving a somewhat brighter smile. 'Jesus Suze, I do believe our Mr Sandford has just stirred up a very hot slurry of even hotter curry!'

'Slurry as in shit slurry?'

'Precisely!'

THE RECEPTION:

'Murray!'

'Nat! Hi! You look great!'

'As do you, darling! Oh, I don't think you've met Howard, Howard Hanover; Howie and I starred in that dreadful television series a few years ago, *Vesuvius,* an embarrassing epic set in Ancient Rome.'

Murray glanced at the strikingly handsome man standing alongside Natalie. 'No, I haven't but I'm delighted to meet you Howard. I'm a great fan of yours. Saw a rerun of *Figures of Eight* the other night. Terrific!'

'Thank you,' came the cool response. 'One of my best.'

Murray stared again at the chiselled features, the artfully tousled hair, the dark, expensive Italian suit and the diamond encrusted evening watch on Howard's slender, lightly tanned wrist, thinking, Howard, my dear, you are one obviously very pampered play thing!

'Murray's in PR,' gushed Natalie immediately picking up the animosity between the two. 'And I know I've mentioned him endlessly to you, Howie darling!' She gave a tinkling laugh. 'I find it simply extraordinary the two of you haven't met before!'

'Well, now we have,' smiled Murray, adding wickedly 'Ah, is that a tray of champagne as opposed to a dagger I see afore me?' Smiling flirtatiously at the pretty young waitress now standing in front of them he added, 'Yes, we'll certainly have three of these. Thank you.' Handing Natalie a glass he held another out to Howard still staring at him intently. 'Howard?'

'Err…thanks,' muttered the actor taking hold of the glass, his fingers lightly touching Murray's. 'Thanks again,' he said, treating Murray to a dazzling smile.

Jesus, thought Murray. Sandford are you *mad*? His eye caught Howard's who was still staring at him while Natalie chattered away nervously, looking at the two with growing alarm. I don't know what's going on in that head of yours Howard Hanover, but you're fucking gorgeous. To his acute embarrassment Murray found himself developing a rampant hard-on.

As if aware of Murray's reaction Howard dropped his glance and leaning forward, pressed his muscular thigh against Murray's bulging crotch. Murray, jumping away as if he'd been burned, grasped Natalie by the arm saying, 'I've just spotted Robin Anderson, the best-selling author whose latest novel, *Still Life,* is about to be made into a film. I've read the book and you'd be simply great as Clytemnestra Jones. Come and meet him, he's a really cool guy! Excuse us Howard.'

Watching the two move rapidly away, Murray literally pulling Natalie along with him, Howard, his eyes narrowing, said quietly to himself, Fuck you, Mic! Two can play at your game and if this chunky, hunky Murray Harbourd is half the fucking stud he looks – and I bet he's even *hung* like a fucking horse! Felt like it anyway; all these polished East End boys usually are! – you can't say, dear Mic, you didn't ask for it. Yes, Mr Harbourd, I think you'll fuck me most satisfactorily so, all being well, let full ream ahead be the call of the evening!

CHAPTER 16:

'How was Wales?' asked Susie as Harry settled himself down behind his paper-covered desk.

'Very Welsh,' sniggered Harry. 'But rest assured, Suze, even though Lenny's castle conversion will, without a doubt – *avec* the brilliant Harry Humphries at the helm – end up a honeymooner's ultimate wet dream, give me good old England any time!' He leaned back in his chair. 'May I simply say whilst Wales is so near it's altogether too bloody, fucking far!'

'Don't forget it gave us the likes of Dylan Thomas, Richard Burton *and* Tom Jones!' camped Susie.

'Exactly! Bring on the Alzheimer's quick!'

'Oh, and there's a *very important letter* for you from Mic Sandford; sent over by special courier earlier.'

'Ah, Mr "Cap in Hand" Mic! Let's see what the dear old thing has to say.'

'Meanwhile…?'

'But of course! After several hours of travelling in the company of Lenny Freed, I certainly deserve one. A gallon of red would be great. Thanks.'

Picking up a paperknife Harry neatly slit open the envelope muttering, 'At least it's a letter, letter and not some shit-filled jiffy bag.' Taking out the neatly folded pages he quickly skimmed over the immaculate penned script, his face breaking into a self-satisfied smile. 'Yes!' he said. 'Oh yes! Most definitely yes!'

'*My dear Harry,*' he read out loud. '*After your most unexpected call last Thursday which, I must tell you, left me well and truly devastated, I was so relieved you called me back from your Welsh venue.*

How right you are and how wrong I was/am to assume your feelings towards me should – or would – be the same as mine towards you!

As I tried to explain – while there is really is <u>no</u> *explanation – I have fallen deeply in love with you. However, in retrospect, this is an attitude of extreme selfishness and I can only trust – and pray – you will allow me the chance of continuing to see you and you getting to know me. If this be the case, let fate then take its course.*

Meanwhile, my word is my bond and I have no intention on reneging on our proposed business venture.

If you and Murray are still willing to sign a mutually satisfactory agreement, it will be my great delight and honour to do the same.

Finally, you have my word I will never attempt to force you into any sort of personal relationship and can only hope, as previously said above, your feelings towards me may change.

As always,

Mic.

Harry reached for the phone. 'M, me. Get your shapely butt over to the Fax machine! I'm about to send through Sandford's latest. It confirms exactly the phone call he and I had over the weekend and what I discussed with you.'

'So, as the mighty Murray advised you, you're willing to sign once we've gone through the contract with him, his lawyer and our Henry and given them the green light?'

'Yes, we sign. Can you confirm our meeting right away?'

'Your word is my command oh, most serene Maharanee of *Muchi-whore*!'

'Fuck off Marharaja My-big-cock-fill-any-jodhpur!'

'You wish, swish!' chortled Murray hanging up.

Harry glanced down at William's letter again. '*So* touching!' he said, giving a small snigger. 'Poor old sod, yet another victim of the Humphries irresistible allure! Irresistible but unobtainable! Count your blessings, Mr Sandford for you've no idea as to what a lucky escape you've had!' Re-reading the letter for a third time he gave a camp, indignant squeak. '*What*? I knew something was missing! There's no mention of dear Howard's little deposit!' Harry looked thoughtfully at Mic's bold signature. 'Hmm, that signature... taking into account the contract where that very same signature is about to reinstate itself, maybe it's better for all concerned if I totally disregard Howard's little *signature* and never refer to it or its source again.*'

THE BARNYARD:

'Hideous Harry's in the news again,' said Paul, pushing the rumpled tabloid over to William, 'Seems he's about to out *Raj* the *Taj* Mahal!'

'What now for Christ's sake!' snapped William grabbing for the offensive paper. 'Jesus fucking wept!' he snarled, his eyes racing across the headline, *The New Star Of India*! *Top Interior Designer Harry Humphries In Multi Million Design Deal*!

'Fuck! Fuck! Fuck!' bellowed William having read the piece in full, 'Who is this fucker Sandford? Furthermore, what is this fucking Sandford Holdings? Find out for me. *Now*!'

Not wasting a second Paul and Nelson scuttled out of the kitchen, their grotesquely distended crotches bobbing obscenely like a pair of twisted red, fun party balloons in front of them.

'And for fuck's sake cover yourselves up! You're fucking disgusting!' roared the puce-face artist after them.

Half an hour later, Paul and Nelson, wearing extra-large, matching track suit bottoms – suitably shortened – and matching Tee shirts bearing the slogan, *Blow Jobs Are Better Than No Jobs,* joined William in his studio.

'What did you find out?' grunted William delicately scribing the letters W.WAN onto the bottom right hand corner of a large, glowing canvas.

'Wandsworth's a closet queen, married to a socialite dyke and has had a long standing on and off affair with an actor, Howard Hanover!' growled a smug Paul.

'Well done, Paulie! Well done, Nelson!' exclaimed William. 'As always, two mines of information!' He gave the two a broad smile. 'And your very canny source, if I may ask?'

'Prince Albert's journalist friend, Cameron. He knows this Hanover creep quite well.' Paul gave a snigger, '*Intimately,* if you catch my fart!'

'Charming hyperbole, Paulie, and yes, one has most definitely caught your pungent point!' William gave a deep chuckle. 'Now, you say this Howard creep is an actor?'

'Yes.'

'An actor being an artist, or *artiste,* correct?'

'Correct.'

'And Howard creepy Hanover is Sandford's lover?'

'Yes, and furthermore Cameron tells there's more to this Mumbata business than meets the eye.'

'There is?'

'Yes, there is,' said Paul, pausing to take a deep breath before delivering his punch line. 'Howard told Cameron that Sandford is now in love with Harry Humphries and Howard is very, very jealous and upset!'

'My dears! You've done it again!' beamed William. He pointed to the recently applied signature on the canvas facing them. 'You see this? W.WAN?'

'Yes,' said Nelson giving William a puzzled look. 'It's your signature. You *always* sign your works like that.'

'Indeed I do and you know who inspired me to sign my name like that, don't you?'

'Yes, Paul Gauguin.'

'Exactly! Paul Gauguin the Dutch painter. Only *he* signed his works – though only some, mind – with the letter P for Paul followed by a dot and then the word GO; hence P.GO reinvents itself as W.WAN!'

'Yes William, said Nelson, frowning, his brother doing the same.

'And who was desperately in love with Paul Gauguin?'

'Vincent Van Gogh!' croaked a smug Nelson.

'Correct again,' laughed William, thoroughly into the game. 'And what did Vincent Van Gogh then go and *do* in a fit of lover's pique to gain the not-at-all-interested Paul's attention?'

'What?' growled the two baffled dwarfs in unison.

'Silly Vinnie cut off his ear and sent it to Paul!'

'He did?' grunted Nelson, his pig-like eyes widening.

'He most certainly did,' chuckled William. 'So, as one artist to another, my lovelies…'

'Who do we get to do it? Who do we get to do it? Can we?' rasped Paul.

'No, my little ones,' said William in his most soothing manner. 'It will have to be done very, very discreetly and' – here he gave a placating smile – 'with those splendid new cocks and balls of yours you'd be spotted in a second! No, we'll have to get Prince to organise this. Oh yes, Mr Sandford, your lover's ear in an envelope will, I sincerely hope and trust, come as quite a surprise!'

LONDON:

'Good morning, Murray Harbourd Associates. How may I help you?'

'Good morning. May I speak to Mr Harbourd if he's available? My name's Hanover. Howard Hanover.' There was a slight pause. 'It's a personal call. Mr Harbourd knows who I am.'

'Of course, Mr Hanover. Would you please hold for a moment.' Fiona Briggs. Murray's chirpy, red-haired secretary, putting Howard on hold, clicked through to Murray.

'Howard Hanover on the phone for you. Says it's personal. Please make this suffragette's day and tell me it's *the* Howard Hanover!'

'You day's just been made, Fi!' said Murray with a laugh. 'Put him through.' There was a silence followed by a click. 'Howard, good morning. This is a surprise.'

'Is it? Oh come on, Murray, as the late Mae West said, "Is that a gun in your pocket, or are you just pleased to see me?"'

'Sorry?'

'Your hard-on the other evening. Don't worry, I was the same. You free for lunch? The Wolesley, one'clock suit you?'

'Err... yes, fine, err...great,' stammered Murray.

'Good, see you there,' laughed Howard. 'And Murray, may I suggest you cancel any afternoon appointments which means we can go back to my place where you then fuck my brains out.'

Murray dropped the phone.

THE BARNYARD:

'Paul Column please, Mac Guthrie. Tommy Tyler's manager.'

'Paul Column at your service.'

'Ah, Mr Column, a slight change in plan, a change which, I trust, will be more fortuitous than inconvenient. Is there a chance we can meet slightly earlier than previously arranged? It's only Mr Tyler has now been asked to take part in a charity concert on that date and it would appear churlish of him not to do so.'

'But of course, Mr Guthrie. Mr Wandsworth, like myself, will quite understand,' growled Paul in his most unctuous manner. 'When are you suggesting?'

'At a push Tommy could spare an hour or so next Tuesday. But only a couple mind, otherwise the whole matter will have to be put on hold until after his German tour which would mean at least another three to four months delay. In circumstances, may I also suggest we postpone our proposed luncheon until another time?'

'Tuesday should be fine, Mr Guthrie and please don't worry about the luncheon. I shall inform Mr Wandsworth about the changes.' Paul gave a snide laugh. 'I am sure he will be only be too happy to venture up to London for so *important* a meeting. The same venue as before?'

'Absolutely, Mr Column. Flemings at noon.'

'Thank you, Mr Guthrie.'

'Christ,' said Mac to the silent phone. 'From the sounds of it, this Mr Column still writes with a bloody quill pen!'

Paul, bursting with self-importance, made his way as quickly as his short, stumpy legs would allow to William's studio where the burly artist stood working on a new canvas.

'It's getting better!' puffed Paul.

'What is?' growled William. 'Not this fucking canvas, that's for sure!'

'Operation Hideous Harry!'

'Operation Hideous Harry?' said William, his former scowl dissolving into a smile. 'I like it Paulie, I like it! What a clever little soul you are!' He looked down at the grinning dwarf. 'And how, exactly, is this Operation-Hideous-Harry, or OHH, getting better?'

'Tommy Tyler's manager's just called. You're now seeing him early next week and not at the end of next month as previously arranged.'

William gave another smile. 'As you say, Paulie, better and better.' Starting to clean his brushes William said softly, 'I must say, whenever asked to do *anything* for me, you and Nelson are the best. Now, even though you haven't mentioned it again, you two must be wondering about my promise for someone or something new for the new, big, bigger two of *you* to fuck?'

'Yes! Yes!' croaked Paul, jumping up and down on his stubby legs with excitement, his enormous package making a giant rippling motion in his adapted track suit bottoms.

'And haven't you and Nelson always been ardent fans of the Lone Ranger?'

'Yes! Yes!' Paul croaked again, his excitement – and his erection – visibly mounting, his twisted lips flecked with spittle.

'Well, I don't know if you noticed but Skids has been busy sprucing up part of the stables.'

'No, not really,' said Paul defensively, clutching his protruding front and looking as if he was about to overbalance. 'Big Nellie and the new big me have been very busy!'

'Of course you have,' said William soothingly, putting out a large, paint-stained hand and grabbing hold of Paul's bloated front so as to stabilise the teetering little figure. 'Anyway, they're meant to have been a surprise but I'm telling *you* now!' William paused dramatically but not in his squeezing and kneading of Paul's now seeping monster. 'You have two Shetland ponies arriving this afternoon.'

'Shetland ponies? You mean like miniature horses?'

'The very ones.'

'And we can ride them?'

'My dear Paulie, they're yours to ride whichever way you wish!' laughed William as Paul, with a guttural cry, came with a series of hot gushes into his track suit bottoms.

CHAPTER 17:

'Mr Wandsworth! Welcome!' said Mac Guthrie staring in astonishment at what could only be described as his dishevelled double. 'Mac. Mac Guthrie, Tommy Tyler's manager.'

Christ, thought William, my doppelganger but a doppelganger straight out of Men's Vogue! Shaking hands William peered curiously around the elegant, marbled lobby of the hotel. 'And our star?'

'Already downstairs waiting for you.' Mac gave William a conspiratorial smile. 'Tommy always uses the Clarges Street entrance to the hotel as opposed to this main one in Half Moon Street. Fans. I don't know if you noticed those few young ladies gathered outside as you came in? Someone has obviously tipped off some fan club Tommy may be here today.'

'And that someone wouldn't be you, Mac, by any chance?' grinned William, giving the beaming Scotsman a broad wink.

'Who knows, William, who knows?' laughed Mac. 'Now, if you'll follow me, you'll be able to see your future subject in all his glorious flesh!'

At Mac's bidding the three made themselves comfortable around the small dining table in the lavish hotel suite. Drinks in hand, William and Mac began discussing the proposed commission and accompanying contract while Tommy – having simply said a formal hello and shaken hands with the big man before excusing himself with a murmured 'I leave this up to the two of you,' while supposedly returning to idly flicking through a magazine – sat glancing across at the two men in disbelief, his wide green eyes darting from to the other. Determined to keep his gaze directed at his immaculately groomed lover Tommy found his glances repeatedly drawn to the pure animal magnetism of the artist. Christ, he thought, he's another Mac but a Mac living on the wild side! A brutal, devil-may-care Mac, crudely *oozing* male aggression and sex!

Tommy gave a gulp, quickly placing his hands down firmly upon his lap where the tiny Tommy Tyler cock was defiantly struggling to stand upright. A sudden vision of a naked William, his powerful hirsute body hunched over him, his massive, turgid, angry-looking cock ready to be rammed deep up inside Tommy's moist, greedily winking, receptive arsehole, caused the young man to give out a sudden cry, one hand flying up from his lap, catching a nearby glass of wine and sending it flying across the table, the contents partly catching William in the face and chest.

'Oh! Sorry! I'm so sorry William!' Tommy cried out, acutely embarrassed. 'I do apologise!'

'No need to apologise, Tommy!' smiled William wiping himself with a grubby handkerchief and ignoring Mac's whiter-than-white proffered one. 'Let's take it as a symbolic; a type of baptism; though one of wine and not of fire! Your portrait is obviously destined to be unique. Just as well the wine chose me instead of Mac, it would have ruined that very expensive suit whereas on this old jacket – covered in paint stains – it can only be an enhancement!' He gave a blushing Tommy a mischievous wink. 'Forget it Tommy Tom! I've got several more even worse stained jackets at home.'

'Tommy Tom? You called me Tommy Tom?' cried Tommy. 'Why, that's what Mac always calls me?'

'Yes, I do,' said Mac in his soft Scottish burr, giving Tommy an uncomfortable glance.

'Well, as they say, great minds think alike, Tommy Tom!' said William, giving Tommy another wink before taking a deep sip of his wine and thinking, Thank you again Cameron for *that* little gem of information. The effect on both has been one hundred percent!

Standing saying their goodbyes in the main lobby a worried-looking Mac, muttering his apologies, excused himself before making his way to the 'Gents.'

'I'll only be a wee moment,' he said, giving a self-deprecating grimace at his pun.

In a flash William homed into the still confused young man. 'Tommy Tom,' he said, taking Tommy's slender young hand in his large calloused one. 'I have a good feeling here. I know, just *know* we're going to become great, if not *intimate* friends.'

Ignoring the few gaping bystanders – both having been instantly recognised – William stooped down giving the startled Tommy a gentle kiss on the cheek. Looking down at the stunned young man he whispered, 'You're quite, quite lovely Tommy Tom and I can see why Mac is so deeply in love with you. But here' – quickly rummaging in a jacket pocket William pulled out a card – 'my private telephone and mobile numbers. Please call me at any time you wish.' He gave another soft smile. 'As a painter of portraits I need to get into my subject's soul, *your* soul. Hopefully you will get into mine.'

'Ready Tommy?' asked Mac, his anxious voice breaking the obvious electric tension between the two. Giving William a wary glance he turned to Tommy. 'There quite a few wee girls outside, the car's ready and waiting so, a few autographs and then we're off!' Mac turned to William. 'Thanks William; we look forward to seeing you at Tommy's first sitting.'

'We?' said William with a frown. 'Sorry Mac, "we" is not allowed when I'm working. It's my subject and me, nobody else.' He turned to Tommy. 'I take it that's OK with you, Tommy Tom?'

'Oh *yes,* William!' breathed Tommy Tyler, pop star supremo, 'Oh, most definitely OK!'

As William had anticipated, the call came through later that night, the light voice that thrilled millions nervous over the static. 'William, it's Tommy… did I wake you?'

'No, Tommy Tom, I was waiting for you to ring.'

'You *were*?'

'I was indeed.'

'William, I don't quite know how to say this… it's never happened to me before …'

'Say it, Tommy Tom, say it,' whispered William.

Tommy's voice came out with a light sob. 'I think I've fallen in love with *you* when I'm supposed to be in love with Mac! Does that sound crazy?'

'Not to me, Tommy Tom, it sounds quite beautiful…' William gave a small triumphant smile, his free hand forcibly kneading Nelson's bloated cock as Paul repeatedly prodded his stubby fingers in and out of his brother's foetid, willing arsehole. 'And Tommy Tom, I think I've fallen in love with you.'

MEGAMIKE RECORDING STUDIOS:

'Tommy, what is the matter?' demanded Mac. 'That's the *fifth* time you've been off key! You're simply not concentrating!'

'Sorry Mac,' whispered Tommy, a sheepish expression on his face. 'Sorry guys,' he said glancing at the small band. He looked back at a worried Mac, 'Can we take a short break and then we'll do it again? I promise it'll be perfect and a print.'

'OK. Ten minutes, fellows,' grumbled Mac, looking at Tommy with a mixture of concern and exasperation. 'He's not been himself since that meeting yesterday,' he muttered to himself. 'It's something to do with that bloody William Wandsworth, that's what it is! Christ knows what the guy's up to. And all this Tommy Tom shit? Where did he dig that private endearment from? Furthermore, last night was the first time – unless it's before a major concert – Tommy has slept in his own room and not ours.'

Making his way to a vending machine in the corridor outside the recording studio, Mac fetched himself a mineral water, standing contemplatively as he sipped his drink. Still muttering, he quietly voiced his concerns to the empty passageway.

'If it wasn't for the fact that there's so much stake – and let's be realistic here, young Tommy Tyler is only *young* Tommy Tyler for a very short career span, teenage fans being so fickle – I'd scrap that bloody portrait this instant. Let's just hope the wee laddie gets back to his former self sooner than later.'

'Now that was magic! Pure bloody magic!' cried Mac, his bearded face wreathed in smiles as he joined the band in applauding the smiling young man while Tommy, smiling back at Mac was sharing his moment with the superimposed image of a wild-looking, rumpled William; a William, his eyes burning with lust, a throbbing, rampant, cannon-like hard-on protruding from his open flies as if about to explode.

'I was singing for you, William!' Tommy nearly cried out. 'I was singing for you!'

The call came through after midnight. 'I've got to see you William, please! I've got to see you!' cried Tommy, his voice choking.

'But of course, *wee* Tommy Tom,' cooed William soothingly. 'And I'm desperate to see you too, my sweet but your career must come first… here you are in the middle of recordings, about to go off on tour and then of course there's the slight inconvenience of Mac always being around…'

'That's just it, William!' cried Tommy brightening, his former sobs miraculously forgotten. 'Mac's away tomorrow,' he added breathlessly, 'he's away in Paris for two days!'

'But your recordings?'

'Apart from tomorrow morning I'm free! My only appointment is a meeting in the afternoon with my designer at my new flat. Oh William, why don't you come along and see the flat? – it's going to be fabulous! – which means you can also meet Harry! He's terrific!' Tommy let out an excited squeak. 'Then after the meeting…'

'We can spend the rest of the afternoon and the evening together,' William cut in, adding, 'if that's what you were about to say!'

'Oh William, you silly, wonderful *thing*!' giggled Tommy. 'Of course, I was!' There was a moment's silence. 'I'm frightened, William,' said Tommy in a low voice, 'I've never been unfaithful to Mac before.' His voice reduced to a whisper, he added, 'I've never err… done it with anyone else. Mac was my first, my one and only…'

'You're not being unfaithful, Tommy Tom,' said William gently, his voice a deep, soothing rumble. 'How can you be unfaithful to someone when you've fallen *out* of love with that someone?'

BATTERSEA:

'It's amazing, Harry and Alan,' said Tommy looking at the model of proposed scheme set up of the display table in front of them. 'It really is going to be the most fantastic place ever! Utterly amazing and utterly fantastic!'

'Simply a mirror or, in other words, a reflection of our client!' laughed Harry. 'You've obviously been an inspiration to Alan and the team's fingers in making the model!' He gave another laugh. 'You really do like it, don't you?'

Tommy, vigorously nodding his head, stood gazing rapturously at the scaled-down, delicately webbed model of his flat-to-be.

'If only we had more clients like you!' chuckled Harry. 'I'm sure Alan will agree we've never seen someone so animated, so enthusiastic so… if you'll excuse such a crass expression – so *radiant*!'

'Do I? Do I really?' cried Tommy, his face breaking into a beatific smile.

'Do you really *what*?' asked Harry.

'Look *radiant*!' shouted Tommy in wild-eyed delight.

'Positively!' giggled Harry, 'To quote you Tommy, utterly amazingly and utterly fantastically *radiant*!'

'Can I let you into a secret?' asked Tommy shyly.

'Of course.'

'I'm in love.'

'You are?' said Harry. 'Who's the lucky guy?'

'Me!' boomed a familiar voice. 'Harry! What an unexpected pleasure!'

CHAPTER 18:

'Jesus! It's two a.m. I have to go!' said Murray adding, as he gave Howard a soft kiss on the cheek, 'I've an early start.'

'Must you?' said Howard with a pout, reaching out for Murray's arm and saying mischievously, 'No time for a farewell fuck?'

'Christ, Howie! You're insatiable!' laughed Murray. 'And as much as I'd love to, my prick feels as if it's on fire, about to drop off and it's literally been rubbed fucking raw!'

'Tell me about it,' giggled Howard, his hand dropping from Murray's arm to his flaccid cock. 'This,' said Howard, holding the limp, plump red length in his hand and bending forward to give it a light kiss, 'is quite something. What a pity you'll never know how good it is to be fucked by your own dick!'

'Perish the thought!' laughed Murray. 'Besides, that'd be some sort of incest, wouldn't it?' He gave another laugh. 'Now, Howie, I really must go. I'll have a shower when I get home.' He smiled down at the grinning young man. 'See you later today?' he questioned.

'Call me,' yawned Howard. 'Apart from lunch with Natalie, I'm open.'

'Tell me about it!' sniggered Murray, now dressed and making his way to the bedroom door.

Howard, having finally got up for a pee along with shitting out Murray's seven deposits of cum in a series of satisfying wet farts, made his way back to the dark bedroom. About to climb into bed he stood, startled by a sharp, distant knocking to the downstairs front door.

'Aha!' cried Howard, a self-satisfied smile appearing on his handsome face. 'You may be raw but you want some more!' he sniggered. 'Once again the lure of the Hanover arse proves irresistible!'

Clambering naked down the narrow stairs Howard raced across to the front door, pulling it open with a flourish. 'The return of the rampant one!' he cried, his voice trailing off as he saw the outline of two darks figures standing in front of him.

'Not the rampant one, I'm afraid,' said a deep bass voice mockingly, 'but the avenging two.'

Giving a loud shriek Howard made a feeble attempt to push the door shut but the figure with the voice beat him to it. In seconds Howard found himself being bundled back into the house, any further screams stifled by a giant black hand.

Mic warily eyed the small, padded envelope, stamped *PRIVATE & CONFIDENTIAL* in red, lying unopened on his desk. 'Jesus,' he murmured, prodding the spongy package with his forefinger, his mouth curling in disgust. 'Don't tell me Howie's gone and done another Harry by posting *me* a bag of his shit!'

Taking a paper knife he cautiously slit open the sealed end while attempting to peer inside. 'It doesn't *smell* of shit,' he said, his aquiline nose twitching, 'so what the hell?'

Lifting the bag Mic turned it upside down along with a vigorous shake, his hoarse cry echoing through the office as a bloodied ear plopped down onto his desk.

An hour later a distressed Mic having dealt with a supercilious police inspector and his sidekick, received a telephone call from a hysterical Howard. Despite Howard's incoherent ranting Mic eventually managed to gather there had been an attempted break-in and Howard, having been viciously attacked was now in a local hospital where he been interviewed by the police. It was only later in a second phone call that an even more hysterical Howard informed Mic about his missing ear. 'I thought my head was bandaged because of the blow that knocked me out,' Howard shrieked. 'I was found lying in the doorway to the house by a neighbour who called the ambulance and the police! But Mic! My looks! My looks! I'm ruined! Ruined! Oh, why couldn't they have just killed me instead?'

'Christ! Howie!' Mic had yelled. 'I think I've just been sent your bloody ear! In a jiffy bag! To the office! The police have just left taking what could be your ear with them! Until now there had been no link up. I'm on my way to the hospital but first, I must report this immediately!'

'What do you mean they sent you *my* ear?' screeched Howard. 'Are you telling me you've got my missing ear?'

'Yes and no,' said Mic as diplomatically as possible. 'What I mean to say is I *think* I may have had your ear but now it's with the police!'

'But it's mine! I want it back!' screamed Howard, adding, 'My looks! My looks! My career is ruined! Ruined! Ruined!'

A calmer Howard later called Murray who, though shocked, quickly diverted Howard's hysterical outpourings of self pity. 'Even the darkest cloud has a silver lining, Howie,' he said soothingly. 'As Ben Franklin said, "*Out of adversity, comes opportunity*!"' he added with a reassuring chuckle. 'Let me handle this for you, Howie. Leave it all to me and watch me turn your *adversity* into the biggest career move you could ever imagine or wish for!'

'You can? You will?' said Howard, his rich, modulated voice returning back to its usual dulcet tones.

'Watch this space!' laughed Murray. 'Look, Howie, when they say you can go home, let me know and I'll come and collect you.'

'No need, dear,' said Howard smugly. 'I called Mic and he's coming to collect me. It's the least the two-timing shit can do! Call me later, action man!' Howard gave a camp laugh. 'I'll make sure I'm ready for my *very* close ups, Mr De Mille!'

'Atta girl, Norma!' cried Murray.

The next day found Howard, his head bound with a rakishly-tied, colourful bandana, posing happily for a battery of photographers, all thanks to the swift machinations of the ever astute Murray.

Heart-Throb Actor in Burglary Horror! Screamed one placard. *A Sabre Tooth Tiger*! Screamed another, followed by the story of how a brave Howard, attempting to protect his home, battled with a sabre-wielding burglar who, in the middle of the violent struggle, had severed the dashing actor's ear. The story ended with a quote from the 'resting' actor.

'*I vowed I'd never stoop to any sort of plastic surgery,' said Mr Hanover, putting on a brave face at his luxurious Chelsea Mews house yesterday. 'But as it now involves a new ear, I'm first in the queue*!'

The fact the ear had been taken by the attacker was never revealed.

The following weeks would see Murray – now Howard's new manager – inundated with phone calls offering new roles for his revitalised star.

HH INC:

'Someone cut off Howard Hanover's *ear* and posted it to Mic Sandford?' chortled Harry looking across at a grim-faced Murray. 'But how *divine*! Teach the fucker to send *me* a packet of shit!'

'You're missing the point, H. Someone *deliberately* cut off his ear and *deliberately* sent it.'

'So you said, twice,' sniggered Harry. 'And if that is a fact, how come it hasn't been mentioned in the press? Unless you're slipping in your new *role,* Mrs Harbourd!'

'Not funny, Harry, not funny at all. Don't you think it a bit too much of a coincidence you receive a packet of shit, blame it on Howard who then just happens to have his ear cut off which in turn is sent to Mic?'

'I'd much prefer receiving an ear as opposed to a heap of shit!' sniggered Harry.

'Jesus, Harry! At times you are too much! For once I hope the mighty Murray is wrong in his predictions.'

'Oh, stop being such an oracular old queen! All I can say is it serves that arrogant prick right!'

'In amidst all your bitchy jubilation at Howard's humiliation has it occurred to you, Harry, Howard may *not* be the culprit responsible for sending you the package? Let's face it, nobody, but nobody, would cut off their own bloody ear and send it to his ex unless he was really off the rails! So the million dollar question; who *is* doing this and, much, *much* more worrying, who's next?'

Harry sat staring at Murray, the blood slowly draining from his face.

TWO WEEKS LATER:

Susie phoned the news through to Harry in Mumbai where he, Murray and Mic were spending a day and night before their flight back to London following their three day visit to Calcutta.

'He got *what*?' screeched Harry into the receiver. 'Hold on, Suze! Hold on! Let me get Murray!' Racing over to the doorway from his bedroom leading into the sitting room of their suite, Harry yelled, 'Murray! Pick up the fucking phone extension. I've got Suze on the line. She's had a hysterical Tommy Tyler on the phone trying to get hold of you, me, the works!'

'What? Why?' gasped Murray looking up from a sofa where he and Mic were sitting going through some papers.

'Just pick up the extension and fucking listen!'

Racing back into the bedroom Harry snatched up the phone. 'Suze, I'm back.' Ignoring Murray's affirmative 'I'm listening,' Harry charged on. 'Now Suze, can you repeat all again but slowly this time.'

'I can't believe it, I simply can't believe it!' muttered Murray gratefully taking the glass of whisky from a solicitous Mic.

'Nor me,' whispered a white-faced Harry. 'Christ M, Christ Mic. What the *hell* is going on?'

'Sorry to ask you lads but can you give me, once again, the gist of what Susie told you?'

'In a nutshell, Tommy Tyler received an envelope this morning containing an ear, the ear's believed to be Mac Guthrie's. Tommy apparently recognised a distinctive mole on the lobe. Tommy's gone to pieces. Quite, quite hysterical according to Susie.'

'Can you blame him?' muttered Mic, his face grim. Adding, 'And where is this err… Mac?'

'That's the cause of more hysterics. According to Suze he and Tommy had some sort of row at the recording studio yesterday and Mac walked out. Tommy wasn't too fussed thinking Mac may have gone down to their flat in Brighton to cool off. It's something he does quite regularly, apparently.'

'Didn't Tommy try and call him?' asked Mic.

'For some reason known only to himself, he didn't.' Harry gave a snigger. 'Perhaps making hay while the sun shines or, in this case, wasn't,' he said.

'And what do you mean by that?' questioned Murray.

'Just a thought, Murray, just a thought.' Harry gave a shrug. 'Perhaps everything isn't quite as rosy in the world of little Tommy Tyler as one is led to believe.' he added, his mind going back to William Wandsworth's unexpected arrival on the site of Tommy's new studio flat and Tommy's ecstatic welcome.

'You know what's going to happen, don't you,' said Murray gloomily.

'Oh oh,' said Harry. The oracle is about to speak.'

'To use an old saying, "Look at home before you look abroad," my friend!' said Murray ominously. 'First there was you – no, not an ear but a packet of shit! Then Mic being sent Howard's ear and now Tommy receiving Mac's.'

'So?'

'So, Harry? *So*? They're all bloody clients or connected to Harry Humphries Inc., that's what's *so*! It only takes a wily journalist to spot this and *voila,* a story to end all stories. *The Harry Humphries Houses of Horror*!'

'No, Murray, I have to disagree,' interrupted Mic. 'It's simply all an unfortunate coincidence.'

'I agree with Mic,' said Harry giving Murray a devious grin. 'But, if someone *does* happen to pick up on this so-called pattern of yours, as you are always saying M, all publicity etcetera!'

Murray, about to reply was interrupted by the ringing of the phone which Mic swiftly picked it. After a few muttered 'yesses' and 'I see' he ended saying, 'Thank you Susie, I'll let the boys know and Susie, may I suggest we all convene at my office tomorrow evening. Our flight lands late afternoon and Hector will be meeting us. Can you please call Marge and ask her to get in some snacks and such? Thank you, my dear and we'll see you then.'

Putting down the phone he gave Harry and Murray a grim smile. 'They've found Mac Guthrie. He's in the Chelsea and Westminster Hospital. Apparently he was attacked after leaving the studios yesterday – he was obviously being watched or followed. From what I could gather he was found gagged and trussed up on a building site – Tommy's new flat to be precise – by one of the workmen when he arrived on site this morning. The poor man was suffering from shock, hypothermia and, of course, a considerable loss of blood and his right ear missing.'

'Jesus,' muttered Harry.

'There's no "Jesus" about it!' snapped Murray. 'Harry, I know you're going to say no but you're moving in with me until this is all sorted out.' He held up his hand. 'No arguments, please, I'm sure Mic agrees with me.'

'OK, two to one. I give in.' Harry gave a mirthless laugh. 'Just as well William Wandsworth *didn't* become a client.' Looking at Mic and Murray he added with a sneer, 'Now there is someone *definitely* mad enough to cut off his own bloody ear!'

'Harry!' cried Murray, his face lighting up. 'I think you may have just answered the million dollar question! Didn't you tell me Wandsworth had turned up on the site of Tommy's new flat? Now why would he be doing that?'

THE BARNYARD:

'It couldn't be better, little ones,' said William, 'but now we must be extra careful. Sandford and Harbourd, especially Harbourd, are no fools whereas Humphries is so up his own arse he's never got time for anyone or anything else.' He looked solemnly at Paul and Nelson. 'I have a nasty feeling this could easily turn out to be a case of the finger of suspicion pointing very directly at me.'

'No!' cried Paul with a grin.

'Never!' croaked Nelson displaying his misshapen yellow teeth.

'So, said William,' equally amused, 'we need a diversion.'

'What?' said the two figures in unison.

'A very good question,' said William. 'It will have to be something major, something to douse any rumours involving William Wandsworth.'

'By *dousing* are you thinking what we're maybe thinking?' giggled Nelson.

'You are a pair of uncanny little buggers, aren't you?' laughed the big man. 'But, as always, on the *dot* as if it were!' He looked at the two. 'It'll be a bit of an upheaval but, as I see it, most fortuitous.'

William held up three paint-smeared fingers. 'One, work on the castle is well underway, all thanks to the manager of the Hotel Splendido whose brother has turned out to be a genius of an architect. Two, the Park Lane development is all on schedule along with planning permissions passed – all thanks again to the talented Senor Marcello Mazzuchelli now having taken over from the uninspiring *Mr Pillars of Light*! – so demolition begins next week and it's now it's full steam ahead. And three, we will have to relocate until we can use the castle and I know just the place.'

'You do?' This from Paul.

'Mazzy-Marcello – says it'll be four to five months before we can move into the *Castello Paradiso* so, in the interim, as Paulie's namesake did, what do you little guys say to a few months on Tahiti?'

'Tahiti!' exclaimed the two.

'Will I be able to wear a grass skirt?' chortled Nelson.

'That's Hawaii!' croaked Paul. 'We're going to Tahiti!'

'I'm sure you can wear a grass skirt, should you so wish,' laughed William. 'However, you'll have to let your cocks deflate a little and drain your balls. You can't very well walk around with a bunch of cocoanuts between your legs!' He gave another smile. 'There's nothing really holding us here, is there?' Affectionately ruffling their unkempt heads William added, 'Sorry the ponies didn't work out.'

'No, we didn't take to them,' agreed Paul.

'Did you ever err…?'

'Oh yes!' exclaimed Nelson. 'But not much fun. They just stood there and we *still* had to stand on a box!'

'Anyway, it was a very shrewd move of yours to sell them to that so-called halal butcher in Camberwell!' laughed William. 'What's more, what you've once again demonstrated to me is your honesty and loyalty not only by offering me all the monies from their sale but paying back *into* the company account all that money you – momentarily – had taken out of it! As if I wouldn't have noticed!' He wagged a thick, hairy finger at the two sheepish faces. 'Naughty, naughty!'

'Sorry, William,' croaked Paul.

''Yes, sorry William,' growled Nelson.

'William?'

'Yes Paulie?'

'Can Skids come to Tahiti with us?'

'*Skids*? What on earth for?'

'Well, we've been fucking *him* with our new willies and he *loves* it!'

William, genuinely taken aback, looked at the two grinning up at him. 'And what about poor Mrs Skids?'

'Oh, she loves them to!' grunted Nelson. 'Skids was quite shocked seeing he thought she only saw sex with him as a duty but, when she saw our new cocks…'

William, slapping his massive thigh gave out a loud bellow of laughter. 'Now I've heard it all! But,' he added soberly, 'you don't expect me to invite Mrs Skids, do you? I don't think I could cope with that.'

'Oh, you won't have to,' croaked Paul. 'For some reason, after being seriously *depraved* with us, Mrs Skids has decided to repent.'

'She has?'

'Yes,' grinned Nelson. 'She's about to become a nun!'

William's loud roars of laughter – if physically possible –would have, without doubt, raised the proverbial roof.

CHAPTER 19:

'Take a look at this,' said Murray handing Harry a morning paper with one hand and a mug of steaming coffee with the other.

'And a very good morning to you too!' yawned Harry, stretching luxuriously in the steel four poster bed dominating Murray's guest bedroom. 'Good God!' he exclaimed spilling part of his coffee onto the leopard print duvet. 'I know I should be saying "good riddance," but shit, what a terrible thing to have happened, even to a cunt like him!'

He looked again at the headline, *FAMOUS ARTIST'S STUDIO DESTROYED*. 'Christ Murray,' he added with a smirk. 'Pity he never did start my portrait then I really would have been an *old* flame!'

'Oh, fuck of Harry! The poor guy's probably lost uncountable thousands of pounds worth of paintings. At the end of the day all the poor bastard did was fall for you – though when you act like this, only Christ knows why!'

Unbeknown to Harry, Murray and the general public, all paintings from *The Barnyard* had been taken into secure storage a week before the fire, William having announced to the owner of his usual gallery the proposed break on Tahiti prior to taking up residence permanently in Italy. Algie Symthe-Tomlinson, the gallery owner had, through his numerous connections, assisted William in finding a suitable alternative place to work, this being an idyllic, old plantation house set on a promontory overlooking a sparkling bay near the old town of Papeari.

'I plan to immerse myself in the atmosphere that so inspired Gauguin,' William had explained to the eager Algie who was in the early stages of organising his forthcoming *Illustrious Illuminati* exhibition for the following year. 'I have now made innumerable sketches of my subjects who will only be required for a final sitting here in London on my return.' He gave a reassuring laugh. 'After all, the portraits are more *illusionary* as opposed to realistic. Pure William Wandsworth in other words.'

'And for these you'll be working in your Notting Hill studio, I take it?' said Algie.

'Maybe, maybe not, Alfie my sweet,' had been William's nonchalant reply. 'Perhaps I may be working in another London studio, a studio destined to end all studios. You'll simply have to wait and see!'

HH INC:

'He's fucking off to Tahiti of all places,' commented Murray. 'Cock, stock and bloody paintbrushes! And yes, he's also got the go ahead for Park Lane! Christ alone knows – and Wandsworth obviously – whose helping finance all that! Talk about a devious old devil! There's no stopping the bastard!'

'And the Italian castle? My *bête noir*?'

'Apparently the same architect responsible for the Park Lane project. Some unknown Italian who, let's face it, Wandsworth is certainly putting on the bloody map.'

'Poor Tahiti! Poor Italy and poor Park Lane is all I can say!' said Harry spitefully.

'Rich Tahiti, rich Italy, rich Park Lane and very rich architect is what you should be saying!' came back Murray's sharp riposte. 'C'mon, an international name like William, the new Francis Bacon, seeking solace in the arms of Gauguin and the greats of Italy? It's pure soap opera, a saga made in publicity heaven! Furthermore, it now appears there were no paintings destroyed in this most convenient of fires. Apparently Wandsworth has been planning this Tahitian sojourn for some time and all his major new works were already in safe storage thanks to the ever vigilant Algie "ooh, give-us-a-sniff-of-your-armpits" Smythe-Tomlinson.'

Harry, cutting into Murray's diatribe, picked up the phone. 'Yes Suze,'

'Tommy Tyler on the phone in a rant!'

'Jesus! Now what? This is all I need. Put the spoilt twat through! Yes Tommy?' Harry listened patiently to the high-pitched tirade before saying patiently. 'Tommy! Tom. *Listen*! The contract *is* on schedule, in fact we're *ahead* of schedule. Yes, ahead, Tommy.' Putting on his most soothing voice he added, 'No, you won't be let down. In fact – and I wasn't going to tell you as I wanted it to be a surprise – on the day after your return from your German tour Harry Humphries Incorporated is planning an amazing party for you in the completed flat. Two months *before* the given moving in date!'

'I love you Harry!'

'And Harry Humphries Incorporated loves *you,* Tommy!' There was a pause. 'How's Mac by the way?'

'Oh fine. Just fine,' muttered Tommy, sotto voce.

'Well on the road to Mandalay – oops! I mean recovery?' quipped Harry. 'Good' he added to the noncommittal reply. 'Well, give him our love and Tommy and, as I've just said, don't panic! Again Tommy dear, remember, Mac mustn't know I've spilled the beans about the surprise party. He was simply going to say he was bringing you *here* for a drink when instead he'd be driving you straight to your new abode.'

'Panic over, Harry,' said Tommy, his voice even softer. 'Err… Harry, there's something I should tell you before you see it in the press and I haven't dared tell Murray. He'll go berserk.'

And what's that?' asked Harry glancing at Murray, alarm bells beginning to ring in his head.

'Mac Guthrie's no longer my manager and PR guy. I've sacked him!' The line went dead.

Harry slowly replaced the receiver.

'What now?' asked Murray, seeing the shocked expression on Harry's face.

'Tommy Tyler's gone and sacked Mac Guthrie.'

'What? But he can't have! Why, Mac Guthrie *is* Tommy Tyler!'

'Not any more, he ain't!'

'But this is pure madness!' muttered Murray, shaking his head in disbelief. 'Did he say who he's taken up with instead?'

'No, but I'm sure a discreet call to Mac may put you in what is becoming a very unpleasant picture.'

'What do mean exactly by "unpleasant picture?"'

'Well, William Wandsworth is painting his portrait, isn't he? Another of these coincidences, *n'est-ce pas*?'

'Mac? Murray Harbourd.'

'Ah yes, Murray,' responded Mac, his soft Scottish burr sounding hoarse with exhaustion. 'I suppose you've heard? That's why you're ringing?'

'Yes Mac, and I'm so sorry. Is there anything I can do?'

'No, not really Murray, but thank you kindly.' Mac let out a deep sigh. 'It's come as quite a blow, Murray my lad, a mighty blow in fact. He was my *life,* Murray, my whole reason for living. I wanted everything for my Tommy Tom.'

'And you gave him everything, Mac. If it wasn't for you he wouldn't *be* Tommy Tyler.' Murray paused for a moment. 'Mac, I know Harry, Harry Humphries, always sends me up about my old fashioned proverbs and predictions but there is an old saying, *"Pick yourself up, dust yourself down and start all over again!"* Are you free for lunch?'

'Could be. Why do you ask?'

'I have an idea. The Wolseley at one?'

'I don't think so Murray, but thank you all the same. I'm not ready for any new ideas yet. Maybe I'll simply let that dust lie a wee bit longer.'

'So tell me super sleuth, did you find out who the new Svengali is?'

'No, I was planning to do so over lunch.'

'Lunch? How come lunch? He asked you to lunch? But why? Tommy's my client! *Our* client to be exact! Mac Guthrie's now old hat!'

'Christ Harry, it was the other way round. If you'd been doing your usual eavesdropping you would have heard it was *me* asking him to lunch.' Murray gave Harry a glare. 'I feel sorry for the guy, OK?'

'Well don't! I'm sure quote – the guy – unquote, is feeling fucking sorry enough for himself and now, if you don't mind, I need to call Griselda. She's all *ears* to hear about the console table I found for her at Rabigh Hagh.'

Murray spotted the announcement in the latest *Spotlight* magazine. 'Who the fuck's this Prince Albert,' he muttered to himself. 'Never heard of him.' He looked at the caption again. *London Impresario Prince Albert To Represent Tommy Tyler.* 'What the fuck is this all about?'

Having re-read the article Murray threw the magazine down in disgust. 'Jesus, Tommy! What the fuck are you at? Reading between the lines this guy's nothing more than a fucking hoodlum. Lap dancing clubs? Gambling joints? *Art* films? You've got to be joking. Bloody porn films more likely. More to the point, who put you on to him or him on to you?'

He reached for his mobile. 'Harry, M. I've found out the name of Tommy's new manager. A guy with the dubious name of Prince Albert.'

'So?'

'Ring any bells?'

'Not that sort of ring, no,' said Harry with a snigger.

'Very funny, Harry! But this Prince Albert – the guy, not the piercing! – I've just done some further research as to what is generally being said. The guy's a fucking mobster!'

'Murray sweet, as I've said Tommy's our client, a client of Harry Humphries Incorporated and not *your* client. Once the new contract is finished – and he's hopefully settled his final invoice – little Tommy Tyler is old hat. He will have served his purposes, lots and lots of lovely money plus lots and lots of lovely publicity. All you have left to do is concentrate on the final shots for all those various design magazines you've lined up. Once these are done, Tommy Tyler is a closed book – or magazine! Take your pick. Then forget Tommy Tyler.'

'For once you're absolutely right but it's Mac I still feel sorry for.'

'Oh, I wouldn't feel too sorry for big Mac,' quipped Harry, grinning at his pun. 'He'll get over it. He's a burly Scot – all those oats and all that whisky! – and I bet he has a massive caber beneath that imaginary kilt which hordes of rampant wannabes will be only to willing to toss!'

'Very funny Harry, but again, you're probably right!'

'Where are you?'

'Having a coffee in Starbucks. The one in Old Brompton Road, along from *The Troubadour* . Why, what are *you* up to?'

'Meeting you in about half an hour for lunch at *The Troubadour*! By the way, when you get back to the flat this evening you'll no doubt find a lead weight envelope waiting for you.'

'Oh no, let me guess. More shit, more ears or – if I'm lucky – maybe a massive cock this time?'

'Nothing so unoriginal. A gilt – and when I say gilt think Fort Knox – edged commission for you.'

'Now what are you going on about?'

'Actually, it's a letter from Griselda Carter – she called Suze and insisted on your personal address. Madam C's been banging on about a surprise anniversary party and needs someone to organise this for her. Naturally – or very unnaturally – I suggested you as you're the man with all the contacts. She wants something spectacular so you'll have to find a venue, the works.'

'What about the house?'

'Don't be daft! A, it won't be ready and B, it wouldn't be at all suitable, or big enough, for what she has in mind. She wants a dinner dance, cabaret turns, you name it, the golden Griselda wants it!'

'Let me guess, a fancy dress bash?'

'Correct.'

'By something spectacular maybe a Bollywood as opposed to Hollywood extravaganza?'

'Correct.'

'Acres of marquees tented in miles and miles of silks supplied from a certain Humphries, Mumbata Worldwide?'

'Correct.'

'Tommy Tyler part of the cabaret?'

'Correct.'

'Jesus Harry, why didn't *you* simply offer to organise it?'

'Because I'm so nice and so considerate. After all, even a public relations man of your calibre needs a challenge every now and then!'

'Cunt!'

'I love you too!'

CHAPTER 20:

ONE MONTH LATER:

'Murray! I was hoping I'd bump into you!'

Murray stared blankly up at the smiling man.

'It's me, Mac. Mac Guthrie.'

'Mac? Good God! *Sans* beard and moustache I didn't recognise you!'

'It's the new me, Murray, the new Mac dusted down and started all over again! No beard, no moustache but, as you can see, a new, longer "Operation Cover Up" hairstyle!' Smiling, the big Scotsman turned to a dazzling, dark-haired youth standing next to him. 'Meet Jamie, Jamie Jefferson about to become the *new* and even more magical Tommy Tyler!' He gave the smiling Jamie a gentle squeeze on his arm. 'Jamie, meet Murray, Murray Harbourd, the very kind and *simpatico* gentlemen I told you about. The one who rescued me from the abyss of despair as if it were.'

Oh really? thought Murray. Looks as if this Daniel Radcliffe lookalike has probably done more to rescue you than I ever did!

'Hi, Murray,' said Jamie, his green eyes twinkling. 'So you're the man responsible for this slave driver! He never allows me a moment's break! Well, apart from the odd treat like lunch today.'

'Mac, I really am so glad to see you!' Murray enthused. 'And I must say the removal of the beard and moustache is remarkable! Why, you're even better looking than before!'

'Tell me about it,' laughed Jamie. 'As I said to Mac, either the face fungus goes or I go!'

'Oh.'

'Absolutely!' grinned Jamie. 'I told him I wasn't prepared to kiss a bush – well, not up there. Down below is different!'

'Oh,' said Murray again, staring at the totally unabashed young man. 'Err… are you guys going straight to your table or have you time to join me for a drink?'

'Mac?' Jamie looked up adoringly at the big man towering above him.

'Absolutely!' laughed Mac. 'Are you waiting for someone? If not, please join us for lunch.'

'I'm meeting Natalie Vine and Howard Hanover.'

'Ah, my soulmate,' laughed Mac. He touched his neatly styled hair covering both ears. 'As you can see, the top now compensates for the beard and moustache due to you know what.'

'Of course,' muttered Murray, his face reddening.

'I'd very much like to meet Howard,' smiled Mac. 'From what I hear he's in much demand, partly thanks to you, if I may add.'

'Simply helping out a friend,' murmured Murray.

'And of course, the lovely Natalie Vine. I'm a great fan.'

'And here they are!' cried Murray on seeing the couple entering the restaurant. 'Nat, Howie, bandana *et al*!'

'Bandana?' whispered Mac.

'Yes!' replied Murray quickly. ''They've been working on rebuilding his ear and the unveiling is in a week or two but, I must say, he certainly looks very rakish – very Johnny Depp – in that head gear!' He stood up from the banquette where he had been sitting. 'Nat! Howie!' he called, waving in welcome. Turning back to Mac and Jamie, he added. 'Do please join us as my guest. It'll be fun.'

'Oh please, may we Mac?' cried Jamie. 'I'd love to meet Natalie. She was fab, simply fab in *Tomorrow's Way.'*

Introductions made and two extra chairs brought to the table, the five sat down for lunch. Having finally got round to ordering their coffees Murray, having already excused himself once from the table to make a few 'urgent phone calls' after a continuous animated, huddled conversation with Howard and Mac, eventually stood up saying, 'Please excuse me but I've got a few things to doubly check.'

Giving Howard's shoulder a friendly squeeze he smiled at Natalie and Jamie. 'Howie and Mac will explain all and hopefully we'll all be meeting back at my place in about an hour's time.'

On leaving the restaurant, a popular haunt for celebrities, the four were immediately set upon by several photographers.

'Natalie! Howard!' one called.

'Natalie – over here, luv!' cried another.

'Ian! How are you?' said Natalie, smiling brightly at a small leprechaun-like figure. Grabbing a bewildered Jamie by the hand she pulled him next to her. 'Smile for the birdie, Jamie! You'd better start getting used to this!'

'New boyfriend, Nat?' asked Ian with a mischievous grin as he lifted his camera.

''If only, Ian!' cried the actress. 'No, this is Jamie Jefferson.'

'Jamie Jefferson?'

'Yes Ian, Jamie Jefferson,' said Howard butting in and placing Jamie between himself and Natalie. 'And Ian, you've got an exclusive! Jamie's going to be singing the theme song for the new film Nat and I are making in the spring! Quick, quick, you two! Our car's here!'

Posing briefly for one more photograph Howard bundled the startled Jamie, a smiling Natalie and a beaming Mac into the back of the stretch limousine which had suddenly materialised as if out of nowhere.

'Now we're being kidnapped!' cried Mac camply.

'Not quite!' laughed Natalie. Smiling at the big man now sitting opposite her and Jamie, a beatific smile on his face, she added, 'Mac, your Jamie is divine. He totally captivated me over lunch whilst you old fogeys, rather like Macbeth's three witches *sans* cauldron were getting up to heaven only knows what!' She gave another laugh. 'But after the tit bit you dropped Ian, I've a pretty good idea and wholeheartedly agree!'

'If this is being kidnapped,' laughed Jamie looking around the luxurious interior of the limousine and the friendly faces, 'then I'm all for it! But will someone kindly tell me what's going on?'

'Oh, it's all Murray,' laughed Howard. 'Tell him, Mac.'

'Well, wee Jamie, while you and Natalie were so busy canoodling during lunch…'

'I wasn't!' cried Jamie, his face turning a bright pink.

'Now I'm offended!' laughed Natalie.

'Oh Natalie, I didn't mean… '

'Shush! Wee Jamie!' laughed Mac, 'and listen to Howard.'

'It's very simple,' said Howard. 'Nat and I are about to make this new film, a romantic comedy along the lines of those old Doris Day, Rock Hudson movies like *Pillow Talk* and *Send Me No Flowers* – way before your time Jamie, I may add! The one we're making, *Mayhem in Mayfair*, will require a hit song to help plug it and, as Murray suggested, why not give you the opportunity to record this? The lyrics will be sent over to within a day or two. Furthermore, Mac deserves it.'

'I thought as much,' laughed Natalie. 'As soon as I saw you three going into a huddle and M's darted looks at Jamie, I knew it had to be the song. The music's great, by the way. A blending of Ricky Martin meets Michael Bublé!'

'Wow!' This from Jamie.

'I don't know what to say, how to thank you three, the magical Murray, you lovely Natalie and you, handsome Howard, bandana and all!' said a beaming Mac.

Think nothing of it,' replied Howard, his face deadpan. 'Simply see it as another Murray-ism and one we've all heard. *Out of adversity...*' he began only to be joined by a laughing Mac, the two carolling '*comes opportunity*!'

'Now,' Howard continued once the laughter had died down, 'Jamie, to put you in the picture – ha ha – Murray not only organised this get away car but those oh so convenient photographers. You can bet on your last penny that Ian will have done us proud and you'll be splashed all over the tabloids tomorrow! So, young man, with Mac's connivance, we're now on our way to Murray's flat for a celebratory drink. Furthermore, garrulous Greg, Nat's manager will also be there. Mac says you've just recorded your very upbeat version of *Strangers In The Night,* which we will be asking you to sing with Mac accompanying you on the piano. Once Greg hears you it's another step in the right direction of getting you to release the theme song.'

'Wow!' said Jamie weakly as he squeezed Mac's hand. 'Wow!'

'May I ask a very personal question,' said Howard as the big car made its way along the busy Chelsea Embankment.

'Depends how personal,' laughed Mac.

'Where did you two first meet?'

'Oh, quite by accident,' smiled Jamie, unaware of Mac's growing embarrassment. 'I'd been to dinner at a local restaurant in Earl's Court and decided on a late night cruise in the Brompton Cemetery. In the dark I made out this big guy standing near a tombstone – it was obvious from what was on view what he was after – so I gave him a blow job! Which was great! Furthermore, we agreed to a repeat performance, same time, same place two evenings later. The rest is history!'

'You mean...' gasped a delighted Natalie.

'Yes! The man was Mac!'

'You're definitely our voice for *Strangers In The Night*!' chortled Howard.

'Furthermore, on occasions, we replay the little scenario. Keeps Mac on his toes and me on my knees, as if it were!' giggled Jamie.

'Oh Mac, Now I can see why you adore the little monster so!' cried Natalie, tears of laughter running down her face.

'I dinna believe he said that!' snorted Mac, his big hands covering his smiling face in mock embarrassment. 'Oh laddie, we'll have to make sure you are never allowed to say certain things to the press!'

SEVERAL DAYS LATER:

'Howie, it's Mic.'

'Mic! This is a surprise!'

'Have you got a moment?'

'Of course.' There was a moment's silence.

'How are you, Howie?'

'Mic, I'm fine, really fine and the ear is nearly there, the skin grafts have taken on top of the new bits of cartilage so in a few weeks there'll be the great unveiling. Literally!' There was another pause before Howard asked softly. 'Did you get my note?'

'Yes Howie, I did. And thank you, it was very sweet of you to write.'

'No Mic, thank *you*!' Howard gave an embarrassed laugh. 'Christ Mic, it's not every day your lover insists on paying for London's most exclusive *and* expensive plastic surgeon to give someone else a new ear.'

'Lover?'

'Oh, slip of the tongue,' laughed Howard. '*Ex*-lover.'

'How sad. My spirits soared for a moment.'

'Mic?'

'Yes Howie?'

'Err… would you like us to see me again?'

'You only have to give me a time and a place! Oh dear, another slip of the tongue!'

'Tell you what, Mic. I'm meant to go to some bash with Nat and Murray this evening, but I can easily get out of this.'

There was another pause before Mic said quietly, 'I hear you and Murray are becoming quite an item.'

'Murray's not only my agent Mic but also a great friend. He's may have been the occasional fabulous fuck but he's not my *lover*!' snapped Howard.

My, my Howie, thought Mic with a smile, You'll never change! 'Oh?' he said instead.

'Yes, "oh" Michael Sandford Esquire! And if you get your big hairy, delicious arse and even bigger cock round to my *other* Mews house – we're well on our way to becoming quite a rich Howard in his own right now – you'll be made to remember who my lover is! Here's the address.'

CHAPTER 21:

'Good morning, Mr Sandford please. My name's Wandsworth, Willaim Wandsworth. Mr Sandford's expecting my call, I believe, following an earlier conversation with my representative, Mr Algernon Smythe-Tomlinson.'

'Good morning Mr Wandsworth, and yes, Mr Sandford told me you may be calling. Would you mind holding on for a moment and then I'll put you through. Mr Sandford's just finishing a call.' There was a slight pause before Marge added, 'Or would you prefer me to call you back when Mr Sandford is free?'

'No thank you, I'll hold.' William sat staring contemplatively at his grubby nails while listening to a muted rendering of Vivaldi's *The Four Seasons* coming over the static. 'Why always those fucking four seasons?' he muttered. 'Still, I suppose it's considerably better than that fucking nonce Vaughan I'm-a-fucking-lark-ascending Williams!'

'Mr Wandsworth?' said Marge, 'Sorry to have kept you waiting. I'm putting you though now.'

'Mr Wandsworth? Mic Sandford. This is indeed a pleasure and I was delighted to receive Algie Smythe-Tomlinson's call. As he says, it's an offer I can't refuse!'

'Thank you, Mr Sandford.'

'Mic, please.'

'Thank you Mic, and likewise.' William gave a buddy-buddy laugh. 'As Algie told you I'm leaving England next week for a few months break staying on Tahiti before taking up permanent residence in Italy. Of course I'll be returning to London on a regular basis and will still be keeping on my studio here in town.' Taking a deep breath, he continued. 'As the wily Algie explained – and a very subtle move on his part I must say – I am holding an impromptu and very select, small private viewing this coming Monday of certain completed portraits due to appear in my next year's exhibition, the eagerly awaited – again all thanks to Algie – *Illustrious Illuminati.*'

William, pausing for a moment in order to let his words sink, then continued. 'Should any of the guests wish to purchase any of the portraits they may do so but on the condition the works remain with the Tomlinson-Haydon Gallery until after next year's exhibition.'

'I'm listening,' said Mic.

'I know Algie has briefed you on a proposition I would like to run past you,' said William silkily. 'Time is the essence Mic as I am leaving on the Wednesday. This is extremely short notice but, as you know, Algie and I only discussed the matter yesterday even though he has been mulling over it for some time. So, we're hoping you too can meet us at the gallery on Monday at noon and maybe join us for lunch afterwards?'

'I'll be there but lunch could be a problem.'

'Well, see how it goes. And Mic, as this is all slightly underhand, as if it were, I'd be happy if you would keep it to yourself.

'Of course William, I quite understand. I look forward to meeting you on Monday.'

William looked across at Prince Albert. 'Got him!' he said. 'Next step we inveigle Sandford into personally investing into the new WW Gallery; nothing to do with Sandford Holdings but certainly Humphries Mumbata Worldwide.'

'And then?'

'Simple Prince my man, we destroy both Sandford and Humphries.'

'You sure about this?'

'One hundred percent, Prince. The two go hand in hand. We slipped up in thinking Howard was the way to get to Sandford but this Mumbata business puts it in a whole new light. It's this Harry Humphries cunt the man's besotted about.'

'Fuck me William but you really *are* out to destroy this Humphries guy, aren't you?'

'Short of killing him? Absolutely!'

'And what about you and Tommy?'

'Like a lamb for the slaughter but saved by the fact I *like* the kid. And your view?'

'Pretty little thing.'

'You fucked him yet?'

'Not until you give me the go ahead, William.' Prince gave a deep, bass laugh. 'But from what you've just said I don't see it happening! Well, not at this present moment of time. *Like* him? Looking at you, William my man, maybe you *more* than simply like him, huh?'

William gave the grinning black man a bemused smile. 'You know what Prince? If you'd said yes you'd fucked Tommy Tom why, for the first time in my long, sordid life I do believe I would have been quite angry with you. Fucking furious in fact!'

'Well, if that's the case I'll be making sure I keep you very, *very* calm!' laughed Prince. He sat staring warily at William for a moment before saying, 'Talking of Tommy, the lad called earlier in a bit of a state.'

'He did? Nothing to do with me, I trust?'

'No, it's about this Guthrie guy.'

'Mac Guthrie? What about him? I thought he'd gone to ground, literally, as if it were?'

'No way, in fact he's very much *above* ground. Here, take a look at this.' Prince slid William one of the day's tabloids. 'After Tommy's call I sent out for a copy. It seems our Mr Guthrie is much tougher than we thought. Not only does he seem to have magically reinvented himself in just a few short weeks but he even has a new star in the ascendant! This group photograph was taken yesterday. The kid's name's Jamie Jefferson and according to the accompanying text he's about to be signed up to do the theme song for the earless Mr Hughes and Miss Vine's new film. No doubt the envisaged hit being what Bassey did for *Goldfinger*.'

'Shit! And Tommy saw this?'

'Hence the phone call.'

William, his face distorted with anger, gave out a snarl. 'I tell you Prince, it *all* leads back to this fucking Harry Humphries again! It's like a bloody fucking pattern! Tommy and Sandford are his clients; originally connected with Tommy was this Guthrie guy who is now managing bloody Jamie jingle bells whatever who in *his* fucking turn is now involved with Sandford's ex in a film! Jesus fucking shit, hell and Christ! What the fuck next? What *is* it with this Humphries?'

'You tell me, William,' said Prince, 'for, let's face it mate, he's certainly got to you!'

'Yes,' said William with a growl. 'He certainly has.' He glared at Prince. 'I said a few moments ago I was jealous of Tommy which for me is a first. What I *didn't* say was that with Humphries it was the first time in my life I've ever been told to literally go fuck myself and furthermore the little bastard screwed up – for me – what could have been a very lucrative deal.'

'But you're about to make millions, William.'

'They say, Prince my friend, money is the root of all evil but in this case, it's this Harry Humphries who's the fucking root! Somehow, and I don't know how, he's certainly got under my skin! Oh, I know it sounds trite but he's become a bloody obsession.' William gave Prince a confused look. 'You know what, my friend, not only – because of Tommy Tom – am I experiencing jealousy but again for the first time – and all due to this Harry Humphries – I'm experiencing complete and utter hate.'

'Jesus, Wandsworth,' muttered Prince, 'No need to remind me again never to fall out with you!'

TOMLINSON-HAYDON GALLERY:

'Mic, how lovely to see you,' simpered Algie Smythe-Tomlinson. 'The divine Cynthia not with you?'

'I didn't dare tell her about our clandestine date, Algie!' laughed Mic smiling at the tall, thin, bespectacled man and thinking, Christ Cyn, why did you ever have say Algie reminds you of a gay tapeworm? 'Some things being better left unsaid,' he added with a wink.

'Oh, Mic Sandford, you're such a *tease*!' squeaked a delighted Algie, his long, pale hands fluttering. 'Now, come and meet William – he's still looking for subjects regarding his forthcoming exhibition so… now your Howard's becoming such a *star* – not that he wasn't before! – perhaps…?'

Leaving the sentence unfinished Algie grasped William's arm leading him over to where the artist was standing talking animatedly to a large black man.

'William! Prince! Meet Mic Sandford! Cynthia, Mic's lovely wife, is the lady who bought your *Foetus Frenzy* for Mic at your last exhibition.'

Shaking hands the three men stood quickly appraising each other.

Big, handsome bastard, thought Mic, and I bet he's got more notches on his bedposts than the Pope's said Mass!

Ah ha! thought William. As imagined. Shrewd, tough as nails but we know there's an Achilles heel there and what's more, we know the *heel's* name!

After a few moments of pleasantries Algie interrupted the three by saying, 'William, the actor Howard Hanover whose name I mentioned earlier.'

'So you did,' said William, right on cue.

'Well, Howard is a great friend of Mic's and I was…'

'What Algie was wondering,' interrupted Mic with a warm laugh, 'was whether you would consider painting Howard Hanover's portrait. Well, would you if I commissioned this?'

'Howard Hanover, the actor?'

'The very one.'

'Well, of course I'd be delighted to talk about this but the portrait would have to be one by proxy as if it were,' said William. 'I doubt if I'll have time for even the quickest of sketches before I leave. I'd be working from photographs while on Tahiti and then arrange a sitting or two on my return.'

'Sounds perfect,' said Mic looking at the smiling artist and the equally smiling Prince. (He would later describe Prince to Cynthia as an even more terrifying macho version of Mike Tyson than Tyson himself!)

'William and Prince,' said Mic, 'I know you very kindly suggested lunch and I wasn't too sure as to my plans but, as I thought, I am as a matter of fact, having lunch with Howard and his agent, a Mr Murray Harbourd. If you are still by any chance still free...?'

'Thanks, but you'll have to count me out,' said Prince in his deep bass voice. 'I have to be at the recording studios by two.'

'And of course, while I'd *love* to join you,' camped Algie, 'To quote you-know-who it's a case of "Duty first, Self second!" Now, if you'll excuse me...' With a flutter of hands the fey man sashayed his way back to join his illustrious guests.

'Duty first? Self-second and you know who?' said Prince genuinely puzzled. 'Who's who?'

129:

'The real Queen,' said William drily. 'And yes, Mic, if I can get away from these few rich wankers Algie's got together – present company excluded! – I'd be delighted to join you.'

Murray, who had never met William, found himself captivated by the big, bluff, larger-than-life artist. At times Humphries, Murray repeatedly said to himself during the luncheon, I truly don't know what you're on about or what makes you tick. The guy's great! Just great! Fuckin' ace in fact!

By the end of lunch it was agreed Howard would liaise with William regarding a quick sitting sometime next day. 'Your photographs don't do you justice,' said William, 'and so I would prefer to catch some actual active facial expressions. If you could spare an hour to come over to Notting Hill for a few sketches, it would be tremendous.'

To William's surprise it was Murray who brought up the subject of his proposed gallery on Park Lane. He was even more surprised when Howard, who had been listening intently to William's enthusiastic description of the project suddenly turned to Mic and, with a mischievous grin, camply said, 'What *you* should be doing Mic is investing in William's gallery so that there could be a special room displaying my portrait and my portrait only!'

'Move over Dorian Gray!' chortled Murray, 'or should that be *gay*?'

The call came through to William early the following morning. 'William, Mic Sandford. I'm not too early for you am I?'

'Mic, good morning and no, not at all. I've already been working for a couple of hours and Howard is due in about twenty minutes. Then it's a case of continuing chaos before I leave for the airport tomorrow evening.'

Mic gave a laugh, 'Well, let me now add to that chaos.' Giving another laugh he added, 'I know it's extremely short notice but could you manage a few minutes at my office sometime today? Any time to suit you. There's something I'd like to discuss and it's something which really can't wait until you're back. It's something Howie and I went on to talk about at length after you left us yesterday. He obviously won't mention it when you meet this morning but, as you are no doubt aware, it has something to do with what has simply evolved from his flip remark at lunch.'

'Straight after I've finished sketching Howard? Say eleven or thereabouts?'

'Splendid! See you then. You've got the address?'

'No,' said William thinking, You're wily enough to put two and two together, Sandford. Of course I have your address or how else would dear Howie's ear have reached you? 'Give me a moment to get a pen and take it down.'

Later William met up with Prince in the impresario's flashy Soho office.

'He actually offered to invest in the gallery?' remarked the big man. 'Offered instead of you asking?'

'Absolutely. Our Howie, earless or not, must have quite a control over Mr Sandford.' William mentioned a figure.

'Fucking hell!' said Prince with a gold toothed smile. 'So I take it he's now on the board of defectors?'

'Very funny, Prince!' smiled William, 'But of course, our Mic is now a bona fide director of the William Wandsworth Gallery.' Giving an evil grin he couldn't resist adding, 'Pity about Howie's ear but he assured me at the sitting this morning the new one will be as good as new. As someone said, "Out of adversity comes opportunity" and our mistake regarding Howie and leading to Sandford inadvertently investing in our little project proves the old saying to be absolutely right!'

The headline appeared several weeks later. *TOMMY TYLER CANCELS REMAINING GERMAN TOUR* it screamed, followed by the brief story. *Tommy Tyler has, on the advice of his doctors and manager, Prince Albert, cancelled the rest of his appearances, due to a prolonged throat infection.* There followed the usual platitudes about exhaustion, the star wanting only to give his fans his best, not wanting to let them down and would be back when well enough to finish the tour.

'It's a good PR stunt,' said Prince glaring at the scowling young star lounging in the chair opposite him, 'and furthermore, I had no alternative for, let's face it Tommy my lad, at the moment your performances suck! Better a clean break and a load of disappointed but still caring fans as opposed to a load of disillusioned ones all wanting their money back!'

An ecstatic Tommy flew out from Paris to Tahiti the next day, having travelled incognito on Eurostar from London to Paris the evening before, his sole companion being one of Prince's trusted sidekicks. To the surprise of Paul, Nelson and Skids the ecstatic Tommy, on arrival, was swept up into the brawny suntanned arms of an even more ecstatic William.

As William would repeatedly tell a bemused Prince in their almost daily telephone calls, 'I don't know what happened, Prince my friend, but I really worship and adore the little guy. Furthermore, did you know he's a bloody good painter? Start thinking Big His and Little His shows, my friend. Just think of all that *feelthy lucre*!'

'Fucking hell,' said Prince to no one in particular after this intimate disclosure. 'Talk about a fucking marriage made in paint box heaven!'

On their return from Tahiti William and Tommy stunned the general public by entering into a civil ceremony. 'It's made more headlines than Elton and Dave!' crowed a delighted Prince. 'More fucking headlines than wally William and his dreary wanton, wantin' waity Katie!'

Tommy's fans instead of being dismayed at their idol's treachery became even more possessive and protective of their star while William's powerful influence as a painter continued to either enthral or outrage. It was inevitable William would move into Tommy's new home turning one of the elaborate guest suites into a small studio as opposed to using the former Notting Hill address now temporarily occupied by Skids and the dwarfs. Otherwise, he and Tommy planned to spend as much time at the *Castello Il Paradiso* as their schedules would allow.

CHAPTER 22:

BATTERSEA – FIVE MONTHS LATER:

William looked across at Tommy. 'Happy?' he asked.

'So, so,' said Tommy, his pretty face going into a pout.

'Only so, so?' said William with a smile, 'And why is that, little one? Here, come and sit on Willy's lap and tell him why it's only "so, so."'

'It's Mac and that bloody Jamie Jefferson,' said Tommy sulkily, moving over to where William was sprawled comfortably on a sofa, his thick, muscular legs akimbo, his dressing gown hanging open displaying his thick flaccid length.

Bending down to give William's cock several light kisses resulting in an immediate response, the heavy shaft beginning to thicken and stiffen, Tommy eased himself onto the big man's lap and resting his dark head against William's chest, his slender hand idly playing with a whorl of William's thick, curly chest hair. 'Especially that bloody Jamie,' he said, his voice muffled.

Jamie Jefferson? But why, Tommy Tom? OK, he's doing ridiculously well with that trite song, *Mayhem in Mayfair,* but Christ, look at you my sweet. The reinstating of your German tour and now there's the O2 Arena to look forward to and maybe Madison Square Garden next year. Forget the likes of Lady Gaga, it's you they'll all be going *gaga* about! What more can you want?'

'I wish them all dead!' Tommy spat out.

'A tall order, Tommy Tom,' laughed William, kissing the young man lightly on the top of his head. 'Even for the world's number one pop star – or diva!'

'I bet Prince could do something!'

William gave Tommy a bear-like hug. 'I think Prince is doing quite enough as it is Tommy Tom and don't even begin to think of going down any other route with him,' he whispered. 'Just don't.'

'But I hate them both,' said Tommy with a whine. He looked up at William, his green eyes wide. 'Can't we just… just upset them a little bit?' he whispered.

'Bit?' William let out a deep laugh, giving Tommy another kiss on his blond locks. 'As in the past tense of bite? Now could very well be an idea,' he said, his mind flashing back to a conversation with Howard during one of the sittings as to how Mac and Jamie had met and how they frequently replayed the scene in the Brompton Cemetery.

William gave William another kiss, whispering in his ear, 'If you just slip off your trousers and sit yourself down on my cock while I think, I'm sure I can *come* up with a solution!'

Several minutes later a flushed William gently lifted Tommy off his glistening prick, the vast canopied room echoing with a resounding plop and Tommy's dribbling wet farts as William's cock slipped out.

'I bet Harry never realised how his Hokusai wave would turn out to be a delicious, decadent echo chamber,' giggled Tommy kissing William's sweaty left nipple. 'And there's another one I hate for being so unfair to you!' he added, giving the nipple a gentle bite.

'Oops! Your bottom's dripping,' observed William glancing down at his spattered thighs. Rubbing his big hand up and down inside the clammy cleft of Tommy's pert arse he gave the young man another kiss. 'Go and get yourself cleaned up, little one, and when you come back bring another bottle of wine with you. Meanwhile I need to call Skids, or Super Skids as the little ones call him. Christ, those three never seem to stop doing it!' He picked up the phone and dialled the number. 'Paulie? William. I have a little job for you. It involves some very boring surveillance work but patience, as you know, is a virtue and can have its rewards. I need you and Nelson, aided and abetted by Skids, to stake out the Brompton Cemetery.'

He glanced up as Tommy sashayed his way back into the stylish sitting area, a bottle of iced Savignon Blanc in his hand. 'See how fucking you always inspires me, Tommy Tom? A fabulous orgasm right up inside you and Mac's immediately sorted out! Again, I have a feeling his little misadventure may have a serious rebound effect on Master Jamie Jefferson.'

'Good,' said Tommy topping up their glasses.

'Now it's your turn, Tommy Tom,' said William, raising his wine glass in a silent toast to his young lover. 'I want you to ask Harry Humphries and Murray Harbourd to dinner.'

'Harry and Murray to dinner? But why!' cried Tommy.

'The final cure of a cancer as if it were.'

'I don't understand.'

'You will. Believe me, Tommy Tom, you will.'

Murray, having been told by Susie that Harry was 'putting the finishing touches to the showroom to end all showrooms at the Chelsea Design Centre' duly called Harry on his mobile but not before remembering to ask, 'How are you feeling Suze, enjoying being preggers?'

'Oh, fuck off Murray!' had been the quick reply. 'Why Harry couldn't have volunteered to be the baby's father I'll never know!' This followed by a sniggered, 'And trust fucking clever clogs Bunti to get her *brother* to donate his sperm so that the brat would look a bit like its she-dad! Jesus Christ, it'll be just our luck the kid turns out to be a raving queen or, worse, a raving dyke!'

Still laughing Murray had hung up and made the second call.

'Harry. Me. Are you ready for this? Tommy Tyler's been on the blower asking the two of us to dinner next week at the Permanent Wave (Murray's name for Tommy's studio complex) along with – and you'd better believe it – William fucking Wandsworth!'

'No way.'

'Ah, c'mon Harry. You've got to face your rival sooner or later.'

'Rival?'

'Let's face it H. Tommy Tyler's certainly replaced you in William's affections. Why, they're even *married* for Christ's sake!' Murray couldn't resist a snigger. 'Talk about swings and bloody roundabouts!'

'There you go again in *typical* Murray Hard-on fashion! Old proverbs and even older sayings!' Harry took a deep breath. 'Oh, alright, you win as you always bloody well do! But if you *dare* say, that's the right attitude, "let bygones be bygones," I'll fucking slaughter you!'

'Then you'll simply "have to learn to live with it!"' laughed Murray, 'as well as letting "bygones be bygones!"' There was a moment's pause before he asked, 'Just out of interest, how *is* the Design Centre's answer to Bollywood coming along?'

Harry gave a long-drawn sigh. 'Let's put it this way, M, at the end of the day this place will be nothing more than a glorified showroom when completed. Apart from the magical *moi* adding the odd extra pattern design or two the place will – and is already doing so – run itself. Julian Markham, the so-called manager and queeny friend of Cynthia Sandford's, is as happy as a pig in shit poncing around the place even in its present state. Dame Julia will be even happier if left to manage the place on her ownsome.'

'If you say so and just as long as you make a royal appearance now and then to warrant your name above the door plus all that investment!'

'You hit the nail on the head my friend, more *oopla* than *ooh la la*!'

'*Oopla*?'

'As in "oh dear" for the uninitiated! Mum-boring-bata would be more appropriate! Oh, the sacrifices one has to make for one's art!'

'As I've already said, dearest, you'll simply have to learn to "live with it!"' chortled Murray before hanging up.

To Harry's surprise – and Murray's relief – the dinner with Tommy and William proved not only a great, fun evening but one which the four were quick to repeat and soon to become a regular feature, whenever possible, within their busy schedules. On several occasions dinner saw only the three together due to William being away in Italy and seeing to the final stages of the castle. It was inevitable that Mic and Howard were soon to become part of the increasingly close knit group.

On one such evening Harry, a mischievous glint in his eye, turned to William and asked, 'William dear, whatever happened to that extraordinary so-called chauffeur of yours and your little helpers? If my olfactory senses serve me well that little group were brilliant in *their* rather unfortunate misrepresentation of Snow *Shite* and the two dwarfs!'

William, much to Murray's relief, appeared unfazed by the question. Giving Tommy a quick glance he wickedly replied, 'I take it by Snow Shite you mean Skids as the dwarfs aptly call him, aka skid Mark Elliot the idiot, our general dogsbody? In answer to your question they're alive with smell and living happily ever after in *Castello Paradiso*!'

'Alive with smell?' said Harry blankly, adding, 'Oh, I get it! Very droll, William. Very droll indeed!' before collapsing into shrieks of laughter.

'What is it Jamie?' asked Murray, his voice filled with concern on hearing the young singer's hysterical voice. 'Mac's been *what*? Shit! Where are you? Stay put, I'm on my way.'

Half an hour later he was sitting with Jamie in a screened off section of the A & E (accident and emergency) sector of the Chelsea and Westminster Hospital waiting for Mac to be discharged.

'Tell me again,' said Murray, giving the young man's hand a reassuring squeeze. 'You found Mac just as he was coming around, having fainted or such, his pants down and a massive *bite* taken out of his arse?'

A choked Jamie gave a faint nod. 'Yes,' whispered, 'more like a tear than a bite.'

'Jesus! Any idea who did this? You didn't see anyone?'

'No,' sniffed Jamie, wiping his nose with the back of his hand. He looked beseechingly up at Murray. 'And Murray, I told them *I* did it! I said we were playing a silly game.'

'But why say you did it?' said Murray, his voice an angry whisper.

'Because I know it's something Mac wouldn't want to get the police involved with,' said Jamie simply. 'The publicity would be too damaging.'

Murray looked at the young singer in astonishment. 'Well, Jamie Jefferson, Mac will be proud of you. Talk about being an old pro! And look, here's the man himself.'

Murray stood up as a sheepish-looking Mac made his way through the screen of curtaining. 'OK Mac?' he asked, giving the big man a cautious smile.

'Aye,' said Mac with a weak grin, 'If you can say being bitten on the arse by a midget at midnight in a cemetery is OK, then I suppose I am!'

'A midget?' cried Murray.

'Dwarf, midget or little person, call it what you will! I just don't know.' Mac put his arm around Jamie. 'Thank you for coming over and looking after the wee lad, Murray. I really appreciate it.'

'No problem.' Murray patted Mac on his broad shoulder. 'Come along. I've got the car outside. I'll give you a lift home and we can talk about it in the morning.'

'No police please Murray and no mention of this to anyone, including Harry.'

'As you wish, Mac.'

'Thanks,' said Mac. 'Jesus, Murray,' he added, his face breaking into another grin, 'Talk about being camp, why, I've no alternative but to spend the next few days – or weeks – sitting side saddle!'

'But the dwarfs are in Italy,' said Murray the next morning, having called by Harry's studio on his way to another meeting, the details of Mac's unfortunate attack concluding with a stern 'And don't you dare let on I told you. Wait until Mac decides to tell you himself!'

'Are they?' questioned Harry.

Murray stared dumfounded at his friend. 'You seriously don't think…?'

'Well, there's only one way to find out,' said Harry. 'We call William and ask him the troglodytes' whereabouts.'

'We can't do that!'

'We can't? Watch me!'

'No way! *I'll* do it,' said Murray gabbing the phone from Harry. 'What's the number again? Jesus,' he muttered as he began dialling, 'the things I do for you, Harry Humphries.' He looked at Harry, 'It's ringing.'

'Phones do have a tendency to do that,' said Harry sarcastically, reaching for his coffee mug.

'William, good morning, it's Murray. William, a question concerning the two dwarfs, one we've discussed before. There's a chance I may need them in a Christmas commercial I've been asked to help organise. A couple of days' shooting and of course I'll make sure the money's good. Sorry, the line's a bit crackly. What was that? Ah, they're already in Italy. I was rather hoping they were still ensconced in your Notting Hill studio. Oh, you've finally given that up! When was that? Two months ago? I see.' Murray gave a shrug. 'Of course it makes sense seeing the final move to Italy is imminent. What? Oh yes, please do William, I'm with Harry at the Lots Road studio.'

'What was that all about?'

'Apparently the dwarfs are now living in the castle and furthermore, Notting Hill hasn't been in use for the past couple of months. Something we can quite easily check on. William's calling us back and that, I think, must be him,' he added as Susie buzzed the extension.

'You take it,' said Harry. 'I'm going to have a pee.'

'Sorry about that Murray,' said William. 'As I was saying, we're off to Italy again next week, this time permanently. The castle has exceeded all my expectations and Mazzuchelli has been a positive genius. Once we've really settled in – give us a several months to go native as if it were, rather like we did on Tahiti – we thought the four of you would like to come out and stay for a couple of days or, if it's more convenient, a long weekend for a wishing us "good luck and a happy future" celebration as if it were.' William gave a deep, friendly chuckle. 'You game?'

'We sure are!' laughed Murray, giving Harry a mischievous wink as he came back into the office. 'I'm sure Harry can hardly wait to see what Mazzuchelli, the positive genius, has created. Let us have a date, or dates, as soon as you are settled.'

'Bitch!' camped Harry.

'I heard that!' laughed William, adding, 'sorry it was a no no regarding the dwarfs,' before hanging up.

'They're in Italy.'

'So you just said,' snapped Harry. 'Strange, isn't it, how everything that should be connected to William is always so conveniently dismissed.'

'Now who's being paranoid? C'mon Harry. Mac seems only too happy to forget about it – those two won't be playing cemetery remembers again, that's for sure! – so I suggest we do the same thing. "Let sleeping dogs" and all that.'

'*We* being the operative word,' said Harry. 'But, as you say, it's none of our business and seeing I've never met this Mac or Jamie, why should it be?'

'You'll be meeting them at Griselda's bash.'

'That tired old thing?' sniffed Harry, 'I mean the bash, not Griselda! When *is* the party to end all parties finally going to take place? You ordered all the stuff weeks ago?'

'Blame it on Terence, apparently he's doing strange things in China as we speak and Griselda can't quite pin him down.'

'The mind boggles!'

BATTERSEA:

'Who was that?' asked Tommy sashaying his way into one of the downstairs perimeter suites of the complex, currently being used as a temporary studio by William.

'The wily Murray checking on the whereabouts of Paulie and Nelson.' William replied. 'They obviously know about the attack on Mac last night. I told him they're already in Italy plus the fact the Notting Hill studio is no longer.'

'Both of which are true,' laughed Tommy. 'Well, almost. The studio was rented out at least two months ago and, if I'm not mistaken, the dwarfs and Skids are on their way to Paris via Eurostar as we speak.

'Just as well we put them up in that out of the way house in Hurlingham for the past two months,' said William. 'No nosy neighbours and, because of the vigilant Skids, no sightings of any strange little folk.'

'Let's face it William, Mac Guthrie's bitten arse is one public relations exercise he won't be using in any promotions of the *wee* Jamie Jefferson!' said Tommy gleefully.

SIX MONTHS LATER:

'Like the outfit!' laughed Mic, eyeing Howard's striped matelot top, light blue chinos and Gucci loafers. 'Still the bandana, I see?'

'Strange, isn't it?' said Howard, giving Mic a tender kiss. 'Although the new ear is perfect I've got so used to the damn thing and, thanks to the photographers it's become a sort of trademark.'

Mic looked approvingly around the small neat Mews house. 'I know I've said it before Howie – and I'm saying it again – what you've done to this place is quite remarkable.' He gave a laugh. 'Should you ever get tired of the acting profession you should really consider going into interior design. With your following you'd have them queuing to be *done* by Howard Hanover.' Mic cleared his throat nervously before adding. 'And between you and me, Howie, there's always Humphries Mumbata Worldwide.'

'Humphries Mumbata Worldwide?' Howard looked at Mic curiously. 'Don't tell me there's already trouble in that little paradise?'

Mic gave Howard an uncomfortable look in return. 'Let's just say Harry isn't quite pulling his weight, not giving it his full attention. He barely visits the new showroom and seems happier with things as they were before, namely working from his Lots Road studio for a few select clients. Now he has his name on a range of fabrics he seems to think he's done his bit.'

'Mic, I'm really sorry to hear that,' said Howard, his concern genuine. 'I really thought Harry would have given it all.'

'No, Howie, not quite. Harry, I'm afraid is a bit of a dilettante and always will be. He's a very much here today, gone tomorrow man. Now, enough of my problems, we've got the "here today" Harry and Murray to collect and a plane to catch.'

'And if I *did* decide to take you up on your offer, the interior design thing and especially the textile showroom?'

'No problem,' said Mic with a smile. 'Humphries Mumbata Worldwide is easily changed to *Hanover* Mumbata Worldwide. Here, let me take that,' he added, reaching for Howard's holdall. 'Hector had to park at the entrance of the Mews.' He nodded towards the arched opening. 'As you can see a dustcart's decided to be obnoxious.' Making their way to the waiting Bentley, Mic looked sideways at his lover. 'Happy?' he asked softly.

'Blissfully, and all thanks to you Mic Sandford,' said Howard, giving Mic a dazzling smile.

'I had a call earlier from Cyn and Nat,' said Mic as Howard climbed into the back of the car. 'They send their love and wish us a glorious week in *Bella Italia*!'

'Pity we have to come back early,' said Howard, 'though you could stay on for a few more days, Mic. It's only I have to be back for rehearsals and, after all, it *is* my West End debut!'

'What, and leave you on the loose in London? No sirree! Having almost lost you once I'm never going to allow that to happen again! Ah, we're here and there they are! Morning you two!' he called from the open window as the car drew up outside the main entrance to the block housing Murray's flat.

'Morning Mic! Well driven, Hector!' called back Murray smiling at the beaming driver. 'We timed you from the time we got Mr Mic's call saying you'd just left Egerton Garden Mews. Not bad, not bad at all! Mr Harry and I have only been waiting at the main entrance for a couple of minutes.'

Sitting in the back of the luxurious motor, the de rigueur goblets of champagne in their hands, the four chatted amicably as they sped towards Heathrow airport.

'To be quite honest,' announced Harry, 'I can't wait to see the *Castello*. If it's anything along the lines as to what is about to go up in Park Lane – those visuals are wild! – it has no choice but to be sensational.'

'That's very magnanimous of you, Harry,' chuckled Mic, giving Howard's hand a squeeze.

'I'm a very magnanimous person, Mic. Or didn't you know?' laughed Harry.

'I'll drink to that,' grinned Murray.

'Me too!' cried Howard, smiling at his three companions. 'As the wise old bard said, "*All's Well That Ends Well.*"' Giving an even a greater smile he added, 'Who would have thought all those months back the four of us would have become such firm friends? Friends now happily travelling together to stay with William and Tommy, now also our closest friends! Quite extraordinary, really!'

'Come on Murray,' cried Harry mischievously. 'You can't let Howard off that easily! Surely it's time for a typical Murray-ism?'

'I know when to give in graciously,' said Murray with a grin. 'And I do think Howie has said it all quite to perfection. *"All's Well That Ends Well."'*

CHAPTER 23:

CASTELLO PARADISO:

A smiling William and Tommy stood waiting on the platform as the Rome Express pulled into the small station at Levanto.

'I don't believe it!' cried Harry, clutching Murray's arm. 'To misquote *Macbeth,* "is that a band I hear before me?"'

'Too right,' laughed Howard. 'It *is* a bloody band! Uniforms and all! Trust William to insist on such a *low key* arrival!'

With whoops and cries of delight the six greeted each other with warm hugs and kisses.

'The great thing about Italy,' laughed Tommy kissing Murray resoundingly on the cheek, 'is men kiss each other all the time and nobody turns a hair!'

'Right,' said William, beaming at the four arrivals, *'Andiamo!'* I've brought along our car and we also have two local taxis in tow – the drivers' handpicked by Tommy Tom! – so you've got Nero but no fiddling with him *per favore* – even though your fingers may be burning! – along with Romeo, more Michelangelo's David in appearance but – according to local *fuck*-lore – boasting a monumental dick!' He gave Murray a wink, 'Sadly, as I am now well and truly betrothed, like my faithful self you'll simply have to accept what is so wickedly rumoured!'

Turning to Harry he gave another smile. 'Harry I'd like you to travel with me, Tommy Tom and the rest in the two taxis,' adding diplomatically, 'I'd like Harry to be the first to see what has been done to the revitalised *castello* as opposed to what could have been his magical input!'

'Fabulous new gate posts,' observed Harry half an hour later as William turned the Fiat into the neat, gravelled driveway. Looking back at the receding gleaming steel structures he burst out laughing. 'If I'm not mistaken have we or have we not just driven between a pair of gigantic metal thighs?'

'Spot on, Harry! Mazzuchelli's interpretation of the Pillars of Hercules!'

'Christ,' muttered Harry, 'I can't wait to see what he's done with the castle.'

'We just have to get round this corner – if you remember – and *chi me lo fa fare*! There you have it!'

Harry sat staring silently at the gleaming complex in front of them before saying softly, 'Why, William, it's not only simply fantastic, it's truly amazing. Your friend has retained the original battlements but how has he achieved that gleaming checkerboard effect? It's quite, quite brilliant!'

William, his face wreathed in smiles at Harry's genuine enthusiasm went on to explain. 'He's faced the alternating blocks of the original stone with plates of polished chrome.' William gave a small laugh. 'Mazzy calls it his checkerboard effect while I call it my open *cheque* effect!'

'By *Mazzy* I take it you mean Mazzuchelli?'

'Correct and, to give you an approximate idea how much that little game of checkers cost me, think one complete W dot WAN!'

'W dot WAN?'

'A William Wandsworth painting,' said William glancing into the rear view mirror. 'Ah, here come the others. We'll park in the main courtyard and someone will put the car away later.' He patted Harry lightly on the knee.' Once I've given my illustrious guests a welcome drink you can then have the grand tour.'

'What's the modernistic grouping in the centre of the courtyard? Fabulous new geometric paving stones by the way.'

'That's our intimate circle,' said William. 'Instead of a traditional fountain Mazzy suggested a pair of semi-circular stone benches where friends could sit and enjoy an *apperitivo* or two; especially late on a summer's evening.' He gave an expansive smile. 'It's then the last rays of sunlight – before the sun disappears completely over the battlements – strike the main tower now sheeted in chrome. In other words another *Illustrious Illuminati* as it were. A prelude to my exhibition to end all exhibitions.'

'William Wandsworth, or W dot WAN as I'm now destined to always call you,' said a laughing Harry, 'One day your power of pure and utter undiluted bullshit will slay me.'

'Maybe even something else,' said William with a sardonic grin. 'Now, out you get, I have other guests to entertain.'

'So, what do you think?' asked Mic as he and Howard sat in their guest suite before joining the others for a pre-dinner drink.

'What do *I* think? Why Mic, it's all utterly fucking bizarre! It's Alice in Blunderland on bloody crack cocaine! The whole place is unreal, *surreal,* call it what you like. Christ, who else but William would have thought of a fun fair Hall of Mirrors in a medieval castle of all places? He says the dwarfs love it as they can go from their proper three foot plus to six foot plus in one little hop and step!'

'Tell me about it,' laughed Mic. 'And what about the two rows of torchère in the main hall? Polished chrome skeletons with illuminated skulls? Give me a break. The only moment of sanity was being served those alfresco drinks in that strange circular seating area plonked right in the middle of the bloody courtyard. At least the stone seating had cushions, unlike those metal benches in the second salon.'

'I can't wait to see the dining room! Maybe we'll be eating inside a giant acrylic stomach or – knowing William – maybe a giant sphincter!'

'Shit!'

'My thoughts exactly! But at least the main sitting room has proper couches, Donghia or somebody like that.'

'Jesus Howie,' murmured Mic giving his lover a mischievous smile, 'William warned us the castle would be a bit of a surprise but I wasn't quite expecting such a major one! Dare I say it but I'm rather relieved we're only here for another two days.'

'You took the words right out my mouth Mic, talking of which, as we have at least half an hour before we join the Munsters would you be so kind as to put something else in my mouth so as to replace those wayward words?'

Further down the corridor Harry and Murray were airing their overall impressions.

'I like it,' said Harry. 'I hate to admit it but I really do like it!'

'Sorry my friend, but I have to disagree with you.' said Murray. 'To me it's nothing more than a futuristic Chamber of Horrors, the whole evil scenario capped by those two dwarfs who served us drinks earlier in that hideous mini Stonehenge or whatever it's meant to represent. Explain *that* little architectural travesty if you will!'

'You were meant to be appreciating the *sfumato,* the soft, reflected tonal light as if it were, gently bathing us from the giant chrome reflector, namely the main tower.'

'Reflections out of Wandsworth's arse more likely!' said Murray with a snort. 'And getting back to the dwarfs, Dopey and Grumpy, in those chainmail getups. What the fuck were *they* representing?'

'Sunbeams?'

'Fuck off Harry or pour me another glass of *reflective* wine instead!' Taking the refilled glass Murray muttered a soft 'thanks' before continuing. 'A week of this and I'll be barking, if nothing else.' Taking a long sip of wine he added, 'And as for Tommy, what's with this painter's smock shit? When I saw him at the station I thought for a moment Susie had followed us here! The idiot looks fucking pregnant!'

'Oh, didn't you know?' said Harry with a smirk. 'Tommy Tyler is now a blossoming artist as opposed to a pirouetting artiste! Hence the smock.'

'Shit!'

'And talking of shit, I haven't seen, or sniffed, that shitty chauffeur, major domo, whatever.'

'Perhaps he's busy helping Italy's version of Jamie Oliver in the *cucina*!'

'If that's the case no doubt the main course for dinner this evening will be proudly named *Germ Warfare*!'

'With a shit *soufflé* as a starter!'

Despite their misgivings the four guests found William and Tommy to be excellent hosts with motor launch trips (William owning a gleaming Riva boat) to the neighbouring, picturesque Cinque Terre coastal towns of Monte Rosso and Vernazza for a lunch and a dinner and a day trip, again by motor launch, to Portofino.

'Sorry you have to be leaving in the morning,' said William to Mic and Howard the evening of their departure, the three sitting in the central seating area.

'It's been great, William. Really great,' said Howard. 'But I begin rehearsals day after tomorrow but, if asked again, we're definitely coming back.'

William gave the two a warm smile. 'I do hope so. As long as it's here, my *casa* is *your casa* or, in this case, my *castello* is your *castello.*'

'Ah! There you are,' carolled Harry from the main doorway to castle tower. 'W dot WAN and his little coterie!'

'W dot WAN and his coterie?' muttered Howard. 'Just what does Cruella de Vile mean by that?'

William gave Mic and Howard a sly wink. 'A severe case of sour grapes methinks! Harry, although he won't say it, hasn't quite accepted Mazzy's brilliance regarding the *castello* and now, of course, the eventual unveiling of the Park Lane gallery. Harry,' he called back, 'We were just about to come inside. We'll join you in the main salon in a few minutes. Meanwhile could you organise a gigantic jug of those lethal Humphries' martinis, please?'

Giving a camp wave Harry disappeared inside doorway.

'And to think I offered him all this,' muttered William to himself, for the moment seemingly oblivious to the presences of Mic and Howard. Still lost in his own thoughts he concluded by muttering out loud, 'Devious, ungrateful little cunt,' causing Mic and Howard to eye each other with alarm.

'That God that's over,' said Howard gripping Mic's hand as the plane lifted off from Christopher Columbus International airport. 'And it's now back to London, to just us and, of course, the play.' He smiled at Mic sitting alongside him. 'I'm so glad Cyn and Nat will be flying over for the opening night. Isn't it great, that – at long last – like us, they're now a proper couple living together in LA where Nat is the toast of the town as we are in London, a proper couple with one exception, I've still got to *become* the toast of this town!'

'Which you will, my darling, which you will.' Mic gave Howard's hand another squeeze. 'But there is one very wrong thing in what you've just said.'

'There is?'

'Yes, there most certainly is.' Mic gave another smile. 'We're not quite a proper couple like Cyn and Nat, not until you move into Chester Square with me. Please say you'll do that for us Howie. Let's make that our proper home together.'

'Why Mr Sandford,' camped Howard. 'I was wondering when you would say that. It's about time – after all it *has* been some ten years or more – you finally made an honest *poule de luxe* out of me!'

Harry and Murray sat facing Tommy and William in the soft, reflected glow of the evening sunlight.

'Enjoyed yourselves?' asked William with a smile.

'Yes, thanks W dot WAN,' said Harry with a smirk. 'It's been quite an education.' He gestured towards the courtyard in general. 'Something I remarked on when we arrived but it hasn't been until now that I've really had a chance to take a closer look at the patterns to the new paving stones. All these endless half circles, triangles and squares? All very astrological, if I may say so. But shock, horror! Unless my beady eyes deceive me, no messy Mazzy chrome insets?' Harry gave a malicious snigger. 'Your Mazzy's mind would be even the most hardened psychologist's nightmare!'

'Now apart from the all your other observations, that last remark of yours about Mazzy wasn't very nice Harry, now was it?' said Tommy in a syrupy voice. Turning to a glowering William he added, 'And I'm sure William agrees with me, don't you William? Not nice, not nice at all!'

'Absolutely my sweet Tommy Tom, as you so succinctly put it, not nice at all.' Giving Tommy a gentle stroke on the cheek William added softly, 'but then, my little one, as you and I have always agreed, Harry is not a very nice person. Never has been. In fact we both agree to him being an insidious, heinous horror in comparison to *Mazzy* – no, I take that back, how dare one even begin to compare Harry Humphries to Marcello Mazzuchelli when Harry Humphries is nothing more than a talentless, queeny fuck up!'

'What?' gasped Harry, his face turning white, 'What did you just say?'

'Considering all your failings Harry, being hard of hearing isn't one of them,' said William giving the shocked young man a brittle smile. 'Something else I should tell you,' he added, sliding his big hand along the smooth arm of the stone bench, 'when you first visited I warned you about a cave-in and how I didn't want you tumbling down into the old dungeons, remember?'

'Yes,' said Harry, his voice reduced to a low, nervous rasp.

'William! Enough!' cried Murray in a horrified voice, his face deathly pale. 'This has gone far enough!'

'Just shut the fuck up, Harbourd!' snapped William giving the startled young man a ferocious glare. Turning again to a stunned Harry he gave a small, hollow laugh. 'Hard luck Harry, the warning no longer applies as I've since changed my mind.'

Pressing heavily down on the carved decoration to the front of the arm to the bench William gave a twisted smile as, with a soft rumbling, the paving beneath the bench on which Harry and Murray were sitting smoothly slid open causing the heavy bench to overbalance, tipping the two startled occupants into the dark void below. Within seconds the heavy bench followed, landing with a squelching thud on top of the two dazed figures.

William and Tommy sat staring silently at the neat hole before William, taking Tommy by the hand whispered gently, 'Time for dinner, Tommy Tom.'

Pressing the arm for a second time the two watched as the faux paving panel slid back smoothly into place. 'Remind me to tell Skids and the dwarfs to organise the replacement bench first thing in the morning.' said William as they made their way to the main door of the gleaming tower. 'Not that there's any great rush but, as you know, Tommy Tom, I do like things being in their proper place.'

'And our recently departed guests?'

'Cue for a new song for you should you ever design to tread the boards again, Tommy Tom!' said William giving out a deep, rumbling chuckle.

'Oh, and what would that be, Mr Impresario?'

'*Dungeons are Forever* perhaps?'

THREE DAYS LATER:

'Mr Humphries, please.'

'Who's calling?'

'William Wandsworth.'

There was a moment's pause. 'Err... Mr Wandsworth, it's Susie, Mr Humphries' secretary, we have spoken before.' There was another pause before Susie continued. 'Mr Humphries was expected for a meeting here this morning – he was due back in London sometime yesterday evening – but the meeting had to be cancelled as Harry – Mr Humphries – didn't show up. I've tried both his flat and his mobile several times but all I get are requests to leave a message. Fi, Mr Harbourd's secretary – he's also done a no show – is experiencing exactly the same.' Susie gave a nervous gulp. 'Until now we were rather hoping both were still with you.'

'With me? Good heavens, no!' said William. 'In fact, there was a change of plan, the two leaving the day before yesterday by train en route to Genoa and then onto Monte Carlo for a night – maybe even Cannes – before flying back to London.'

'Oh.'

'Which means they'll probably be back sometime today.'

'I hope you're right Mr Wandsworth, no, I mean I'm sure you're right,' Susie gave a light laugh. 'Harry, Mr Humphries can be a bit of a flibbertigibbet at times! Can I give Mr Humphries a message? Get him to call you?'

'If you would, please err... Susie. Get him to call me, that is. Tell him I've been thinking over his clever suggestion of turning one of the old dungeons into a recording studio for Tommy, Tommy Tyler the pop star and my partner.'

William gave a small chuckle. 'A very witty man, your employer, if I may say so, Susie.'

'Oh, he most certainly is, Mr Wandsworth!' Susie couldn't resist a giggle. 'May I dare ask what he's said, or gone and done, now?'

'It was his name for the potential studio that literally *cracked* both Tommy and me up!'

'Oh, and if you don't mind me asking, what was that?'

'Harry called, he called the project, seeing it was to be in a dungeon and a recording studio' – here William began to chuckle – 'oh, dear, you've started me off again, young lady! He called – ha ha – he called the project "Crypt Cacophony!"'

'Crypt Cacophony?'

'Yes, like loud noises coming from a crypt or coffin, as if it were.'

'Typical Harry, Mr Wandsworth!'

'As you say, Susie. Typical.'

The news concerning the mysterious disappearances of Harry Humphries and Murray Harbourd would have made bigger press had it not been for the sensationalism brought about by a mysterious fire at the *Castello Paradiso de Insprirazione* which saw the untimely deaths of world famous artist William Wandsworth and his partner Tommy Tyler, the former pop star. Along with their charred remains were those of the two dwarfs employed by the artist.

CHAPTER 24:

PRESENT DAY:

'Algie, good morning, it's Mic Sandford. Everything geared up for tonight's big opening?'

'Up and running, Mic,' came Algie's light voice purring camply over the static. 'The building looks magnificent. Such a pity *Himself* isn't here to see his lifelong ambition come to fruition!'

'Knowing William, he'll be up there watching and just waiting for someone to make a cock up!' laughed Mic.

'Oh Mic, I just *love* it when you talk dirty,' simpered Algie.

'And sadly Algie, it has to remain just talk!'

'Oh, wicked Mic! Now, put my marcel-waved mind at rest. You, the divine Howard – *Mein Got*! Hasn't *he* taken off as designer to the stars! I know he was distraught when his play folded after only three performances but then, if that hadn't happened one would never had realised what a brilliant designer he is! A man of many *hidden* talents if I may say so!'

'You may say so and yes he is, a man of many, *many* hidden talents, Algie.'

'Oh, there you go again! Twisting every innocent little thing I utter! And the divine Natalie? The *real* queen of Hollywood! Have she and Cynthia arrived?'

'Yes, they're happily ensconced at Claridges.'

'Divine!' Algie gave out a high pitched giggle. 'And finally, your last two guests, the *divine* Jamie Jefferson and his big Mac?'

'We'll all be there Jamie and we're expecting you, when you finally manage to tear yourself away from all your worshipful admirers, to join us for dinner at the Savoy later.'

'We wouldn't miss it for the world! See you later! Love to the Dazzler! Mwah! Mwah!' Algie hung up.

'I gather from that little conversation our Algie is flying?'

'He's just bypassed Mars!' Mic smiled at Howard. 'You look great, a dinner jacket suits you and I must say that sequinned bandana promises to be quite an eye-opener!'

'Being London's leading interior designer one has simply no alternative but to live up to as well as look the part!' camped Howard, reaching for the proffered champagne. 'To us,' he said, raising his glass.

'To us,' whispered Mic.

'Strange how it all turned out, isn't it?' said Howard to Mic as they sat in the back of the Bentley on their way to the opening of the William Wandsworth Gallery and what there had been finished as part of the exclusive *Illustrious Illuminati* exhibition. (It having been the wily Algie's decision, as director of the new gallery, to delay the viewing of the portraits until the spectacular opening of the magnificent gallery building itself; a move which had generated much publicity and almost hysterical interest in the event).

'In what way, darling?' asked Mic, giving Howard's hand a gentle squeeze.

'Well,' said Howard with a comfortable laugh. 'There's you and me definitely riding into the sunset together as a blissfully happy pair of old fogeys; Cyn and Nat living in equal bliss in LA and Jamie and Mac now our greatest friends but, even more extraordinary – bizarre even – is the emergence, or "coming out" of Algie who finally not only *got* his man but got his man to *marry* him!'

'I take it you're not referring to William Wandsworth,' said Mic drily. 'Though, by God, Algie also got him! Imagine William making Algie sole executor of his estate; responsible for all his unsold works going to the nation; curator of the new gallery etcetera.'

'Let's face it Mic, it was Algie who discovered William, took faith in him and gave him his first exhibition. The rest is almost fairytale history.'

'Just as he's now found his *mark* with this Mark,' laughed Mic.

'Yes, just what *is* his story.'

'Algie's always been extremely vague about how they met. All I've ever been able to gather is this rather striking man came into the gallery one day – I can't remember whether to have a general look around or have a drawing or painting evaluated – they got talking and the rest is history.'

'Good looking bugger, isn't he?' said Howard mischievously.

'Who? Algie?' cried Mic, feigning astonishment.

'However vivid one's imagination,' laughed Howard, 'Algie's the gay tapeworm of the couple, remember? *No* dearest! His other half, the dazzling, rugged, clean cut, immaculately groomed, smooth, craggy-chinned James Bond, Daniel Craig lookalike!'

'True,' smiled Mic.

'Just remind me before we get there, Mark's full name again?' asked Howard.

'Elliot, I think. Yes, Mark Elliot,' came the nondescript reply.

ABOUT THE AUTHOR

Robin Anderson, an internationally known author and interior designer was born in Scotland and brought up in the former Southern Rhodesia (now Zimbabwe) and South Africa. Before attending Rhodes University (the Oxford of South Africa) he hosted his own radio programme in Rhodesia ('The Golden Voice of Teenage Half Hour!) and worked as a cub reporter on 'The Bulawayo Chronicle' during his gap year.

Leaving South Africa, he spent the early Sixties working with interior design companies in Paris, New York and London. He set up his own design company in London in 1970. Although interior design had been his first interest, the designer never stopped writing. Nowadays he makes numerous television appearances and is a regular guest on selected radio programmes, gives regular lectures on his writing.

His first novel, REGINA, A NOVEL OF SOME EXTREMES, was published in 1998. The novel gives a salacious look 'behind the scenes' of the glamorous but bitchy and competitive world of interior design, following the path of the unpleasant but talented Reginald Forbes as he cuts a swathe through the lives of his many unsuspecting victims.

Though London-based, the author travels extensively and the benefits of this are apparent in the various settings to his books. The Amazon, the Yucatan, Borneo, Myanmar, China, Russia, Japan, Sri Lanka, India, Egypt, Morocco, Kenya, Australia, The Maldives, Mauritius, Central Europe, Canada, North and South America plus the majority of the Caribbean Islands have also been visited. He has walked the Inca Trail in Peru; climbed Mount Kinabulu (Borneo) and Mount Kilimanjaro (Tanzania).

The author is a strong believer in the protection of endangered species. In 1959 he took part in 'Operation Noah' which involved the rescue of hundreds of animals from the rising waters of the new Kariba Dam built across the mighty Zambezi River in the north/western part of Zimbabwe.

He is also the proud 'foster parent' to four Orang-utans living at the famous Orang-utan Sanctuary in Sepilok, Borneo plus two elephants, Marlene and Marlon, who live happily on a ranch in Zimbabwe.

In a total contrast to the above, he also helped with the salvaging of precious works of art and manuscripts in Florence, Italy, during the Sixties when the River Arno burst its banks and flooded a major part of the ancient city.

In between his travels Anderson lives mainly in a spacious studio 'overlooking a glorious, leafy square' in London's exclusive Chelsea and a small hideaway in the Cinque Terre in his beloved Italy.

'Have laptop, will write and will travel!' is his mantra. *Paul Dot Go* is his eleventh novel. In addition he has published a collection of short stories, *Thirteen Tales of Textual Arousal*.

ROBIN ANDERSON 2011
www.robin-anderson.com

www.ingramcontent.com/pod-product-compliance
Lightning Source LLC
Chambersburg PA
CBHW051658260626
47170CB00004B/1562